WEIRDO

Sara Pascoe is a highly acclaimed comedian and writer. On TV she has performed her solo show *LadsLadsLads* (BBC2) as well as hosting *Live at the Apollo*, appearing on numerous panel shows and fronting the much loved *The Great British Sewing Bee* (BBC1). She also wrote and starred in the autobiographical sitcom *Out of Her Mind* (BBC2). *Animal*, her lauded first book, was a personal and evolutionary exploration of the female body. Her second book, *Sex Power Money*, examined porn and transactional sex and was a *Sunday Times* bestseller. The accompanying podcast garnered millions of listens and multiple award nominations during its run.

Weirdo is Pascoe's debut novel. The *Weirdos Book Club* podcast is a sisterly offshoot celebrating the perceived outsiders in literature, hosted by Sara with Cariad Lloyd.

SARA PASCOE

weirdo

faber

First published in 2023
by Faber & Faber Ltd
The Bindery, 51 Hatton Garden
London EC1N 8HN

This paperback edition published in 2024

Typeset by Faber & Faber Ltd
Printed in the UK by CPI Group (UK) Ltd, Croydon CR0 4YY

A CIP record for this book
is available from the British Library

ISBN 978–0–571–37454–0

Printed and bound in the UK on FSC® certified paper in line with our continuing
commitment to ethical business practices, sustainability and the environment.
For further information see faber.co.uk/environmental-policy

2 4 6 8 10 9 7 5 3

SARA PASCOE

weirdo

faber

First published in 2023
by Faber & Faber Ltd
The Bindery, 51 Hatton Garden
London EC1N 8HN

This paperback edition published in 2024

Typeset by Faber & Faber Ltd
Printed in the UK by CPI Group (UK) Ltd, Croydon CR0 4YY

A CIP record for this book
is available from the British Library

ISBN 978–0–571–37454–0

Printed and bound in the UK on FSC® certified paper in line with our continuing
commitment to ethical business practices, sustainability and the environment.
For further information see faber.co.uk/environmental-policy

2 4 6 8 10 9 7 5 3

For Gail
(am I your favourite now?)

I would rather go on reading myself
as a fiction than as a fact.

JEANETTE WINTERSON,
Why Be Happy When You Could Be Normal?

My body recognised him first: the hairs on my arms prickled. Then so did the rest of me when I turned around. His eyes were empty, though, as he ordered two gin and tonics.

'Chris?' I checked, even though it was definitely him.

'Yeah?' His tone conveyed no curiosity. He already didn't care how I knew his name.

I fetched his drinks, held out the machine for tapping and asked no more questions. I didn't panic. As he walked away I assured myself this wasn't over. He'd probably warm up when he'd had a few, like he used to.

My view of Chris is obstructed now he's sat down. I do get glimpses when the obstacle leans forward on his stool. I see a woman drinking the gin and tonic I made. Her dark hair is curly and shiny and she's laughing without covering her mouth. I've still got his jumper at my house. I used to sleep in it and he doesn't even remember me.

The obstruction's name is Pete and he's a 'regular', if I'm being polite about him. I can't feel sorry for him because he takes up too much of my time and energy. The police station is next door and he comes in after work and drinks and talks at me. I say things like 'Watch it, cheeky' when he starts being disgusting. It's better on Friday and Saturday when it's busy and there are more ears around. Weekdays I only chat when he's sober – how was his day, what new crimes are happening? Then when he starts asking *his* questions I fake-laugh and do my job. He's on his second pint and telling me about an old lady who died in the bath and wasn't found until days later, after all the water had evaporated. Pete, waiting with his next sentence while I served Chris, wanted my full attention. I turn back to him to signal that he can continue.

'I had to wait for the coroners . . .'

I nod at Pete but another customer is approaching and it's an easy choice. I wonder how long I can avoid the ending of the story. I wonder how Pete will die while I milk the optics of a double Baileys.

With my arm in the air I catch my own eye in the mirror behind the bar. My roots need doing and my concealer isn't rubbed in properly. I look unimpressed. I wish I'd done something different. If I'd known Chris was coming in I could've worn a nicer top or had a smaller nose. I hate looking at myself because all I see is my mother. Her disappointed jowls waiting in my cheeks. I should've had my own face, not this mash-up mess of my parents'. I hear someone calling, 'Abi.'

Leave me alone, Pete, get lost with your dead old bath lady.

'ABI!!!'

I've overfilled the glass and Baileys is dripping down my arm. Oops.

I turn carefully around and put it down in front of the customer. He's a young man with a blue suit and a horrendously pubic blonde goatee. I smile at him.

'Four fifty.'

He doesn't smile back but glances warily at his overfilled tumbler in its creamy puddle.

'Happy Christmas.'

I smile again to make it all fine, take his fiver, swap it for a coin and he retreats. Walks over to Chris and the woman like this is destiny or something. I knew something was going to happen today. Blonde Beard raises his overfull glass like a toast. I can't hear what he says but their three faces look at me and laugh. I spray the bar and wipe and focus on seeming like how a normal person would seem after a small spillage in their place of work. Maybe I'm ditzy, or a klutz – something with a z in it. Maybe I've got more important things to think about and that's intriguing and you should fall in love with me. Maybe the Baileys wasn't an embarrassing mistake but an indication that I'm an interesting character with hidden depths?

If you need to know what the pub is like, it's called The Slipper. The carpet is navy-ish, to be like a night sky, the chairs and tables are brown wood, the ceiling is painted white and has large bulbs hanging down. It's a bright place, with no music cos it's part of a big chain and those are the rules. We're across the road from the rail station so we hear trains and announcements if it's not busy. When it *is* busy all you hear is chat. I've worked here for two months and I hate it and thought I was here as a punishment because of my stupid bad life decisions, but then Chris walked in tonight and now I understand this has <u>all</u> been destined. I got a credit card bill this morning as well. The planets are aligning or something.

I hear someone say my real name and turn around but no one's looking at me.

'So she seems fine, not all withered or anything. We don't know exactly how long she's been there.'

There's nothing else to clean. I throw the cloth in the bin.

'The plug was in the bath, though. That should have been a clue.'

I reach down and get the cloth out again. We're not supposed to throw them away.

'Her body had absorbed all the water while no one was looking. She would have swollen up but because she'd been in there so long she'd shrunk again cos all the water evaporated. She looked fine when we got there, she didn't even look dead.'

I sigh but I don't mind this story, if I'm honest. I used to like the Darwin Awards, when people tripped over and drowned in vats of cabbage or shepherd's pie. There is something about ridiculousness that cancels out the horror of death and it's a relief not to be sad or pretend to be sad.

'So they lifted her up, these two paramedics, one at her feet, one at her head. But because she's been in water all her skin is stuck, it's stuck to the bath—'

I laugh like a cute ditz would. Pete radiates pleasure that I've reacted while behind him the woman with Chris is looking over. She has such dark skin. She's done her make-up really well; her lips look smooshed, like fruit hammered in half. I wonder if she does a YouTube tutorial. She must mix a gloss with a rich, heavy colour. I wonder if that colour would work on pale lips on pale skin, then I wonder if gloss ends up on Chris's dick and then wish I hadn't thought that.

'—and the worst thing isn't all the organs and everything flopping out of her, it's the smell – cos your intestines rot, you know, all gases and putrefying added to the shit that's in there, because it's all in there . . .'

I decide to laugh again, but this one doesn't sound very

human. I've forced it, it's yelpy, like fox sex, which stops
Pete. I'm about to consider what will happen next when
it's happening already. Chris's woman with the red mouth
has come to the bar. She smells very clean, like a candle
or a hotel. I think she's older than me, or maybe she's just
confident.

'Two G and Ts and half a pint.'

Her voice is loud and Irish and I want to know everything
about her.

'What of?'

'Not Baileys!'

I love her.

'We're gonna have to pour Steve into a cab!'

I love her so much.

'I'm sorry. I got distracted, I wasn't concentrating—'

'Don't blame you.'

Red Mouth rolls her eyes towards Pete and then away so
perfectly, so derisively. I control the impulse in my facial
muscles who want to copy, suppress the urge to see if I
could do it too.

'Probably do us some waters as well?'

I set about the drinks, doing my best, conscious brain
giving motor-skill orders so I'll seem capable. Pour plonk
pour arrange. Her body is facing towards me like she's
open to chat. Women never do this. I spray water in pint
glasses and consider if I could be a lesbian before I get
goosepimples and realise it's a trick. Chris has told her
everything and she's come to humiliate me.

'Want a tray?'

'You've got such long eyelashes.'

What the heck is she playing at.

Red Mouth sashays away like she's made a friend and I study her return to the table in case she's feeding back about me, but Chris and Blonde Beard carry on talking and ignore her. So it'll look like they weren't watching us, maybe? Maybe. Difficult to know how to play this. I wipe the bar again and try to ignore how big my body feels. I knew something was going to happen today and this is it – I just don't know what it is yet.

Pete gestures with a pointed point at his glass that he wants serving and he's moved on to rum so it's downhill from here. He asks if I've seen *Line of Duty* then spews his opinion of *Line of Duty* in my direction.

'No spoilers, Abi . . .'

Pete's holding his hands up like *I'm* the policeman. His fingers are fat and orangey. I'd kill myself if I had sausage hands. Or I'd get very precise liposuction. I wouldn't wave them around; I'd be rightly ashamed.

'No spoilers,' he repeats while continuing to spoil my life. I look away from Pete but accidentally land right on Chris, who turns his head like he's felt me see him. I concentrate on looking around at the other customers, the ones that aren't Chris or his friends. It's mainly couples or small groups, all chatting and focused on each other. And of course because of the time of year there's the odd snowman or Rudolf jumper, minimal seasonal effort mirrored by our lamely decorated windows.

Last Tuesday a man in a boiler suit came and sprayed white snowflakes out of a can. They're all around the edges of the main window, and in the middle is a Christmas tree with a pint on top. There's no carols playing or whatever because of the music rule, which is good because I hate this time of year. I had to make that window-paint man a latte. I thought we were getting on okay so I asked him how much he gets paid to spray windows and he acted like I'd been rude or mean and didn't speak to me again.

I hear the closed-circuit camera whirring behind me and wonder if Nadia's watching me in the office on her break. I look for my cloth and can't find it. I open the glass wash, which is empty, but I switch it on anyway, then I see my cloth in the bin again – whoops, when did I do that?

I don't like that Nadia uses the camera to check up on me. It's supposed to be for evidence after fights. When I was a child I went through this paranoia that my mum was always watching me and could see me wherever I went. She always seemed to know everything or guess what I was thinking. If I lied, Mum knew. When I stole, she always found it. I was little so I didn't know how she was doing it. The only explanation was that she had secret invisible cameras that floated, following me around. If I needed to do secret stuff I had to do it under the bed covers or inside my clothes, which is how I set fire to my pyjamas. When I was older I realised invisible floating cameras were probably logistically impossible, and even if possible, prohibitively expensive for a single parent in a two-bedroom flat.

'The story swings between completely unrealistic, offensively so—'

Pete's still critiquing *Line of Duty*.

'—then sometimes real. Too real.'

I never told him my name was Abi, by the way. Pete assumed it because of my badge. He is a *professional detective* so it's no wonder murderers are carrying on willy-nilly.

'Never in between.'

'What's in between?' I ask Pete, and his face lets gravity take over for a bit. I elaborate. 'If there's "not-reality" and "reality", what is in between? What else is there?'

Pete deflects by telling me I'm clever, which I'm not. Chris called me clever once too. I'd lent him a book and when he gave it back he pronounced the author's name wrong. Chris said that he thought Came-Us had a lot of sadness in him and I said, 'Yes, that's true about Cam-Moo.' And Chris said I was clever but it didn't sound like a compliment, it sounded like he was never going to sleep with me. Which he didn't/hasn't. I only knew how to pronounce it because we did *The Outsider* for A-level.

I can't stare at Chris. I don't want to be obvious, but I think reckless thoughts about what I *could* do. I could call him to the bar and he'd walk over here with a confused look on his face. I could shout at him in front of everyone, 'I'VE STILL GOT YOUR JUMPER YOU WERE DRUNK YOU KISSED ME I WAS COLD.' There is this powerful energy between us – invisible but absolutely there. Like in the book *Matilda* when Matilda can move things with her eyes. I always understood that force, even though I couldn't do it. I really like *Matilda* and that's not a clever book, is it? It's for children. But she's my favourite main character because she comes from an awful family and likes reading, like I do. Those special powers must've made her life a lot easier, though. She wouldn't be working in a pub at thirty-two.

I find Chris's reflection in the fat gold Foster's tap. His hair is longer, and really curly now all over his head. His face is beautiful, I think, but when I first saw him I thought he was ugly. He has a tall shiny forehead and a pointy chin. Long nostrils too. He's only about my height, so quite short. He's pale at the moment, like the inside of an almond, but his skin goes so brown in the sun and then his eyes become bluer. His mum is Iranian – I don't know what effect that's had on his face but he has cheekbones like a model so maybe that.

I can't believe he's really in this pub, in real life. If he'd come in the first night I worked here that would have been too suspicious, too obvious. Whoever's in charge had to wait until it seemed like a coincidence. But it's not, is it? It's plot.

Customer Collection Team
Barclays Bank
Level 21
Churchill Place
LONDON

21 December 20—

For the attention of Miss Collins,

Further to our previous correspondence dated 1 October and 4 November, we have received no response from yourself about the missing payment instalments, and no repayment has as of yet been received. I must remind you that all lending is dependent on regular repayments, and your failure to meet this requirement may result in your debt, £4,235.50, being passed to a debt collection agency who will be instructed to retrieve this amount in full. Your credit card remains frozen as late payment fees have resulted in your being well over the agreed credit limit of £3,000.

This is the final approach to be made on behalf of Barclays Bank. If we receive no payments or correspondence within 14 days this matter will be passed to the CRB agency. You must be aware that this will affect your credit rating and your ability to borrow in future, as well as incurring increased costs.

I urge you to contact us immediately.

If you have made a full payment in the last 48 hours please disregard this letter.

Yours sincerely,
Peter Synguard
Barclays Debt Advisor

I got over the 'Mum can see me' stage by the time I got to secondary school. I had a brief phase of believing the whole world was watching me on television and then a term of thinking a boy called Abbas could see me through my cat. I know that sounds mental now, but it is important to query things – for example my name badge.

The plastic rectangle pinned to my chest has allowed Pete to assume something about me. He's never asked so it's not like I've lied about it. I know who he means when he says 'Abi', which he does a lot, and in two different ways. One way is when he wants my attention: 'ABI', like he's calling a dog in the park. The other way is more like a salesman in a pitch. He'll pepper the name into his sentences: 'So the thing is, Abi, Millwall fans aren't *more* violent than Arsenal fans' etc etc. It's a tactic for creating familiarity but it's unsuccessful because Abi doesn't work here anymore. She got a job at Center Parcs, which is better because you get to live all year round in Center Parcs. Also the customers are only there for three or four days or maximum seven if they're millionaires. Also I bet they have more interesting things to talk about, like archery or having seen an owl.

I'd LOVE to go to Center Parcs. I can really imagine myself cycling through the trees like on the advert. I only need a completely different life and then I'd be rich. I know I deserve it; I know I should have a lot of money, which is why it hurts so much to have none. Minus none really because I'm still paying off the flight to Australia. I took out two credit cards to get there and see him. I pay them £45 each a month just for remembering I owe them three grand and now Chris has walked into my pub and doesn't even recognise me. Or he's pretending. I don't know which is worse. The thing I'm sure of is that this is TOO BIG to be a coincidence – there are millions of pubs in Essex. He must've been looking for me, going into each one. Or were they waiting until I stopped thinking about him before sending him in? Because I had stopped. He hadn't crossed my mind for ages until I got the credit card bill this morning.

I like being Abi because it makes me not me. It's like I'm a stripper using a fake name. I always wanted to go to a strip club because that's the coolest kind of girlfriend, one who buys you a lap dance and then has sex with you when you get home even though she knows you're thinking about strippers instead of her. My ex-boyfriend James, his ex-girlfriend Sasha took him to Spearmint Rhino on his twenty-first birthday and did that. I can't take Ian to a strip club because it would scare him; he doesn't enjoy female sexuality. Or at least he thinks it should be dormant and not in anyone's face. I wouldn't go by myself because I worry the strippers will think I fancy them even though I'm not a lesbian. And what happens if I *do* fancy them?! Strippers are superior beings who know all about men like Pete who use your name as a leash or a sales technique and they don't even bother pretending. Call me Cherry Tree, call me Glitter, call me Domestos. Imagine getting paid to dance because you're so lovely it's a treat to watch. I have a lot of respect for that. I respect the beautiful people. Like Red Mouth with Chris. We want beautiful people to like us – we can't help it, that's how humans are made. Dogs don't care, though. I've seen loads of ugly people with dogs who love them.

Chris is one of the beautiful people, but I didn't notice at first. Maybe because he's the same height as me? We were going round on the bus. How you train for being a tour guide is you go on the tour again and again with different guides until you remember what to say and then you get a mic and a bus and off you go. I never saw London until it was pointed out to me. On your left-hand side, look, that's London. And if you turn to the right, more London over there. I liked learning it all and I liked pointing at it and sometimes when I gestured at a statue or a church I would see Chris as well, on his bus coming the other way, and eventually I did notice him and I never really stopped wanting him to notice me back even though I haven't seen him for three years. And all of a sudden he's in the same room, right over there, and inside me all my cells are pointing and pointing like he's St Paul's or Westminster Abbey. I'm jittery with it.

Nadia comes back from her dinner break and her badge says 'Nadia', very honestly. She smiles and jokes with Pete and he starts to tell her about the old lady in the bath and her face gets tense but she's still listening. I complained about him once, anonymously, to the police station. I typed up a letter explaining that a member of the constabulary was saying sexual things to staff at the pub next door and then they sent a detective to investigate but unfortunately it was Pete. Nadia asked if I wanted to make an official grievance but I told her I could handle it and smiled like it was fine. That night Pete told me he was just having a laugh and he thought I liked banter and I told him it was Nadia that'd sent the letter. So he doesn't ask Nadia about her knickers anymore or what she sounds like when she orgasms. Just me.

This is the worst job I've ever had. The job I had before this, I thought that was worst at the time. It was in a dungeon. Something that happens in London is that if tourists go and see something, like a bridge or some waxworks, they want people in ripped clothes and face paints jumping out at the end. It's called 'scaring' and everyone who worked as a 'scarer' went weird. They made us stay down underground the whole time. We weren't allowed out on breaks as that would ruin the 'illusion'. If tourists saw us queuing for a meal deal at Boots they might realise we weren't real zombies and want their money back. So we didn't see any sunlight or breathe any air, we spent all day under the earth like potatoes. Consequently all our conversations were horrible. About Myra Hindley or what drowning feels like or whether we could eat a human leg. That's where I met Ian. He'd worked there for two years before me and he loved scaring. Ian was proud if he made someone wet themselves and would take you to see the patch on the floor. We weren't supposed to touch people but sometimes Ian and the others would. They'd lie in nooks and grab at ankles and skirts or wait in the tunnel to stroke an arm or blow on a neck. They thought it made the experience better if it was actually scary, otherwise it's just actors in the dark with some clanging noises and it cost £18.

The only positive to hating your job is that it makes you

really enjoy the drink after work. Ian bought me drinks sometimes even though usually we all bought our own drinks. We couldn't do rounds because there were always at least three people who had to drink soda water because they were skint. If anyone asks for soda water here I put vodka in unless they are blatantly pregnant. It's so shit that we all have to buy things and then our money is gone. Head Office let us have one free drink after work while we are wrapping the cutlery in napkins for the next day, which sounds nice until I tell you we don't get paid to wrap cutlery. We don't get paid after the pub is closed, but there are some jobs we're not allowed to do in front of customers so we have to do them after closing time for free. Sometimes I sneakily have double drinks, like putting Tia Maria in a Guinness or pouring a pint of wine and pretending it's pale ale. Only if Nadia isn't looking. The other manager is Brandon and he spends all night in the office unless he sees a fight on the cameras and then he'll come out. Brandon likes to be called Kermit. He's an overly thin man, very sallow with a beard of acne. I like him, he's funny.

Wrapping the cutlery is, if I'm honest, and I hate to admit it, fucking wonderful. It makes me a tiny machine, with repetitive purpose. It calms and cools me and I look at my hands that for once feel like mine and think 'Is this happiness, then?' But it's actually relief. Relief that work is done for now, relief that the not-happiness is over. The absence of pain is not pleasure. Except, contradictorily, it is. So I'm angry they don't pay us and I'd like to get revenge one day but I don't refuse to do it or choose a quicker job like mopping.

Woah. She smiled at me. Red Mouth is smiling at me because I accidentally glanced at her while waiting for a stout to settle. Stupid eyes of mine. I smile into the stout, not on purpose, and when I pass the pint to the waiting customer *he* smiles, taking what is not for him. I turn quickly to catch my smile in the mirror behind the bottles but it's gone. But look. Look who else is in there, reflected perfectly. It's Chris, talking and sipping.

Oh boy.

I started taking extra shifts on the buses because the days I didn't work felt pointless. James made comments when I started doing my hair in plaits and putting on mascara and stuff – he was my boyfriend before Ian. He didn't know why I was putting this new effort into getting ready. I didn't tell him I was preparing to be seen in the distance. Men don't like to imagine their girlfriend is chasing another man on her bus all day, willing red lights and green lights with her heart beating like crazy. If I managed to catch up with Chris our break times would overlap and I could sit near him. There was a stationary bus near Piccadilly where guides were allowed to eat our sandwiches and read the free paper. I brought in big books about London to try and be impressive. Chris never spoke to me, but I would listen to him talking with the others. Even the drivers. Maybe he thought I had too much reading to do. One day, though, I walked onto the lunch bus and it was just him. And now me, now I'd arrived.

I hadn't been chasing Chris that day because I hadn't seen him or known he was in. Even on days he wasn't there I never gave up trying to find him. Even when I wasn't at work. Even if I was somewhere else like the cinema or a

shopping centre I'd look around hopefully. If *I* was somewhere else then there was always a chance that *he* might
be too.

So I stepped onto the lunch bus and Chris said 'Hello'
and because it was just the two of us I knew he was saying
hello to me. I stroked my plaits to check they were there.
My face is long and apparently having long plaits hanging
around makes it seem wider. That's what a hairdresser'd
told me. She said I wasn't allowed a fringe because of
my chin but she didn't explain why. 'What are you reading today?' he asked. I wasn't a ghost; he could see me. I
showed him Peter Ackroyd's *London: The Biography* and
he said, 'I've had London up to here' and saluted above
his head, and I resolved never to read about London ever
again.

Later that day Chris passed in the other direction near
Parliament and we waved at each other. Little gestures,
nothing unprofessional. Still talking and pointing. I was
showing the tourists on my bus the Winston Churchill
statue and then I spotted Chris and his wave. I waved back
a little and then that became my life. All I would do is try
to find him so that I could pretend not to see him until I
saw him see me and then we'd wave.

The next time I'm on the lunch bus I've brought in a
smaller book. About loneliness and murder and being too
hot. So hot you can't hear your brain, so you make mistakes. And maybe you didn't care about your mother and
didn't cry at her funeral. That's the bet Camus made with
his friends. They were having coffee, and a cigarette probably, and he bet them that society would execute a man
for not crying at his mother's funeral and then he wrote

L'Étranger. That means 'the stranger' in English but Camus didn't call it that because he wrote it in French. Also nor did the English publishers, they called it *The Outsider*. In the book Camus proved his point: the main character didn't cry at his mother's funeral and he ended up executed, but, er, not to criticise, it was *mostly* because he shot someone. They punished him for that rather than his dry eyes at the mort of Maman.

I try that experiment too sometimes. Imagine Mum's funeral, how it will feel, if I will cry. It's a bit twisted really, because thinking about Mum being dead doesn't upset me, but thinking about myself crying about Mum being dead does. So at Mum's funeral I'll probably have to imagine myself crying at someone else's funeral to stop society executing me. I can't take it seriously! I don't believe she can die or that she will. My mum will always be around, haunting my face even though she's not dead. I *can* imagine myself dying, that's much easier. I hope I die in the bath and become an awful mess. That will be my revenge. One day I'll be nothing more than a gross story in a music-less pub.

Chris's table are the loudest group in here, which means I can hear him talking. He's explaining how he overstayed his visa and was working illegally before the Australian authorities made him come home. I turn my head to ask a question and remember he's not talking to me. Now Chris is saying that his girlfriend wouldn't marry him, which is *crazy* – he's psychic – I was just about to ask about his girlfriend! He carries on telling Red Mouth and Blonde Beard about Australia and it's so weird that I'm not one detail in his story when he is the whole reason I went. I take a walk around the pub's perimeter collecting empties so it seems like I am busy instead of earwigging. Blonde Beard starts talking about a trip he took somewhere and I have no interest so return to the bar.

I was pretending not to listen when Chris told our co-workers that lunchtime. I was sitting a few seats away staring down at my book. Chris told Andy and Connie that he was bringing sandwiches from home because he was saving up: he was going to live in Sydney and chill out for a bit. He said there were dolphins and amazing wine and that his mum had gone when she was young. He was leaving – my plaits and mascara had been for nothing. A week later he sketched a flyer on the back of a handout about road closures and tacked it on the lunch bus window with chewing gum. 'Chris's Leaving Drinks' in bubble writing, and he'd drawn a really good picture of himself in our uniform with a mic and exaggerated his curly hair and his pointing hand.

Chris left about two weeks after I lent him the Camus book, just as we were getting to know each other. His drinks were on the night of his last shift and I got stuck next to our manager. His name was Phil and I was listening to everything he said so I could remember it and make fun of him with James when I got home. Phil was a DJ at weekends even though he was short and ginger. He carried his work folder in a record bag all week, which either meant he had to take his records out every Monday and put them back in every Friday or maybe he had two record bags. One for records and one for letting people know he was a DJ when he wasn't DJing. I was drinking soda water and working out who to ask for a cigarette when Chris said he was going outside for a rollie and I asked for one and he passed me the pouch and so we've always had it, this connection.

Someone had abandoned a half-drunk wine outside on the windowsill so I drank that while we smoked and Chris told me he was nervous but excited and said I should add him on Instagram so I could see his photos. I told him I had always wanted to go to Australia, which was recently true. 'Oh you should, you should,' he was saying; he was insistent. He was tapping my arm sometimes when he was talking and his cheeks were flushed and he was looking right in my eyes and I was making myself look right back, even though my eyes are brown and not good to look in. Then we went back inside and I sat next to Phil some more and then next to Connie who was too old to be touring – she forgot all the facts and just pointed out postboxes and Pret A Mangers. Connie was telling me about her son's failed marriage, which was so boring I wouldn't even be able to make fun of it later, when suddenly Chris got up. I stared at the table to act like I didn't notice him putting his phone in his pocket and then the pouch and lighter in his rucksack. When he announced he had to go home and finish packing everyone else stood up too, hugging Chris or cheers-ing. I needed a wee from all the fizzy water but I couldn't get up because Chris was leaving, he was walking away and waving. Then he says, not to everyone, just to me, 'Let me know if you do come out', and I nodded in a casual way like 'That's a new thought I haven't had before.' After Chris was gone there was no point me being at his leaving drinks but I couldn't go home or it would have been obvious to everyone that

I was in love with him. So I stayed until 2 a.m. drinking discarded drinks and smoking discarded fags and I was sick on the night bus and had a big row with James about not texting when I'm out.

Without me ever directly looking at the part of my brain that was plotting, I came up with a plan. I wanted to break up with James – we'd become very unhappy, very toxic. Two bad things'd happened that poisoned the rest of our relationship. I'm still upset about them. I didn't know how to talk to him so I decided it'd be simpler if I went to Australia then broke up with him from there. I really focused on putting the distance between us first, then ending things second. I am now wondering how I ever thought this was sensible.

So I looked into flights and accommodation and costs. I decided to save up and I tried to, but it didn't work very well. Buses paid £12 an hour so I put aside £40 a week for a month and then the season ended. It took me three weeks to get temp work and in between I had to borrow £600 off my sister for rent. That was my worst mistake, getting her involved. I've paid her back now.

She really overreacted about a few hundred pounds.

So while I was temping I took out a credit card and then another one and then a store card at a clothes shop. What I did was I took them all out at James's address because I was moving out of my flat. That was the reason. I put the stuff I wasn't taking in Mum's garage. I told her I was going to Australia to work on my relationship with Dad, partly out of spite, partly because I *was* expecting to see him. The thing no one ever mentions, I don't know if Australians even know, is that Australia is too big. You presume you can

go to Bondi and hang out and then pop to your dad's on the
way home. Then you find out Perth is a five-hour plane ride
and you've run out of money. Luckily my parents don't
speak so Mum never checked. My only worry was that if I
died they might talk about it at my funeral and then Mum
would get angry that I'd lied.

When I got back and had to live in my old room at
Mum's, she waited for a while before asking her questions:
'How does he seem? Does he say he's happy? Does he look
old? Is he still an arsehole?' I kept thinking maybe she knew
I hadn't seen him and was trying to trick me. I managed
to equivocate. I said, 'Mum, promise that when I die Dad
can't come to my funeral.' And that was the right answer –
I'd found it by accident. Mum loves banning people from
her funeral, it's the ultimate punishment. They'll regret
what they've done and how they've treated her.

The other reason I used James's address was that I didn't
want to get rejected. And, honestly, the debts wouldn't
have been a problem. If you move abroad they stop chasing you after eighteen years like with student loans, so all I
had to do was never come back. It just gets written off and
added to the interest rates or whatever. There was absolutely no need for him to react like that.

I stack the dirty glasses from my walkabout in the
washer. I love this machine because everything comes out
hot and steamy with a subtle lemon flavour. When I open
it it's like being at a spa or something. I use this relaxing
chore to get a handle on myself. If Chris leaves, I don't
know if I can track him down again.

I stay crouching, looking at the line of glasses in the top
rack. A realisation dawns . . . Chris's mouth is currently

squishing around something that I've handled repeatedly; filling, collecting, washing. We are intrinsically interconnected. Then suddenly, without preamble, it's happening. Chris has walked over to the bar and is leaning over it talking to me.

'I remember you – you've changed your hair. From the buses.'

Okay.

In college we learned about situational dependent memory. How people remember things better if they're in the same state they learned them: happy, sad, caffeinated – drunk. It seems Chris only knows me at a certain blood alcohol level. I stand up and I'm waiting for him to ask for his jumper back but he's paused now. He's looking at my name badge with his hairy eyebrows scrunched. I raise mine like 'What?' Chris laughs. I don't laugh in case it's a trick, but I feel nice, not suspicious.

'I don't think that's your name.'

Chris is pointing at my chest and now Pete is looking at it too.

'Sophie,' I say, and then—

'Sophie,' says Chris straight afterwards. Well well well.

Red Mouth has come over but I don't even mind. She is juicy-smiling and saying that they want to go somewhere dancing and don't the clocks go backwards tonight? Chris laughs and tells her they went back ages ago, and I join in and say, 'They don't go back again!'

Pete is scowling and waiting for me to notice but I'm busy. I tell her beautiful face that they should go across to The Pilgrim because they have music until 1 a.m. And I wasn't trying for anything, I don't have a strategy. I think

I'm actually living in the moment and maybe that's why it works because:

'Come meet us there when you finish,' Chris says.

And I say yes.

After Chris and his friends have left it's like being in the cinema after a film. Ejected. All the characters and story gone somewhere else and forgotten you already. The lights come back on and you're nowhere except a chair, surrounded by snack litter. Every good film should have a dull fifteen minutes or so at the end to help you reacclimatise. The last scenes should show people in traffic jams or buying stamps in the post office. But I guess then they wouldn't be good films anymore. Everyone would say 'It started okay' or 'Could've been quarter of an hour shorter.' I am always so impressed when people criticise films because it's like they have an actual personality and thoughts they can be sure of.

'Is your name Sophie?!'

I do not want a confrontation with Pete. All I want is to finish work, wrap some cutlery and go to The Pilgrim. I might get half an hour to dance and I'll grin at Chris and his friends and it will feel like This Is Life, This Is Living. And maybe we'll have a rollie outside and we can talk about what happened in Australia and I can say 'Oh we were so drunk, just a mistake, let's be friends' and then I won't feel bad about it anymore and carry that heavy shame remembering that he didn't turn up the next day or reply to my text.

'Sophie?! **Sophie??!**'

Pete's being sarcastic now, and too loud. There's another man waiting at the bar; he's wearing a green duffel coat and pretending not to notice Pete so I do the same and pour him the red wine he wants. It's £7.60 and I mentally tell him to give me a tip or say 'One for yourself' because sometimes that does work. I wish very hard and look in the man's eyes as I tell him the price and then again when I give him the change and I think he gets scared because he walks away really quickly. Matilda could've done it. But I don't mind because I've realised how to deal with Pete. I step over to him and lower my voice.

'Witness protection.'

I straighten Abi's name badge.

'I'm sure you understand.'

Pete's reaction is gormless and not worth describing. I turn away and open the glass washer. I enjoy my lemon steam and remember the programme *Stars in Their Eyes* – Tonight, Matthew, I am going to be grown-up and in control. I respect myself for a moment then feel sad and sorry that some people are so lonely and there isn't enough love in the world for everyone.

To whom it may concern,

Last week we received an 'anonymous' letter purporting
to be from a member of staff at The Slipper claiming to be
concerned about the behaviour of one or more of our officers.
The Metropolitan Police take all such allegations extremely
seriously.

However, as we have so few details to go on, there is no
way of taking this complaint further, especially as no officers
were mentioned by name.

I must stress we do not doubt the anonymous letter-writer,
especially as they were in possession of unpublicised details
of several recent local cases. We would be grateful if all
pub staff understand that anything overheard from off-duty
police officers remains strictly confidential and should not
be repeated or shared under any circumstances. We have
reminded our officers that they represent their position in the
community even when decompressing after work and feel
assured that no untoward or unprofessional behaviour will
occur in future.

If any of these measures are found to be unsatisfactory, I
would urge the complainant to visit us at the station and be
more specific about their allegations.

Yours in service,

Patricia Cornish,
Deputy Assistant Commissioner, Ilford High Street

I've never wrapped cutlery so fast – I'm hardly even enjoy-ing it. I sip my second black sambuca and laugh at Kermit as he clears the tables doing Alan Partridge impressions. Nadia let me have her drink, which is why I got two. She is mopping with one hand on her belly and I know I can't ask but I also know she's being pretty obvious about it. 'Oh I mustn't, I <u>CAN'T</u> have mine,' she said when Kermit offered, not even making an excuse about antibiotics.

I don't join in with Kermit even though I know all of Lynn's lines. I'm refreshing my memory, going over what happened in Australia. I'm worried I'll be caught out if Chris asks me something later. I was there to visit my dad (lie) who lives in Sydney (lie). I really liked the beaches and wine (true). I was enjoying my freedom after a hurtful break-up (lie, but later true) and then all the icky stuff after the kiss but I won't bring that up and I'll pretend I don't know what he's talking about if he does.

After all the chasing on buses it didn't feel odd to be fol-lowing Chris on a plane. When I landed I felt relieved to be in the same country as him again; I checked the locations of all his social media posts and marked them on a guide-book. I was a love detective and my heart beat so forcefully the first night I couldn't get to sleep. My blood reverberat-ed through me and the bed and shook the walls. I had too much emotion for my body – it was earthquake-sized. It was as powerful as lightning and very uncomfortable.

I started to get unsettled my second day in Sydney
when it occurred to me that Australia might be a trick.
The people could be actors putting on stupid voices and
the different streets and shops just set dressing. Maybe I
was still in England but they'd redecorated the place while
I was on the plane? But that was the jet lag and eventually
I accepted that Australia was real because financially the
trick would have cost many millions and why would anyone invest all that money just to humiliate me?

Unfortunately – here is the problem with my brain –
even though I knew I probably *wasn't* being watched,
I couldn't escape the feeling of being in some kind of
experiment. That's why I waited for five days before finding Chris. It had to seem accidental or *incidental* to anyone
observing.

Over those five days I used my acting to play the part of
'woman who wants to be in Australia (and believes Australia is real)'. I went for loads of walks. I looked up when I
heard parrots and told myself, 'Hear that exotic noise, wow,
okay', and waited to be filled with the sublime. I faked
smiles and expressions of wonder when I thought I should
and I gasped to myself like 'That's quite profound' when
I saw the sea or a mountain. I thought a lot about what I
should do with my face if I ever saw a dolphin.

Inside I was numb and I was bored. There were cockroaches everywhere, even restaurants and public toilets. I
stayed in a hostel and didn't shower for four days because
they can run up walls and across the ceiling and they're
loud, their feet clack like they're in heels, and they can
fly!!! A massive black one came out of the toilet when I
was about to sit down and if that's set dressing then it's

gone too far. I omitted cockroaches from my diary because I was telling it fibs about having an amazing time. The thing about my diary, I realised a few years ago, is that it isn't for me, it's for my future biographer. That's why I keep lots of supporting documents, receipts, important emails, letters and stuff like that. Also, there are so many details I leave out – because I don't want them in my biography. For instance, there was a girl in the bunk above me who farted in her sleep through the night. It's hard to feel you're a romantic and brave adventurer living an exceptional life when a stranger is blowing off above your head.

I was so lonely I started fantasising about getting murdered. Mum and James and Dana would be sad, thinking I'd gone all that way to heal my heart and been stabbed in it instead. Dad would be destroyed, surely, believing I was on my way to see him and so it was all his fault. Chris would find out – someone from the buses would DM him saying 'Weren't you friends with Sophie did you hear she's been murdered?' Or maybe a local paper would have my picture on the front and he would see it when he popped to the shops for a tobacco pouch and regret that he hadn't known I was so close by and that he could have protected me.

Tears are prickling behind my eyes imagining Chris wishing he'd got to know me better, which is stupid because I didn't even die. I unwrap the knife and fork I'm holding and leave them naked on the table while I dab my eyes. I'm not crying anymore, I'm smiling because I'm going to see him in a minute and this is *crazy*. I love black sambuca.

I wrote my diary every day in a café that put coffee in glasses. When I'd finished I would use the computers at the back to email James. I spent ages on the language of my self-expression, telling him about my emotions and how complicated they were. How the decision to come away had been hard but that it was making me grow, which was both painful and good. I was working towards the break-up but I wanted to see how it went with Chris first. I thought, and I know this is selfish, but I thought I'd come across as more confident if I still had a boyfriend. James replied with curt spiky sentences – 'Okay then good luck with your dad' – because he was upset with me. James was angry that I'd gone without him and hadn't told him I was going til the day before. But I'd been worried about him being pissed off or asking how I could afford it and stuff.

I found Chris in a bar on day six. He was with three male friends. The bar had green leafy plants and chairs in leopard-print patterns. He was expecting me – I'd messaged him, super-casual, deft and brief: 'Am in Sydney, let me know if you're still about, Soph from Buses.' He'd replied saying come for a drink and so I had. He was incredibly tanned and had adopted a dog; it was all so relaxed and easy. He was drinking pale ale with fruit floating in it and giving me his full attention. He couldn't believe I was in town alone – ah, he was sorry to hear about my break-up. He teased me about the big London books I used to read and I told him all the goss about how Connie had been sacked cos Phil caught her napping through a tour. I put all our drinks on my credit card and Chris was really grateful because he was skint and hadn't been working. I told him my dad had given me money and he asked, 'What does your dad do?' I couldn't think of a good lie so I said he was a drummer for The Rolling Stones. Chris thought that was amazing and told me all about the music he liked while occasionally touching me on the arm. His friends left and then the bar was closing. Chris wasn't leaving, he was still looking at me and talking, and he said we should meet at the beach tomorrow to swim and play with the dog and he put his 'Aussie' number into my phone and then we walked outside.

I wish I could see the CCTV; I wish I could know how it happened. What I did, or whether it was him – how we went from not kissing, because we weren't, not each other, not anyone, and then suddenly our mouths were squashed together. Did I see him coming, what did I think, was I surprised? Victorious? Why didn't it go slow-motion so I could remember all the details? But I didn't even notice until it was already happening and then it was a bit like with the parrots. I told myself, 'Experience this, you're kissing Chris, that mouth you saw in the distance by St Paul's, here it is close up on your face.' He was a good kisser, I remember that, but I don't know if any kiss is worth a trip to Australia. Maybe I only think that because it all got tarnished by what happened afterwards?

I wrote up the kiss in my diary. I stayed up in the common room of the hostel getting every detail down so that I'd never forget it. Then I tore the pages out of the book and wrote a completely different version, just in case. I was worried that my future biographer might judge me for cheating on James and not want to be my friend – I want my biographer to like me. I haven't worked out what I'm going to achieve yet, to warrant this biography. Poor little Past Sophie scribbling away full of joy in that common room with no idea of the shitstorm that was about to descend.

But now I'm getting ready to go and see Chris again. I've come to the customer toilets to put make-up on even though we're not allowed in here. I've been granted a second chance, another chapter, a different ending. Or beginning? No, ending ending ending, make it all better. I only have mascara and blusher with me but I do what I can. A bit of blush for eye shadow and on my lips and smudge mascara like eyeliner on my bottom lashes to accentuate that I've got eyes. I'm considering going for a wee but I don't wanna disturb the equilibrium down there – the sambuca has taken the edge off. I think the problem with haemorrhoids is that they're too much of a reminder. Of what I am: a skeleton with meat on it, a gristly tube. A winding, meaty tube from mouth to bumhole. Inside we're all basically a worm and that's why it's so hard to be confident or feel pretty. I hope it *is* haemorrhoids and not itchy cancer because I'm too humiliated to go to the doctor.

Nadia comes in and says, 'These ones are for customers only' – but in a nice way, like she's acknowledging how silly the rules are and that sometimes even staff deserve a toilet with mirrors and a hand dryer. Nadia glances over at the open cubicles but doesn't go in, probably because she doesn't want me to hear her piss. She's standing by the sink right next to me and I'm embarrassed to look in the mirror in case it seems like I love myself. I was planning to take my hair down and fluff it around a bit, but I don't want to look like I reckon I'm in a hair advert or something. I want to leave but I don't know how so we're both trapped. I root through my bag as if I'm searching for something, find some broken headphones and put them in my coat pocket.

'Thanks for drinking my drink for me.'

Did I not thank her enough? Why bring it up again? I tell her cheers very much and that I'm going out, so it's much appreciated. Then I ask if she's got any chewing gum because we're still both in here and I don't have anything else to say. Nadia shakes her head no.

'I can't drink at the moment.'

I take my hair out of my ponytail. I didn't decide to, my hands did it of their own accord while I was thinking 'One of us needs to leave or we'll both be in the toilets forever.' I've noticed this happening more and more ever since Ian told me there is no free will. I argued with him, of course, and said there definitely *is* free will. People decide stuff every day and have opinions and make choices between things. Ian's highly intelligent, which used to be attractive. He smirked as I was getting worked up and said that they know, the scientists, from watching on machines, that the brain gives instructions to do things <u>first</u> and then thinks up the reason why afterwards. They watched which parts of the brain were lighting up and the first stage was like the muscles and physical instructions for something, e.g. MOVE ARM. Then the second stage was the explanation: YOU MOVED ARM BECAUSE YOU ARE ITCHY AND NEED A SCRATCH, or because you were dancing or whatever. It's do first, make a reason afterwards. I don't agree with this, by the way, but Ian says no one is really making their own decisions, we just think we are. That really it's bacteria. They live inside us in every nook and cranny and all our lives are for them and what they need and want and now my hair is hanging down limply in a ponytail shape so I hope they're happy.

'You can't tell anyone . . .'

I look at Nadia but not in real life, in the mirror. Like how hairdressers talk to your reflection and you talk to theirs. I think this makes it easier for them to criticise people's faces.

'I got pregnant.'

'Oh, congratulations.'

'No, it's shit, it's so shit. I feel sick.'

I tell poor Nadia how sorry I am and I am so sorry but I also want to run away and take big gulps of air and maybe even leap while crossing the road or waiting at the traffic lights because I'm so glad I'm not her. She says she has to wait three weeks til she can get the operation on the NHS and all she can eat is crisps because she's so nauseous.

'But the worst thing is the not drinking.'

It occurs to me that if there really wasn't any free will then biographies would all just say 'They went over there because bacteria made them, they did this and that because of the bacteria' and no one would read them. I must remember to say this to Ian later.

Nadia is looking at herself in the mirror now, into her own eyes, all miserable. I wonder if she is thinking 'So this is what I look like when I'm pregnant and wish I could have a Pinot Grigio.' She's very pretty with her shiny blonde hair. A round little face and straight white teeth like an albino piano. She looks like a baby herself, a sexy, grown-up one. I want to ask who got her pregnant but that feels rude. It's like asking 'Who put their penis in you?' I wonder if it was Kermit and that's why she doesn't want the baby. I accidentally start imagining Kermit and Nadia having sex on the floor by the glass wash with all the steam

rolling out above them, then I remember I'm in a conversation. I pat Nadia on her shoulder and she grips my hand. I explain that she can drink if she wants, that it doesn't matter – but she interrupts.

'You're not allowed when you're pregnant—'

'But that's only if you're keeping it.'

Nadia doesn't believe me; she's being super-dumb. She's absorbed this piece of information and cannot let it go. All the propaganda about women not drinking in pregnancy has gone too far – this is ridiculous. Nadia can't compute that you don't need to preserve the health of a baby who will never exist. I fluff my hair a bit now, meet my own eye in the mirror and a zap of nerves hits my belly: I'm going to see Chris.

I carry on the conversation because I know what I'm going to do with it.

G'Day Mate!!! As the locals say.

Sorry we missed you this morning, we left for the airport really early and tried to be quiet not to wake the rest of you.

I'm glad you stayed in the bar for a bit last night and we got to know a bit about you — you've been so mysterious scuttling to and from the internet café. And I'm sorry if we seemed insensitive.

It's just that all the stuff you were saying about this guy being 'a leap of faith' and 'your destiny' was a bit unhinged. You did sound like a religious fanatic or something. But perhaps we should have been kinder because you are clearly going through something. So please accept my apology.

And I've left $12 of currency because we wont need it.

Love Freja (the girl in the top bunk) xx

'And so she's saying, "I don't wanna harm the baby!" and I'm saying, "What d'ya think the abortion's gonna do?!"'

Chris, Ella (lips) and Steve (goatee) are really drunk now and laughing at my story. I've got a glass of wine that Steve bought when I arrived as a 'thank you for all the Baileys' and we laughed then too. This is going so well, I can't believe how natural it feels but also like something from a film. I have a tiny niggle that if this was edited together, me promising Nadia I wouldn't tell anyone and then crossing the road to make fun of her, it does look bad. I'd be one of the two-faced people on *Big Brother* or *Love Island*. I would not come across well in my montage. I look around in case Nadia has followed me and notice someone has taped mistletoe above the till, which must be hell for the bar staff, especially if any of Pete's colleagues drink here.

The Pilgrim is a nice pub. In the daytime there are lots of places to sit and it's quite normal – people eat jacket potatoes and read newspapers. Fridays and Saturdays they move the tables at 8 p.m. and put on disco lights and loud music and then people lean against pillars or stand up unassisted. No one actually dances, or if they do it's a man completely off his nut going for it on his own. Sundays there's a pub quiz at 6 p.m. which I come to with Ian and that I used to come to with James and I suppose I'll bring my next boyfriend too. It's quite good for conversation, a pub quiz; it's all 'How did you know that?!' or 'How did you not know that?!' and they explain 'I did my work experience at the British Museum' or 'I'm number dyslexic' and then you know each other a bit better.

I've never been here on a Friday night before. I've walked past after work and looked through the window. Some people find being alive effortless, that's what I think. Especially people viewed through windows eating meals or drinking drinks or even watching TV if you're looking into a house. They don't mean to make you feel an outsider, you just do because you're outside. But tonight I'm an inside person. I try to look out the window but it's too dark, I can only see inside reflected. I see me leaning on a pillar holding a wine glass. I can see the back of Chris and Ella, and Steve's grinning face between their shoulders. I wish I could walk past and envy me.

I look down at my feet, at my flat sensible work shoes. A wave of shame wriggles through my guts. Then I see my right foot is tapping to the music, which doesn't make sense – I hate Christmas songs. What a traitor my right foot is. Christmas is a lie, and the catchy songs are propaganda. Yes, we promise life is magical and cold weather is magical and you are treasured and reindeer fly. My parents did the decent thing and refused to gaslight me. At school they told us about Jesus and Father Christmas and we came home and Mum and Dad said, 'No, absolutely not, it's all bullshit.' I wonder if society would execute a woman who said she hated Christmas?

Steve is staring at me. 'I'm Jewish,' he says, like it's an explanation.

Was I talking out loud? I'm surprised he could hear me over the rocking around the decked halls. The only good thing about the seasonal music is that it's so loud we have to shout, which makes what we're saying seem really important, like it's triple-underlined. Chris and Ella are shouting about their job. It's at the golf club. I've never been there and Ella shouts, 'OH YOU SHOULD COME DOWN SOMETIME.'

I imagine myself turning up with all the kit and checked pantaloons like a lonely businessman. They laugh when I laugh. Ella isn't with Chris, by the way. I didn't ask, but twice she's mentioned her fiancé so she must have a fiancé. Steve I know nothing about except that he has a goatee, he's Jewish and he's not particularly good at conversation. He stares for ages then shouts a question like 'DO YOU LIKE DOGS?' or 'WHAT ARE YOU ALL LAUGHING ABOUT?'

I am going slowly on the wine. Pacing myself because I don't want to say anything stupid and I don't want to need the loo in case they leave without me. Also I can't afford another one because I don't get paid until New Year's Eve. I know I should text Ian but I worry if I get my phone out he'll already have texted saying 'Where are you?' or 'Do you want pasta?' and then I'll have to deal with that and feel bad. It's only twelve-ish. We could have had a police incident at the pub again and had to give statements.

'I DO LIKE DOGS,' I shout at Steve, keeping it simple. But it's more complicated than that. I have a long history with dogs, and it's love not like, or not *love* but deep, deep guilt. I don't know how much to tell him – I can't say the full story as I know how Ella and Chris will look at me like 'Woah, this woman is fucked up.' Then they'll always remember and make fun of me down the golf club whenever a dog comes in.

I think about a dog in checked pantaloons for a second and then change the conversation, keeping it light.

'I USED TO THINK MY MUM COULD SEE ME THROUGH THE CAT.'

Steve smiles while Chris and Ella laugh again and I'm encouraged. I know this is a funny story so that's alright, this is fine. Chris laughing is so magnificent – he throws his head back like a pony and his nostrils tremble and it feels like we're friends, who exist, and everything embarrassing is undone. I must have imagined how awkward it was in Australia. I've been carrying that cringe around in my stomach for three years. I make myself remember it now and nothing happens; I don't shudder and want to die. Because Chris is here – right there! – his face flushed and crinkled as he listens to my story.

'WE HAD A CAT CALLED SOOTY AND WHENEVER HE WAS WITH ME I WOULD BEHAVE AND NOT STEAL OR LIGHT FIRES BECAUSE I THOUGHT HE WAS A ROBOT WITH CAMERAS IN HIS EYES THAT MY MUM WAS USING TO SPY ON ME.'

Ella says she's worried about where the story is going.

'YOU DIDN'T CUT YOUR CAT OPEN DID YOU?'

I laugh to reassure her.

'NO NO IT'S FUNNY BECAUSE SOOTY WAS ALWAYS LOOKING AT ME WHEN I WAS ON THE TOILET OR GETTING CHANGED WHY WOULD MY MUM WANT TO SEE THOSE THINGS?!!'

Chris says something to Ella but I can't hear because he has forgotten to shout.

'AND THEN I NOTICED ABBAS IN MY CLASS HAD EXACTLY THE SAME EYES AS SOOTY.'

Chris thinks he's guessed what was going on.

'ABBAS WAS A ROBOT TOO?'

I tell him he's wrong. Then Ella's worrying again.

'YOU DIDN'T CUT ABBAS OPEN DID YOU?'

'NO I JUST GOT CHANGED IN THE BATHROOM AND DIDN'T LET SOOTY COME IN SO ABBAS COULDN'T PERV ON ME.'

I knew the story was funny but not *this* funny. It's because I've taken out the sad bits like when my mum stroked Sooty and said if she'd known cats were so affectionate she never would have had us.

They're all laughing and even nudging each other a bit and it's going so well I decide to tell them about the old woman who died in the bath but I make it me who found her, not Pete, and I make the old woman my grandmother, but that one doesn't go as well. I think that's a story for a quieter venue like The Slipper.

Chris is shaking his head thoughtfully, like 'Wow', taking it all in, and then Ella is shouting it's her round.

'I'M GOING TO THE BAR WHAT DO WE ALL WANT?'

I look away as I'm not expecting to be included, and I should probably go in a minute or at least check my phone, but Ella points in my face and shouts, 'WHITE?'

My gosh she really is the loveliest woman I've ever met. I've not even finished the last glass so I'll have one and a half wines now. I'm so happy. I celebrate by walking off to find the toilets.

I sit down and fold over, elbows on knees, head in my

hands, and look down at the floor while I piss. I'm checking for cockroaches, a habit that has never left me. They will never surprise me ever again because they're always there, crawling hypothetically in my peripheral vision. Haunting the edges of my life with their potential appearance. I wipe carefully, getting away with it, it's not hurting. I flush and accidentally open the door too hard and it crashes on the outside of the cubicle and swings back in at me. The toilets are empty. I avoid looking in the mirror because I'm feeling brilliant and don't want to ruin it with the truth of my face. I don't wash my hands since there's no one here to judge me. I walk back up the stairs two at a time and then quickly through the bar, thinking about Chris's face when he laughs and then about that black horse on the banking advert whose hair trails in the wind as she gallops up the beach.

I get a **jolt** of adrenaline because they've gone—

—but then I see Chris. He's moved to a different pillar; it has a ledge on it for drinks and there is a big new white wine next to my half-drunk old one.

'I'M A HALF-DRUNK OLD ONE!' I shout as I approach Chris. I thought it was a funny play on words, but when he doesn't react I realise the joke only works if you were in my head hearing the words used in their other context. I pick up the new glass and swig like this has all been intentional and then Chris comes out with something stunning. I am stunned.

'YOU CAME OUT TO AUSTRALIA DIDN'T YOU?'

It's happening.

'YEAH.'

I leave it at that. Maybe that's all that needs to be said.

I look around for Ella and she's at the bar with Steve. They're talking intently and I'm worried it's about me or maybe Abbas. I turn back to Chris and his head is quite near mine and he's looking at me. I can smell his soapy aftershave and it's the same one from before and I can't believe my nose is allowed to suck it in, for free! I'm going to ask what it is and buy it for Ian, but not yet, it will have to be casual. I ask him something else.

'DID YOU HAVE A GOOD TIME OUT THERE?'

He grins like *finally* someone asked him about Australia and he starts telling me about Sydney and how he had a dog called Jasper and spent all day on the beach and how he learned to surf and made so many friends. He tells me he was there for over three years like I didn't know, like I don't know all of this. Ella and Steve come back over and Steve jokes about how Chris is off on one about his time in *Australasia* again and he draws out the word Australasia and is putting on a funny voice but it's not funny because he's trying too hard like someone in a sketch show. Chris shouts, telling Ella and Steve, 'SOPHIE AND I HUNG OUT IN SYDNEY.'

I'm stunned again and I'm wary. He remembers everything and I am not on safe ground.

'Ohhhhhh YEAH . . .'

I handled that really well, I think; the wine is helping my brain by dulling it. I take a big swig from the old glass and remember my manners. I thank Ella for such a nice big new wine and I thank Steve again for the old warm one. Being grateful makes me happy. I am the correct size and in the right place. I'm flooded with assuredity, assurity? Assuredness that I *can*, I can handle this. It's just a short conversation with someone that I thought I was in love with, but I wasn't, it was just obsession. A short chat and then the matter is done, put to bed, close the drawer, slam the toilet lid, done. And I'll never think about it again. I won't need to. I can just enjoy his smell on Ian and move on with my life.

'I WENT TO SEE MY DADS.'

Oops. I'm sure no one will pick up on it.

'YOUR DAD IS GAY?'

Okay, Chris picked up on it, and then Steve.

'TWO DADS?'

So I'm telling them all about it and how hard it was at first but how happy I am to see him settled and in love and true to himself and they are both nodding and believing me and won't guess I accidentally said 'dads' because I'm drunk now. Which I don't know when that happened.

'MY DAD LIVES SO FAR AWAY BUT WE'RE STILL CLOSE.'

I *am* close to my dad because I really love him even if he doesn't know it. So I'm not lying. And I don't worry about him being invited to my funeral anymore because Mum won't remember that I asked. I know she will invite Dad because she wants him to see how much taller Ron is than him. In my opinion, Ron is horrific. He's a duty solicitor, which means he goes to the police station and gets criminals off, even if they did it. Which is fine if it's burglars or whatever but even if it's a rapist he still saves them. So that they're free and still out there – and Mum doesn't see anything wrong with that. I think Ron is the one who should go to prison. Of course Dana likes him and is always telling him about her 'legal background' even though it was only an A-level. And one win in the small claims court.

Ella has been quiet since all the Australia talk and I can see she's reassessing me. No, I'm not just a barmaid, Ella, I am someone Chris *knows*. I put my arm through hers so we're standing arm in arm. I don't remember deciding, this is bacteria again – maybe they get more confident with wine, or louder with loud Christmas songs. Ella's pulled me in by squeezing with her elbow and I squeeze back and we are laughing and Chris shouts, 'WHAT?' And we get hysterical and I hope we're laughing at the same thing, which is that Chris <u>cannot be trusted</u>. Stick together, girls, and don't wait around on the beach in Bondi because he won't turn up and you'll get sunburn on your scalp and ears and the tops of your feet and you'll cry for ages walking home feeling made of heavy grey and still looking around and hoping to see him and find out he had a good excuse like his dog ran away or he got run over. And now I know she does like him, fiancé or not, because she's being weird like me.

Chris was rolling a cigarette while I was talking but I didn't notice because I am intentionally not looking at him – I'm watching Ella Red Mouth to see how often she looks at him – so I don't notice til he waves it in my face: Chris has rolled me a fag and I think that is the most *thoughtful*, sweetest thing anyone could ever do. Ella drops my arm. Not annoyedly, no, but definitely on purpose. If I were her I would just start smoking. It's so lame and I hope no one ever finds out, but Chris *was* the reason I started smoking. I used to watch him through the window of the lunch bus and try and think of an excuse to go out there and one day

I realised the excuse was right there in his hand. But now it's now and we're walking out to the smoking area and we each push a door and suddenly we're outside and on our own. There's only about five other people out here and we don't know them.

The music is quieter here. We're at the back entrance of the pub where there are cars parked, it's probably where the staff park their cars – a car park. But this corner near the door has some orange cones in a square to let us know where to stand. Or maybe to protect us if the cars come to life.

'I WONDER IF CARS WOULD RESPECT THE HIGH-WAYS CODE IF THEY CAME BACK TO LIFE?'

I don't need to shout but I'm so used to it. Chris asks if I think cars used to be alive and I don't know what the hell he's on about so I use his lighter. Fetid hot ash dust is in my mouth and my tongue and lungs are regretting this decision so I swig wine, puff again, and now we're talking. We are actually talking; about bus tours, and Jack the Ripper theories and global warming, and then Chris says:

'So Sydney.'

Oh shiiit, I'm talking to Chris about what happened in Sydney. I've had this conversation over and over again in my head and now it is happening. Unless I'm insane and merely imagining it happening but more realistically this time. This is the problem with really wishing for something a lot, because if you do get it one day, after thinking about it over and over again, you feel mad.

What I wish I knew – I can't ask him, of course, obviously – but what I wish I knew is how it happened. One minute we were in Sydney, he was talking and I was checking about for cockroaches, and then suddenly we're kissing. I want to see the camera footage. I want to know HOW. How you can get so near to someone that you're kissing them.

It must be the bacteria; they must take over at opportune times and drive people like we're mechanical diggers. The bacterias are invested in our physical connections as that is how they make more peoples for them to live in, it's like building houses for themselves – I will tell Ian when I get home it's my new theory.

From: ianhoughton@gmail.com
To: sscollins@gmail.com
Subject: Where u?

Beastie-

have texted & called & I'm getting worried now. You should have been home over ninety minutes ago & u r not answering your phone. Can u just message me back so I know where u are? I don't know what to do or where else to check. I keep thinking about that creepy police bloke and hoping he hasn't offered u a lift or something and then u got in his car. Doesn't matter what u r doing as long as I know & then I can go to bed. I xxx

The driver (Jackson, 4.2 stars) has the windows open and is singing along to 'I Want It That Way' by the Backstreet Boys. The other three are in the back together. I can't hear what they're talking about. I take some deep breaths, sucking cold air up my nose like refreshing water that smells like car exhausts. What am I doing here, apart from trying not to be sick? I said I'd pay for the cab to say thank you for all the drinks, thus inviting myself onwards with them, although, I think I was invited. Or at least Ella presumed. I'm so far over my overdraft the fare will definitely be rejected but we'll be out of the car by then, so it's the least I could do. This is fine, I'm having fun. I need to text Ian. I'm allowed to go out, and have friends and do things, I've done nothing wrong, no, just say hey mate, I'm out, chill sleep I'll see you in the morning— Where's my bag? I put my phone in my bag where *is* my bag I had it when we waited, when, in the toilets – hang on.

'Where's my bag is my bag with you?'

Chris, Steve and Ella check under their legs and Jackson sings a bit louder.

'I've lost bag, my bag can we go back?'

Ella says we're nearly at hers like that's my answer.

'I don't have my door keys . . .'

No one says anything else. Jackson presses a button when the song finishes and it starts again. Steve joins in, then we all do.

When we pull up, Ella, Chris and Steve get out, exclaiming 'Thanks' and 'What a legend' and for a split second I think they mean me. I get out. I don't shut the car door properly and have to have a second go. They're already walking up the path a few feet away, talking and laughing.

I can't get another Uber because I don't have my phone.

I'll walk. I'll walk back to The Pilgrim and it'll only take half an hour or an hour and if I get murdered at least Ian can't be annoyed with me. And I have a good excuse now: I lost my bag, or my bag was stolen. Maybe I'll walk all the way home and say I was mugged and—

'You can sleep here.'

Ella's hanging out of her front door.

'Don't stress about your keys, we'll call the pub in the morning. I'll drive you down.'

I don't know how to reject her offer so I'm walking towards her on automatic-pilot legs. I tell my face to smile.

Once we are in her living room Ella is flitting around lighting candles with Chris's Zippo. Her flat is nice. Really nice. I'm sipping the pint of water she made me, trying not to compliment everything my eyes land on. She's got a table pushed up against the window in the corner; it's got a lamp on it and a massive ceramic bowl on a pile of arty books. Chris is sitting there skinning up. I hope he doesn't think I shouldn't be here; I hope since our chat he thinks I'm normal. I told him I was several times. Steve is on the sofa, which is creamy leather and has a grey wool rug folded over the arm. Does Ella snuggle there drinking tea, looking at all of her things and knowing how lucky she is? Where is her telly? I look around but all I see are books on shelves and a blue-tiled fireplace and bunches of flowers in vases and who lives like this? Even her Christmas tree is classy – all the tinsel is white and all the ornaments are silver.

'Your tree looks like she's getting married,' I tell Ella, but she doesn't react. 'Or like she's a friend of Princess Diana.'

Ella gives Chris back his lighter and he squeezes her hand without looking at her. Steve is staring at the place their hands touched, the air their hands met in, even though it's empty now. What's he thinking about? I wonder if he's secretly interesting. I should have asked him a Jewish question because I don't know anything except the sex-through-a-sheet thing and apparently that's not true. I could ask him if *he* knows it's not true, then Ella says, 'Let's get this party started' and fiddles with her phone and then music comes from somewhere – it's some kind of French rap, which I didn't know was possible. Chris nods approvingly. Steve moves to the table next to Chris cos he's noticed the joint is ready. I hope this *is* a party and not an orgy. I hate orgies. That was James's kinda thing.

I'm standing here not knowing what to do. The candles smell very heavy and oily. I don't have my bag. Ella says, 'Let's go make some cocktails' to me and I follow her to the kitchen, where there is yet another table. I lean against it but it wobbles so I sit down while she's opening blue cupboard doors. I wonder if I'll ever have loads of stuff.

'Are you feeling okay?'

I tell her the water is helping, that I'm fine, just tired. Ella is grating ginger and bragging about what she's going to make and how it's going to perk me right up. I tell her how much I like her lipstick and thank you for being so nice to me. She says, 'Anything for a friend of Chris's.' Then there's an empty silence like I've done something wrong.

I don't know how to get the conversation back on track. Ella's chopping a lime with her back to me; I'm watching her shoulder blades sliding around under her silky black top. Shall I ask about the golf club or how she got so rich or if she knows Samantha Mumba or The Corrs?

'We came in specially to see you tonight – he saw you through the window a couple of weeks ago.'

My brain is too slow for this, I can't absorb what she's saying. She's still saying it.

'He was a dick pretending not to remember youse – I think he was just nervous.'

I'm not mental, this is real. Unless I'm *really* mental.

'But he didn't tell me about Australia . . .'

Ella turns her lovely face to me now. It's like I've known her forever. I really trust her. She only just met me yet she really cares and looks out for me.

'It's really embarrassing,' I confess.

'Tell me.'

So I do. About how I met Chris on the buses and then we bumped into each other on the other side of the world, and we had a drink because that's the friendly thing to do, and then we kissed.

Ella frowns as I say that part, so I know she's on my side.

'Just kiss?'

'Yeah, cos then he said he had a girlfriend—'

Ella and I say 'Irina' at the same time. The ice is melting in the glasses she's lined up.

'I never saw Chris again until tonight, until he turned

up by accident and pretended not to remember me, and now here we are!'

I thought Ella would laugh but she turns back to the drinks and starts pouring ginger beer and I think it's funny how the night has come full circle and now the customer is the bartender and I'm about to mention it but I've lost all my confidence. I'm floating deeper inside my brain, behind where all the words are.

Ella and I take two glasses each into the living room, where Steve and Chris are talking intently by the window. I give Steve a glass and try and give Chris the other one, but Ella already has her arm out and he chooses the glass in her hand. Which is fair because I've drunk from this one. It's a very tasty drink; I'm choking on it slightly, the ginger burns my throat. Chris takes a sip, passes me the rollie and gets up out of his chair so I can sit there and exhale out of the open window onto the shrubbery and the garden path.

I don't turn round to see where he goes. I'm sitting in his smell. I inhale and breathe out, craning my head to look for the moon, and tasting the smoke I realise this disgusting thing is a joint and how did I forget that? I saw him roll it. Shit. I don't want to make a fuss but I can't smoke any, I know what it does to me and I'm already so far from home without my bag or keys or phone. Steve is looking at me so I smoke a bit more and then pass it to him, hoping he won't pass it back. I swig instead and stand up. The room lurches a bit. My torso feels very heavy and precarious.

Chris and Ella are on the couch. My body starts plodding over there – stupid legs. Or bacteria. There's no room, where would I sit, abort abort. I grab the grey blanket and pretend that's what I wanted. Pop my glass on the coffee table and lurch across the room, drop down and make a nest in the far corner where a TV should be.

I close my eyes to come up with a plan. I won't fall asleep because once at a house party Hannah, one of the scarers, fell asleep on a beanbag and then she did such a long loud fart that it was louder than the karaoke and everyone laughed so much and Hannah didn't even wake up and Ian talks about it all the time and tries to do impressions with his mouth of how the fart sounded. It was more like quacking than farts. Like a row of angry ducks making themselves known. I always thought I should tell Hannah, but then I always thought why? Why do we need to know all these terrible things about ourselves? I think of the girl in the bed above me at the Sydney hostel. What was *she* doing there – was she looking for someone? Or sorting things out with her dad? She was so good at making friends with everyone by asking questions that she never said anything about herself.

What if everyone in Australia was only there because they loved Chris?

I wake up so I must have been asleep. I wince in horror about what my body might have done in my absence before an alarm goes off in my chest. Chris and Ella are talking. About me. It's darker in here now, only one candle left. I close my eyes again. I'm being paranoid. They're just whispering. It could be about anything; he could be telling her about the Great Fire of London or explaining how to pronounce Camus. Ella is easier to hear, less rumbly.

'I told her you'd come and found her in the pub on purpose.'

Rumble rumble. I can't make it out.

'She's clearly obsessed with you . . .'

More rumbling. He sounds pissed off, but very quietly.

'I think she's in love with you.'

'No, no – we hardly know each other—'

'You kissed her.'

'No I didn't—'

'In Australia.'

I've stopped breathing, I've given up on it forever. I pray for Steve to change the conversation with a parade of quacky farts.

'Fuck I forgot about that. It was so awkward. She tried to come home with me. Said she had nowhere to stay and had run out of money and—'

'God that's so awkward . . .'

'I was living with Irina so I had an excuse.'

'SO embarrassing . . .'

'She forgot I knew her dad lived in Sydney, I knew she had somewhere to sleep so—'

Then he's back to rumbling. Even she's rumbling now. My heart is loud and manic and I'm thumping with adrenaline while pretending to be asleep and wishing I was dead. And this is so shit because Chris is lying, or if not lying he's missing out important details. Like when he lent me his jumper and hugged me and rubbed my arms as we walked along. And the bit when he said, 'Let's meet up tomorrow yeah, we'll hang out on the beach all day and have a mini holiday romance while we can.'

He would not come across well in his montage.

I must have fallen asleep because I wake up again. I stretch my ears around to see if it's safe to move or open my eyes. The French rap is gone. There is breathing. I lift my head and see that Steve is curled up on the sofa, still wearing his shoes. I feel embarrassed for him. I get up and shake the blanket off onto the floor. It's lighter in here – there's white morning light streaking through the blinds and I'm going to go now. I swallow some curdy spit, concentrating on one foot then the next foot. Steve is watching as I walk towards the door. I'm trying to remember where I put my jacket. I can't think of what to say.

'Bye.'

That'll do. And then, oh. And oh no. And oh god. And panting. A different kind of rumbling. Steve's facial expression tells me he can hear it too. We've turned to each other like people in a film when they realise a herd of velociraptors is thundering over the hill and heading this way. 'What shall we do?' our eyes ask each other. So because I don't want him to think I'm obsessed with Chris, or even that I fancy him, I lower myself down on the arm of the sofa like that's where I was heading all along.

From DANA COLLINS
124 Arden Crescent
Gants Hill, ESSEX

COMPANY NAME

Place your text here

Date: 23 October 20—

To SOPHIE COLLINS
c/o Pippa Collins
124 Arden Crescent
Gants Hill, Essex

Subject: Summons and Complaints Letter

Respected Sir/Madam,

My plaintiff, Ms Dana Collins, has filed a complaint against you on the grounds of unpaid funds owed since May this year.

My plaintiff gave clear instruction that the loan was to be repaid in a timely manner and has time and again brought your notice to the owed amount and asked for assurance that it was to be repaid. When the loan was made an informal agreement was set as to repayment (as you are sisters). Since no effort has been made to refund Ms Collins on your part, the small claims court will be instructed to create a schedule for recompense of the full amount (£600) plus interest (£25) and reasonable administration costs (£60).

We expect a reply within two weeks of the date of this letter. I have attached the following documents with this letter:

1.   CC of emails from Dana Collins to Sophie Collins wishing to discuss repayment of loan.

2. CC of text messages from Dana Collins to Sophie Collins requesting small contributions towards loan repayment as goodwill gesture.
3. Bank statement showing transfer of £600 between Dana Collins' and Sophie Collins' bank accounts.

The date of the first court hearing has been set for 9 January 20—. We will proceed with formalities of depositions and investigations before the date of the hearing.

Thank you, yours faithfully, Dana Collins.

FREE LETTER TEMPLATE

Small Claims Summons and Complaint

I remember when I read *The Celestine Prophecy* it properly affected me and I kept telling people about it, but I can only remember a couple of bits now. I read it when we were in Lanzarote on holiday, James and I. Obviously I don't like my mind to wander back there, but it *was* a fantastic holiday. Everything in the hotel was free – everything behind the bar, everything spread out on the lunch buffet. You just asked for a drink and filled your plate and felt like you were consuming about six times more than you'd paid for. I was very relaxed, which is maybe why the book felt so spiritual. Also because Lanzarote really looks like the moon.

So one of the things I do remember from *The Celestine Prophecy* is that it described how some people grab your attention because they have a message for you. Not literally, like they're holding a fax or a telegram, but metaphorically. They're a kind of divine postman and by talking to them you can learn something important. The book said if you're catching someone's eye in a restaurant or a bar you should probably go over and say hello, because your energy is sparking with theirs. That's why I decide to listen to what Steve is saying, in case the universe is speaking to me through him.

'. . . and it was my brother's stag so a pretty big deal . . .'

I don't even know if I believe in energy, except to annoy Ian.

'. . . and my brother, he was excited to be taking me to his favourite place, his favourite place, it was a big deal . . .'

Steve's repeating himself a bit and I can't tell if he's angry or sad or just drunk.

They're still at it in the bedroom upstairs. They must know we can hear them, or they must not even care. It's positive, though, it's good that this happened. It proves to Chris that I don't fancy him, doesn't it? Otherwise I would've gone home or knocked on the door and asked them to stop. I decide to pretend it's a play. One of the promenade ones where you walk round and watch the acting close up. I once sat in a fake bedroom with a crazy woman who was suspicious of everyone and thought her wallpaper was moving. It was very realistic, reminded me of Mum.

'In the cab on the way we'd all got out and gone to the cashpoint and I'd withdrawn all my money, two twenty-pound notes, forty quid. My brother was proud and he was telling me the rules, he said enjoy yourself, don't touch them unless, well no, don't touch them, and at the end of the dance you give 'em the twenty, either in their hand or if you want you can fold it up and tuck it gently . . .'

Steve is miming tucking now but it looks more like using a tiny saw.

'When she, when we got in there the table was a booth, with all the padding on the seats, you know, and some girls – women, ladies – come over and sit with us, loads of them.'

What if it was a real mad woman and the theatre company were just pretending it was acting and charging people to go in and stare at her? She was saying how she was locked in the bedroom and trapped and maybe that was true. I'm trying to remember if her hair was dirty or only messy like an actress would do it.

'My brother's mate Daryll is ordering champagne and grinning and his eyes are glistening and I've never seen— like, his eyes are *glistening*, I've never seen anyone seem so happy!'

I don't know how we got on to strip clubs. This is weird cos I was thinking about them earlier and the name thing – maybe I brought it up and what he's telling me makes sense? I'll say the name thing again in case I haven't already.

'We're sitting on the table and drinking and three girls are talking to all of us. And they know our names and that my brother is getting married and that Daryll is best man and they've got a tequila bottle just for us and little glasses—'

'Strippers use fake names.'

Steve nods but doesn't react so I don't know if I said it before.

'My one was called Beryl.'

That sounds quite real, to be fair. I've got a cousin called Beryl.

'She was whispering in my ear . . .'

Steve is tickling his own ear now, his fingers a baby octopus.

'I'm leaning so close so I can hear her, she's saying I'm cute, I'm cute and handsome and no one young ever comes into the club and it's her lucky night. I'm thinking I'M LUCKY. I'm so lucky, I'm eighteen years old and I just met the love of my life and my wedding speech is going to be so funny when I say how we met at my brother's stag

– although Siobhan, his fiancée, she banned us. She didn't want us to go to a strip club and she bawled her eyes out and she's oh shit she's going to go bananas when she finds out at *my* wedding that we still went.'

The sex grunts have stopped. Steve is quiet for a moment. A door opens in the hall above us. The footsteps go along over our heads and then another door shuts.

'Beryl was asking questions about me, about what I liked and what I did, and I was telling her about my architecture degree, I was about to start an architecture degree in Southampton, I'd been predicted really good A-levels, and she was saying she'd never had such an interesting conversation.'

Steve sits up so he's looking forwards instead of at the ceiling. Maybe the story is about to get good.

'And Beryl says that she's having such a good time talking to me and feels such a connection—'

He's just bragging really, while I've accidentally started to picture my cousin Beryl in the story, which does change it a bit. She's about forty-three and five foot tall and drives a red Alfa Romeo. She works in Barclays, so if she's stripping on the side it'd be because she wants to not because she needs the money. She did get a boob job, though – maybe that's why she wanted it.

'—but she's going to get in trouble if she doesn't dance, her boss will tell her off if she doesn't dance, so can she dance for me?'

Steve's singing now. And clicking his fingers. He is a much much worse singer than I would have expected. It's all coming up through his nose like when a man on TV is pretending to be a woman, all high-pitched and unrealistic.

'That's her song, "Chandelier" by Rihanna.'

I should check if it's the same Beryl.

'Did she mention Barclays Bank at all?'

Steve doesn't hear me.

'She waves at the DJ and it suddenly comes on and my brother is watching her swaying between my legs and his mates are clapping along and cheering—'

I wonder if he got an erection.

'Did you get an erection?'

'No.'

The sound of water flushing quiets us again. A door opens, footsteps return along the hallway. A creaky door-swing and more footsteps. Mopping up, I expect. Or brushing their teeth. I wonder if we'll all have breakfast together in that nice kitchen. I think Steve's finished the story. He lies back down, but on his side this time with his head on his elbow. I wonder if he'll try to have sex with me. I don't want him to try cos I'm worried it'd be difficult to say no. It's happened to me before – too far from home and having to go along with it.

'It should have been embarrassing but Beryl made it fun. She was smiling at me, I was smiling back. She was dancing more softly than the music . . .'

Baby Octopus is back but swimming around this time, gliding in front of Steve's enraptured face. In my mind Cousin Beryl does the Macarena in her pants.

'. . . more like undulating. I closed my eyes with the bliss of it all. Finding each other, finding LOVE in this hellish disco. I felt the breeze of her moving in the air around me. She smelled of shampoo, and a bit like aniseed from the Aftershock we'd done.'

More footsteps above us but clompy this time, with shoes on. The feet descend the stairs and we both freeze, wondering what's coming. Then the front door slams and we both pretend not to care who's left.

'When the song changed she touched me here . . .'

Steve strokes the palm of his own hand while I feel sick. My head is hurting.

'We're smiling at each other and I've decided I'll ask her out, but not yet, I'll, I'll, when I'm leaving I'll write her a note—'

It must be Chris. Ella wouldn't leave her own house. Unless she's cycling to the bakery like in a cartoon? Maybe they'll have breakfast in bed while Steve and I are still sitting here in this awful real play.

'I thought it would be romantic. I thought she'd show all the other strippers and they'd be jealous that she'd found a good guy who was going to respect her and rescue her.'

Steve's laughing now, but in a choking way, like he hates himself. Maybe he is interesting?

'I thought I could invite her to come to Southampton with me. I decided to take her to Paris when my student loan came through. And Beryl is still smiling at me and touching my hand, and I see my brother is looking at me so I remember—'

The little-saw mime again.

'I know it's weird but I don't want her to get into trouble so I get out my wallet, and I hold it up quite high so the manager can see, wherever he is, or she is, and I get out the twenty and I fold it up tightly and I try to—'

He's tucking into the air.

'—but she swings away from me, and she's <u>furious</u>.

She's yanked her hand away and it's loud in there, but she's hissing at me: "IS THAT ALL? I'VE BEEN SITTING WITH YOU FOR NEARLY AN HOUR, IS THAT ALL I'M WORTH?"'

Steve is sitting up again now and he's rigid with tension. This does feel like an important message from the universe, something I wouldn't know unless I had met Steve, although I'm not sure what it is yet.

'So I get out the other twenty and she's like "Is that all you've got?" and I look at my brother but he's enjoying a dance and not looking at me and she, Beryl, just takes it and I said, "Sorry, that's all my birthday money" and she doesn't even say goodbye, she just walks off.'

We sit in silence for a bit now. There are far-away noises, like traffic. I decide I'm going to leave my coat, I don't even like it or need it. I'll say the muggers stole it. My mouth is clothy and I need water but I need to get out of here more.

'And that's the last time I trusted a woman.'

I strongly disagree with that – I feel defensive. Not just because she's my cousin but because she wasn't being a woman, was she? She was doing her job. So I try to be funny because Steve looks saggy and broken.

'You owe me at least *sixty* quid for listening to that story.'

It doesn't work.

We're sitting in silence and now I don't know how I can leave. I'm scared Ella will come downstairs and tell us to get out or about what Chris's penis looks like. I need to cheer Steve up so I can escape, so I tell him what Pete told me about the old lady in the bath. Steve says I told him that earlier and that I'd said it was my nan, which I don't remember but that does sound like me. I'm trying to think of another story but mostly about how to escape. Then footsteps start coming down the stairs towards us and the door opens.

It's Ella. She's in a dressing gown and looks flushed and amazing. She asks if we want tea and says, 'Open the window, it stinks of smoke.' And Steve gets up and goes over to the window and as Ella walks away towards the kitchen I whisper to him, because I really want to know:

'I thought she had a fiancé?'

And Steve says:

'Yeah.'

Without looking around, he pushes the window up and says:

'We got engaged in May.'

So now I understand what the story was about. It's even worse than I thought.

Steve goes out into the hall then into some other room and if I don't leave now I'll be stuck forever in this horrible theatre piece so I walk really fast to the front door and I open and close it slowly and quietly.

Then, as I'm walking down Ella's street trying to work out where I am, I take a deep breath of outside air and suddenly become me again. Like *Quantum Leap* except I'm jumping back into my real self, remembering a whole night that happened to someone else while I was in her head and seeing through her eyes but in possession of no decision-making power whatsoever.

Hello Sis,

I didn't want to send an invitation without speaking to you first, but then I didn't think this was a conversation for the phone and I didn't know when I would see you. So I just wanted to say, Yes, we are getting married, he proposed when we went to the Canary Islands for our anniversary and it was really perfect and wonderful and I hope that you can be happy for us? There is a bit on the invitation where you RSVP and tell us what you want to eat out of the options. It's not for another year and a bit but it really will help us organise everything so please don't ignore this like you do your bills as that would be a massive inconvenience.

On that topic there is still some mail of yours going to James's flat although we return it all to sender and hopefully it will stop if you contact the Post Office? Also you still owe me about £100 because you left the scaring job before the instalments were completed. Mum says I should forget about it and I have been thinking a lot about that, but it's not about the money, it's the principle. You made a promise and have to honour it, and actually, it's out of order of you to make me ask again.

Please don't think I'm annoyed though!!! I am the happiest I have ever been and can't wait to share the best day of my life with you and the rest of my family. Even Dad has said he will come but we will see eh?

Love Dana xxx

(Invitation and FAQ sheet enclosed)

When I'm hung-over I try to imagine being old and looking back fondly on now, on this bit I'm currently living, and how in retrospect it might seem adventurous. In the future when I only ever sit in a chair because I'm too gnarled for pleasure or movement I'll remember when I stayed out all night and had life-changing conversations and walked all the way home because I lost my phone. Maybe I'll like me in the future and think I was bold, or brave. Maybe I'll tell the young nurses how I used to be audacious. They'll be changing my bedpan and tucking a blanket around my rickety legs and I'll tell them about the sad boy who thought a stripper liked him. About how I chased a colleague all the way to Australia. Maybe I'll have a picture of me in my thirties on the mantelpiece and male residents'll tell me I used to be a beauty because they're senile and I'll believe them because I'll be senile too.

If I was a fictional character people might think I was aspirational. 'She doesn't even care about the consequences,' the reviews would say. 'OMG she is so free,' teenagers might tweet about me. I'm free I'm free, that's all I was doing: I was just following the night and the breeze. I'm like the people who went to Woodstock or who go to Burning Man. But in my work trousers.

I've decided to walk home, that's a start. Exercise. I don't deserve the comfort of public transport. I'm going to walk the whole way even though it's raining; I don't deserve to be dry, do I? Also I don't have my phone or card. Also this is being alive, weather. And blisters.

Walk walk walk, step step step. I'm trying to make this like a movie. I decide to play some music but remember I don't have my phone and that my headphones are broken anyway, in the pocket of the coat I've abandoned. So much loss. If I had music I could do it. Opening credits under my feet, sad sky, sad girl, boring suburban roads with small shops and blank people. I try to remember the words to 'Paradise' by Coldplay – that would fit perfectly. False hope and failure. I'd be dressed like Pegasus, or not him, the other one who caught fire on the sun. My hand looks for my phone to google before my brain re-remembers I don't have it.

Oh I'm sorry. I'm sorry now, that's the thing. Why didn't I text Ian where I was going or why didn't I just go home from The Pilgrim? But there's nothing I can do about it. It is done.

Walk walk walk, it's so slow when you concentrate on it, left right left right. I'm looking down at my dirty black trousers and sensible black shoes as they swing along on the pavement. I'm barely moving. But I must be a kilometre away now, if not a mile. I am moving. Away from last night. I will never see them again and eventually I will forget. Ian Ian I'm sorry, I'm coming.

I read a book once about something – Aboriginals, I think, and Australia. Oh yes, on the plane. And it said walking is good for the brain, grows more cells because we see new things, and when we're in the womb we rock relaxingly when our mother walks – and so it feels good now or something? Although thinking about being inside my mother is too strange a thing to consider, it shouldn't happen. It is something that, if you found out it was a lie, that would make more sense. If babies actually did get brought by a stork or even aliens, or were found underground like potatoes, that would be less weird than having to hang around with someone who created you from their genitals.

I'm reading the street names that I pass, looking for a clue. Florence Road, Beatrice Road. Maybe I should go to Italy, or Stratford-upon-Avon. Start a new life and make completely different decisions. Nurture myself, eat whole grains and drink litres of water. I'll ask Ian to come. We can go wherever he wants. Here is ruined. Here is shit and it's no good for us.

When I'm old I'll think today was glamorous. I'll forget my acidic breath and fluffy teeth. I'll forget my hollow chest and choking on a passer-by's smoke. I'll forget how my stomach flipped, tightened and—

I get to the bin just in time, covering a newspaper, an apple core and a baby's nappy with my runny bitter puke. The upwards clench of my diaphragm pushes tears out of my eyeballs. I'm crying for me because I hate being sick and I did this to myself. And because I have a creeping feeling, under the carpet where I'm not looking, that it's over. That he'll be gone. Ian I'm coming home I'm sorry. I lost my phone and my mind – it's not my fault.

It's not fair because if I *was* a fictional character – in a film, say – my boyfriend would like me *more*. He'd think I was flighty and unpredictable and kept him on his toes or something.

I need to blow my nose but I wait til I'm walking. I try

to do it surreptitiously but I'm using my sleeve so it's a bit obvious, if anyone's looking. There's sick up there. Don't know if anyone saw because I'm purposely not looking around, I'm avoiding everybody's eye. I'm a zombie scarer. A ghost of the night before haunting the high street. I'm very very sorry. I don't know why I do this. I should've gone for one drink then gone home like a normal person with a nice life who doesn't make all this mess and smell so bad in the morning.

If I was in a film I'd be better-looking and that's why men in films like women in films even when they're terrible people.

If he's gone this is my fault, if I've done it again like with James. Although that was my sister's fault. He wouldn't have known anything if she— I don't want to think about . . . about endings. I want to get home. And water. I'm plodding my legs and the backs of my shoes are rubbing and hurting my heels and I'm trying to feel that my life has expanded with new experience and I'm trying to find the rain romantic but it's just wet.

I once puked on a train – I'd forgotten about this but I've just remembered (situational dependent memory). I had to go into work at the sexual health clinic, which was my job before buses. Come to think of it I hated that job *much* more than scaring and there wasn't even anyone to drink with after work. Or to work with. I was on reception and no one ever wanted to chat to me because they'd either just found out they had HIV or herpes, or they'd just got the all-clear and wouldn't want to hang around with me, a stranger who knew they'd needed the tests in the first place.

The night before I'd been drinking with my friend Leanna after receiving some bad news. I'd had wine and vodka and prosecco and I was standing on the train from Romford and it was all commuters and proper people and I threw up between stations. I didn't know what to say and I was squashed, there was nowhere to go. I aimed between my own legs – as politely as possible and crying, of course. But when the train went round corners it made the liquid move, so it wasn't my fault, it was physics. It was running along the runnels in the floor and people were tutting. A middle-aged woman threw some newspaper pages down onto it, but they're not that absorbent and the sick slipped underneath. No one was looking at me but their hatred was emanating from wherever it's made, their spleens and gall bladders, wafting in my direction. A few more papers were thrown down in passive-aggressive attempts to dam the tide. But this just made it spread out, like a tributary, is that the right word, into lots of little streams. It trickled along the whole carriage and reached the door at the end between the side-by-side seats. There was huffing as well as tutting and even though no one asked I said, 'I'm pregnant' quite loudly. I don't know if they believed me because the sick smelled of booze, but I was. That had been the bad news.

I'm only a mile from my flat now. Our flat. I've passed the station and the Londis. A French bulldog is going past me in a pram, like a baby. He's staring at me, which is weird, but I don't look away. The dog's eyes are so human and old, deep brown and calming. This dog has seen it all and I'm nothing to worry about. Once he's passed I feel calmer too for a bit. It will be okay, I just need a bath and sleep and maybe I'll let myself have an apple. Then I remember the one I covered in sick and change my mind.

The good thing about the sexual health clinic, or not good, but handy, was that the computer had records of all the people who'd come to get tests. You could put in anyone's name – like for instance my ex from drama college, Mark Watts – and then the computer'd tell you if he had gonorrhoea or warts or any STDs at all. It's illegal to do this, by the way. That was literally the first thing they told me when I got the placement, which is what gave me the idea. Every day I searched for people from school or college and most of them weren't on there, but sometimes I just made it up. Like I told Dana that Mark Watts had an ingrown pube that went septic but that it was a secret – because that's how to get her to tell everyone.

Sometimes people weren't on the system and I'd be surprised because they were so sexual all the time, like Sasha, James's ex. I was sure she'd at least have had hepatitis but apparently not . . . or she just never got checked out. And sometimes people weren't on the system but someone with exactly the same name was. Like I looked up James and I found a sixty-three-year-old also called James Laycock who was taking antiretrovirals for HIV and James didn't find that funny. James didn't find his surname funny either. He also wanted to keep the pregnancy, which is where it all went wrong. No. Actually I should have broken up with him after what happened with Sasha, and then I'd never have got pregnant in the first place.

As I slowly get nearer to the flat I'm getting sadder and sadder. My vision is going blurry and I like it. The world in front of me is melting, postboxes and bus stops and the tinselly decorations at the tops of lamp posts. I'm passing a crocodile of children in navy uniforms. I don't know what school they're from but they're too loud whenever I see them on the bus. I'm always worried they'll try and fight me and I'll have to get off before my stop. Or they laugh and I know it's about me but I don't know why. I mean what. What about me makes them snigger so nastily? I blink to send some fat tears over the edge and the feeling of them on my cheeks makes me sadder and brings more. This is good.

I start planning the video I'll make to be played at my funeral and by the time Ian answers the door I am bawling and it doesn't even feel fake. This is the saddest I've ever been and I didn't ask to be alive and I've fucked up everything and I need to make it better. Although I only tell him the last part and now he's about to cry and says he thought I was dead.

I don't push my way in; I wait on the doorstep as if it's his house and I'm a desperate beggar asking for help. Ian's skin is blotchy and his eyes are red and tired. His rubbery bottom lip is trembling as he asks me where I've been. He looks like shit but it suits him. Ian is one of those people who is so nearly good-looking. He's got a manly forehead and chin, wide and blocky. But it's all undermined by his little nose and freckles and the gingery hair he's really defensive about. He's also defensive about his chest, which is inverted between his ribs – you could easily use him as a bowl for soup if he'd let you. Of course he's *most* defensive about his penis, which is thin and slightly curved, and having to reassure him about it is exhausting.

Ian takes my hand and leads me inside and it's relief

at first. My relief that he hasn't left, that he's still here and glad to see me. And Ian's relief that I'm okay. He gets me water from the filter jug in the fridge and brings the duvet from our bed into the living room so I can lie on the sofa. The cover's got dried Crunchy Nut Cornflakes on it, which is so gross but I can't say anything because it was me that spilled them.

I sip my water and everything goes quiet. Ian is looking at me, but his eyebrows are too scrunched. I put the glass down and lower my head, like a sorry nun. A nun who is apologetic and also has no self-esteem. She's made herself so small, and hard to be angry at. I might have made it worse. Ian's voice is serious.

'So where have you been?'

I hate this bit. I *am* sorry but I didn't do anything wrong and I don't want to talk about it or have to explain myself and be told off. I'm picking flakes off the duvet and pretending to listen. He's been so worried, apparently. He walked to The Slipper, saw it was all locked up. Assumed I'd been murdered.

'By who?'

'You always talk about that policeman harassing you.'

That's true. I'd hate to be murdered by Pete though, that would be so lame. I've always pictured my murderer as thin and Latino, like an evil Ricky Martin.

'You can't just not come home.'

I've come home. I'm home now, but I nod instead of pointing out the obvious.

'I lost my bag, my phone, I didn't have anything . . . I couldn't—'

Oh that's good, I'm crying again – I must be rehydrating.

'Were you with someone? Fucking someone?'

'NO!'

I feel guilty and am acting like a liar even though I wasn't and didn't.

'I would never do that to you. EVER.'

I go on a bit about how I would never do that to anyone, especially after what was done to me. Ian has heard this speech before. When I've finished he starts on *his* speech about how I should respect him and all he expects is a call or a text. We both know our lines for this scene.

'I'm not saying you can't have a giggle with your mates—'

I hate that phrase. Who has a giggle? I don't. I'm finding it hard to respect Ian, actually, because he's sitting on the chintzy armchair. It's cream and puffy with big pink flowers. The furniture came with the flat and often emasculates Ian during rows. The sofa I'm on is quite macho, I suppose, brown with a rough fabric on it, like corduroy. Maybe that's why I feel so composed and uncaring.

'Come here.'

I lift up a corner of the duvet. I smile.

'I've been told off enough.'

I shouldn't have said that out loud. Ian does an exasperated double-arm movement with accompanying harrumph. It reminds me of those inflatable tube men outside car garages when the wind billows them up. It's not well suited to this situation – a bit over the top, truth be told. It's what people do in sitcoms before they exit dramatically. Perhaps he thinks there's an audience watching and they will all agree with him that I am TOO MUCH and very unreasonable.

Ian storms out and I wonder for a minute if this is a TV show. Then James pops into my head again even though I am trying really hard to avoid thinking about him.

It's all consecutive, that's the trouble. I saw Chris so I'm thinking about James who if I hadn't met Chris I probably would have married. If I hadn't liked Chris I wouldn't have taken out the credit cards to get to Australia. If James hadn't gone mental about the credit cards he wouldn't have been texting and meeting up with Dana. If Dana hadn't been annoyed with me about money then she wouldn't have been helping James and – and if I'd known Dana was hanging around with James I wouldn't have told Mum about kissing Chris and then Dana would have had nothing to tell James to make him break up with me and we'd still be together. So it's all consequential, that's a better word, because I probably wouldn't have liked Chris if I hadn't hated James because he got me pregnant.

I don't want to be thinking about that. I close my eyes and remember hearing Ella and Chris talking about me last night. I don't want to think about that either. Ian pops his head in through the kitchen hatch. I keep my eyes squashed shut but I say the right line in case this is a TV show.

'Sorry, Ian.'

He says he's running a bath for me. I cry. I want to cheese-grate my skin off. Ian walks in and sits down in the middle of the sofa and I curl around him like a worm. I pull the duvet over his head so we're both in the dark. We're both breathing. My head is on his legs and he lays his torso down so his head is on my belly, which gurgles a greeting.

'Hello.'

Ian always pretends he can converse with my intestines. It's very nice, as is he. I'm going to have a bath and it's going to be okay. I'm going to give up drinking and run marathons and volunteer at a food bank. I'm going to join a book group that reads *Ulysses* over and over again and discuss it and understand more every time. I am going to learn to speak Italian and how to play the piano and have a measured life, a contained life. I am going to keep a dream diary and pay attention to my subconscious. When I die they will play 'Paradise' by Coldplay and no one will cry because even my death will be tidy and unexceptional.

From: jay.laycock@hotmail.co.uk
To: sscollins@gmail.com
Subject: Re: I'm coming back baby (and I saw a Dolphin!)

Alright mate, so I got your email about flying back. I think
that's prob for the best we got a lot to talk about. Not least all
the bills coming to my house, it's gonna effect my credit rating
and my dad says its actually illegal to do what you did, so you
need to stop acting like its not serious amd actually deal with
it. There's some other stuff, but its best we talk about that face
to face somewhere neutral. I actually can't believe you went
all that way for two weeks when surely you could have saved
all that money and just spoke to yourdad on Skype like a
normal person. Or waited and we could have gone on holiday
or something, but that's all in the past now. Still, am glad you
seem to have sorted something out that was weighing heavy
on ya or whatever. And thank you for your apologies, I think it
is a start, but – let's talk about it when I see ya. JL.

Ian is telling me about some experiment but I'm not even pretending to listen, I'm on my phone – it was *Icarus* that flew too close to the sun. That was bugging me but I've only just remembered to look it up. My phone bings a text alert and I quickly click it asleep without reading and shove it back in my coat pocket. Too quickly? Ian hasn't noticed; he's looking at the road and droning on. He *is* clever and I should be grateful, I suppose. It's grey and drizzly and doesn't feel Christmas Eve-y at all. I don't know what I expected to feel. I usually like being in the passenger seat with Ian while we chat but the drive to Mum's is so depressing. I want to stop at McDonald's and get a Diet Coke. If Ian stops there without me asking him that means he is The One and I will marry him.

'—two of these robot monkeys, well, they weren't robots but that's what the scientists called them, one of them was covered in prickly wire—'

I got my phone back a couple of days ago when I went back into work. There were thirteen missed calls from Ian so I did feel bad. But then some of the messages were really nasty like how fucking dare I and I've always been a selfish bitch etc so then I was glad I'd stayed out and it started to feel like a victory. We've been getting on well, though, and even had sex, which we don't normally because it's such a minefield. I've learned to lie there and basically pretend to be asleep to avoid doing anything wrong or knocking his confidence – but unfortunately it does make me despise him.

'—the other one has soft warm fur on it like a real monkey, or not a monkey because they're chimpanzees, so they're actually apes—'

I dare myself to say 'Who cares?' to Ian but I can't. I can't face Christmas without him – I need a witness. They'll be there, all loved-up and planning the wedding. I wonder if I should try and get Ian to propose to me on Christmas Day? No. It's all off – we just sailed past the Drive-Thru so no Diet Coke or husband for me.

'Did you want to stop?'

I must have craned my head too wistfully.

'No.'

'You are going to eat at your mum's, aren't you?'

I smile my big fake smile at him.

'Tell me more about the monkeys—'

'Chimpanzees.'

I get a surge of irritated fury even though I knew he'd correct me. I look in my rucksack for some Nurofen and pop three out. I push them down my throat with my finger, one at a time.

'Isn't it supposed to be two at a time?'

That's why I took three, you dumbwad, so you could be the police and tell me what to do with my own body, fucksake.

The rage is always worst on the first day. The only positive is that my period cramps are drowning out the throbbing of my haemorrhoids/cancer, lucky me, happy birthday Jesus.

My phone repeats its bing, needily reminding me that

I've got a message. I know it's him. He took my number when he came into the pub to apologise and we've been texting since yesterday. We're discussing *The Outsider* of all things because he brought me a copy as a gift – which I assumed was a joke but he doesn't seem to remember. Told me the book meant a lot to him and that it had made him see the world in an unusual way, and then he said this stunning thing. He said he thought *I* saw the world in an unusual way. And he pronounced Camus correctly. All these years I've been thinking 'What if I hadn't corrected him, what if *that's* where it all went wrong?' But now it all feels perfect and the right size. It was messy and circuitous and painful but now we're messaging each other all these properly deep texts. I didn't ask about Ella or mention her at all but last night he brought it up and said how intense she'd been and that it was a mistake and he feels really bad about Steve. I have to read my phone in the toilet with the door locked because I don't want Ian to say anything. I'm not doing anything wrong. Chris and I are just friends, finally, after all this time. And that's all I ever wanted.

I get my phone out of my pocket and put it on silent. Ian tries to see the screen.

'Who keeps texting you?'

'Mum.'

I look out of the window to seem nonchalant. Essex is all out there and is cement and terrible, even worse than usual in this pathetic wet murk. The road is punctuated by feeble Christmas shapes: bows and shooting stars and snowmen, but they've hung them under street lamps.

'Why would you put lights up on a light?'

'Your mum doesn't normally text.'

Alright, Sherlock.

'She wanted us to bring her McDonald's but you've already passed it.'

Ian offers to go back but I ignore him. I'm calling everyone we pass a cunt in my head, everyone walking along the street or pushing a pram or looking in shop windows. I hate everyone. Ian says, 'Jesus!' and I don't ask him why. I carry on hating out of the window. I don't trust myself not to say something, and I can't say anything or he'll leave and I can't deal with my family alone.

'Sorry. So they *are* monkeys—'

He's on his phone. That's actually against the law while driving but I can't be bothered to care if we crash and die or get arrested and spend Christmas Day in prison. I fake a yawn. Then I feel actually tired and it's a relief. Ian is still talking.

'—weren't chimps, they were rhesus monkeys. The Harry Harlow experiment—'

'Did you say Jesus before? Or rhesus?'

'Rhesus.'

I don't know why we are talking about animal testing on Christmas fucking Eve so I look out of the window again. It's some fields now as we're getting away from Ilford and there is no one I can see to hate. Ian's still telling me about this experiment I couldn't give a shit about.

'—so it's called "wire mothers" or something like that, what they did, two groups, the first group of monkeys, all of them were newborn, they didn't get to bond with their real mother—'

Human beings are appalling. I can't believe I have to be one.

'—first group went to a, I guess like a robot or some- thing, made out of wire, but it had teats, and could feed milk to the baby, as much as it wanted, all day long. And the second group, their robot had no milk, or only a very small bit, so they starved, BUT, that robot monkey had fur on it so it was softer and it could give the little baby hugs. So the point was, the scientists could find out what was worse – like, being starved of affection or actually starved.'

I don't know what he wants me to say.

'So?'

I think that it's not a good experiment. And I don't mean for moral reasons – I'm not just feeling sorry for the monkeys. It's not very realistic, but I won't get into it with Ian because he'd find the discussion interesting.

'You're not supposed to google stuff while driving, by the way.'

'It reminded me of your mother.'

Okay, maybe it is relevant. I look at the side of Ian's face while he drives. He throws me a little smile. The Nurofen is softening the ache down my legs and in my belly and I'm so relieved. I suppress the urge to stroke Ian's arm and be kind but I feel some niceness emanating out of my pores against my will and floating around the car changing the mood.

'The interesting thing is what happened when the babies grew up and had their own children.'

'Yeah?'

I guess I am invested.

'The ones who were starved but had hugs and affection, they were typical mothers, normal, no adverse effects or whatever—'

'Well, they don't know that, do they?'

'They watched them all the time, so they do.'

You can't tell anything about what's going on in some-one's mind just from watching them, you can only guess. I'm starting to get pissed off with how stupid scientists are.

'And the ones who had loads of milk but no affection, they seemed normal enough all through their develop-ment—'

How the hell would anyone know.

'—but then when *they* had babies, mostly, they ate them.'

Deck the halls with bells of holly fa-la-la-la-la la-la La-La.

Ian's sulking now because I'm not engaging enough in this great conversation about animal cruelty.

We pass an Esso garage and I remember how I used to walk there for Pringles and Mars drinks with James. We're getting closer to Mum's and there are memories unbidden in the dismal landscape and buildings. I lean my head back and close my eyes to avoid them.

'Why is that like my mother?'

I can hear Ian's leather jacket as he shrugs. I feel like I should defend her.

'She didn't eat me.'

Ian starts telling me how it wasn't a literal parallel. He's um-ing and ah-ing so I can tell he's worried about upset-ting me and choosing his phrases carefully. I feel really intuitive with my eyes closed and wonder for a second if I should stab them out like an old man in a Greek play. But I don't want to be blind because I'd never know if I had food on my face or in my teeth. I finally realise what Ian meant, what he means.

'*I'm* the one who seems normal but eats its baby?'

'You had a functional childhood, but you were emotion-
ally . . . y'know . . .'

'I'm not a Jesus monkey—'

'Rhesus.'

'Are you saying you don't think I should have children?'

Ian shrugs and he's stopped smiling. I don't think I'm
upset, I can't tell, but maybe I should be. This was rude, he's
been RUDE to me, I'm insulted. But I'm also numbishly
content from the painkillers working. We're nearly there.

'Have you ever had a Mars drink?'

I've changed the subject. Ian starts telling me about a
long walk he went on with his dad and they got rained on
and when they got home his dad melted Mars bars into
milk to make hot chocolate. It's a very boring story and
he's adding unimportant details like how old he was and
what car they had at the time. My ears are listening but
I'm contained now. My personality or whatever I am is in
a box inside me, and I'm just meat hearing and breathing
and then getting out of the car and opening the boot and
carrying bags towards the house.

HM Courts & Tribunals Service

EX323 – Attachment of Earnings Order

For the attn of Miss S Collins

Following small claims court litigation you should be aware that an attachment of earnings order has been requested by creditor Dana Collins.

If you believe that you earn less than the 'protected earnings rate' please return the enclosed form: N56 Statement of Means, detailing all your outgoings and financial responsibilities as soon as possible. This would need to be received within eight calendar days.

If your income exceeds the protected earnings rate an order will be sent to your employer in exactly one calendar month with details of the amount to be subtracted from your PAYE. The order will be sent by the Centralised Attachment of Earnings Payment System (CAPS) in Northampton which will be responsible for collecting payments. You will be sent a copy of the order, as will Ms D Collins.

You may be aware that you can ask for the order to be suspended if you do not want the court to contact your employer 'London Scary Dungeons'. If the court agrees, this would enable you to make direct repayments of the debt instead, not to avoid them altogether.

It is also important to note that you do not have to accept the court officer's decision. As you were not present while your case was argued you may ask for a district judge to decide what would be a fair way for you to repay your debt.

I hope this is all comprehensible. There is a helpful website on understanding these orders: www.wageattachment.gov.uk if you wish to undertake some research.

Geoff Coates
Small Claims Court Official

My mum's got twigs instead of a Christmas tree. Big tall twigs painted silver and standing in a glass vase in the corner of her living room where a tree should be. I don't care except she's so proud of them. She's told Ian twice how much more sophisticated they are than a Christmas tree, and when he joked that she'd been 'raiding the woods this year' she smugly corrected him that they were from TK Maxx.

I can't help remembering Ella's tree. I think about describing it to Mum but I can't find the energy. The TV is on so I'm looking at it, holding a dark rum and Diet Coke that she made without asking what I wanted. I take a sip.

'There's virtually no carbs.'

And there it is, the explanation.

'Thank you.'

I don't actually care about calories from drinking.

Ian's gone for a bath upstairs and then he's going to put on his 'snuggly pyjamas', his words. Mum seemed really pleased to see him, which reassures me that she isn't secretly watching us. She definitely would have been a bit frosty if she'd heard Ian diagnosing her as a robot monkey who breeds infanticidal carnivores.

'Dana won't be here til the morning.'

I nod and sip. I <u>know</u> Mum isn't watching me, I know that's not how the world works, so why does that thought keep repeating, why does my mind keep looking for evidence just in case? I flash-think about stabbing myself in the head to shut my brain up.

'They're going to have a "betrothed breakfast" at his dad's – you heard he's got engaged too? To Stephanie? So lovely for all of them.'

My mum loves marriage. That could be the most ironic thing about her. Imagine living through an earthquake and then being excited for other travellers heading to the danger zone. Imagine wanting to go back yourself, to the exact location you were reduced to rubble.

I can't even process Dana at James's dad's flat. Dana talking to Stephanie. The fact that I used to sit there and eat and talk has been tippexed out – only I remember and it makes me feel psychotic. I worry for a second that Mum is about to ask about me and Ian, but she doesn't. Her programme has ended in what would be an intense cliffhanger for anyone suspending their disbelief. I look at Mum to see if she's been moved by the character's tearful revelation but she's blank, reaching for the remote to change the channel. One theme tune is exchanged for another, her soap schedule all memorised. I wonder what she gets from them; I wonder what's going on in her head.

If I were a scientist watching her, what would I write down as the results? Woman who had neglectful/scary childhood finds comfort in fictional representations of families? Or maybe something like: Woman with dissociative tendencies finds fictional representations of humans easier/simpler company than real ones? She did try and go to therapy after Dad left but she couldn't get on with it so there are no explanations. Woman loves soap operas more than own child. I'm feeling sorry for myself now but

I know it's true because she once hung up on me because I called during *EastEnders*. She *is* like the Jesus monkeys – she seems normal unless you're her daughter.

Looking around Mum's beige-and-white living room, I wonder where the cats are. They are usually in here, purring on everything and being hairy and clingy. I get distracted by a new thought: 'Do you remember that dog?'

'Yes. What dog?'

From the old house, I remind her. The next-door neighbour had a dog he kept in the shed; she used to bark and bark all night, and I was allowed to walk her sometimes. She was black and white but I can't remember her name. Mum nods but she's engrossed in *Coronation Street* so I stop bothering. I'll ask Dana. I don't know why it matters so much all of a sudden but I've been feeling really guilty about it, like there's something more I should have done.

'He killed himself.'

I think she's talking about the TV so I look to see who she means.

'Aiden. Our old next-door neighbour.'

I'll try and feel bad about that as well, I guess, but there's not enough room in my brain right now.

I sigh without meaning to; I'm fighting a kind of frustrated boredom. I feel homesick but I don't know where for. It's not for where I live with Ian and it's not for the past.

I remember my phone exists and take myself and my glass downstairs to the kitchen, where I left my rucksack. As I stand by the fridge holding it I can hear the taps running two floors above. Ian's submerged in there, he's not going to come out and find me, but I take my bag into the downstairs toilet anyway.

There's a photograph of me and my sister above the loo. It's been blown up too large and is slightly pixelated. I'm about fifteen, Dana is eighteen months younger as usual. She's smiling, genuinely beaming at the camera. Good little girl, making her mama happy. Fifteen-year-old me is tense and tight. Resentful eyes, distrusting ugly face. I hated that photographer, calling us 'love' and 'That's it, babycakes' and telling us to 'watch the birdie'. He flirted with Mum, which she fell for, of course, completely charmed by his clichéd 'But you're too young to have grown-up kids' and 'You all look like sisters.' How is fifteen grown-up? I hated being told I was grown-up. I also hated being told I was young and had all my life ahead of me. I've hated all my ages and every unnecessary and unasked-for comment upon them.

This photograph is from early in the shoot. The rest have Mum in them, even though that hadn't been the plan. It was supposed to be a memento of us kids. Mum'd told us we'd always be 'preserved' in these photos so I thought she meant in case we died – but when we were getting out of the car at the photo man's studio she made us look at our reflection in the car window. I was distorted, all wide and frowning. Mum informed us: 'You'll never be as attractive as you are now' and then marched us inside. She was upset about something. She was muttering about how we couldn't possibly understand what it was like to be forty. Then, once we started, the photographer told her to get in as well and she said, 'I suppose I am paying' and cheered up.

Once when I was much younger, probably twelve or something, I was doing gymnastics in the garden and Mum got hysterical with me. She said Darren, her fiancé at the time, had been looking at my legs and I had to get dressed properly before 'flaunting myself around the house'. I was wearing a nightie. I didn't know how to make it better because I didn't know what I'd done to upset her. When she broke up with Darren months later she told me he'd come back for me when I was sixteen. She was drunk but she still said it and I worried about that for a long time. I had barely spoken to the man – what was he coming back for?

Dana knew how to comfort her. Give Mum what she wanted. It came easier to her, maybe because she's younger and doesn't remember a lot. Or maybe it's genetics and she's got rainbows and sunshine built into her DNA, whereas I have toxic pus in me. But also, it's not that, she's not nicer, she's better at manipulating. That was the bit that came easy to her, the fake love she can manufacture as a survival tactic. Whereas I freeze.

It is weird that the same two parents can come together and make two such different people. Not just that Dana's hair is lighter and her face is rounder. Not just her limbyness and energy. I look above the toilet at her smiling face next to my sour one. Is she beautiful? I can't be objective. She looks very healthy. Like a Nazi who's never had to worry about their own safety.

I sit down on the toilet and look in my bag for my phone, preparing myself to read the text from Chris. I try not to be excited because it might very well be mundane. It could just be an emoji or say 'Happy Xmas for tomorrow' or something else impossible to start a conversation with.

There's a knock at the toilet door and I jump, thinking it's Ian, but it's Mum's voice.

'You're not making yourself sick, are you?'

I flush the toilet and come out. She's in the kitchen switching on her red kettle.

'Ad break,' she explains, and then offers me a sachet of hot chocolate by shaking hers towards me. 'Options. Only forty calories?'

I point to my dark glass on the table.

'I'm still going on that.'

I sit at the kitchen table and put my phone in front of me on the wicker place mat. I feel nicely smug about not having replied to Chris yet. About not having even read his message. And he will know. No blue ticks. I haven't opened the app since before we got in the car, which must be nearly two hours ago. It says what time you were last 'seen' up at the top near your name. I wonder if he's checked our thread and noted that time. I wonder if he reads back over our messages like I do. I wonder if he picked up his phone to see if I'd replied and what he felt when he realised I hadn't. The idea of him noticing my absence is fortifying.

The cats' bowls are gone from the corner of the floor. As is the litter tray.

'Mum, are the cats okay?'

She doesn't look at me, concentrates on intently stirring hot water into powder. Her mug says 'GIRL BOSS' on it.

'Oh I am *not* in the mood to be judged, Sophie.'

I was just asking. I was actually being nice. If I wanted to be a bitch I'd ask where Ron is.

There are footsteps coming downstairs. Mum shakes her empty sachet at Ian as he sits down, offers him the same low-calorie deal. His pyjamas are red-and-white-striped and slightly fluffy. Ian asks if we have any Mars bars and says he'll make us a 'real hot chocolate'. Christmas feels too long already. They are definitely girls' pyjamas.

'I'll go and have a bath now.'

I'm relieved to be getting away from Girl Boss and the dweeb and a step closer to bedtime. I turn at the door and grab my phone from the table and I feel Ian note it without him moving a muscle.

DEBT COLLECT
───── UK ─────

13 November 20—

Dear Miss Collins,

We are writing to request immediate payment on the amount
owed of £6,215.11 which is more than 180 days past due.
This total includes all interest, late fees, and other charges.
This amount was originally owed to Lloyds Bank PLC and our
company is now handling this account.

Please call **0-800-916-8800** immediately to make your
payment. If you need to set up a payment plan, enquire about
that when you call.

Thank you for your prompt attention to this important matter.

Sincerely

Fiona Schultz, Debt Collect UK

I'm awake but I don't want the day to start. Our old room doesn't have curtains; I'm staring at the white-grey sky outside the window and trying to feel alive. A bird is tweeting, some shit sparrow or something. The motorway rumbles in the distance although it can't be that busy, it's Christmas Day. I think of Steve – what does he do with his Jewish self? Does he have dinner and wear a paper hat and go along with it? Or wait in his house for it to be over? I decide not to think about what Ella is doing today. I bet she goes skiing or hires a big farmhouse.

Across the room Ian fidgets and breathes, his red pyjamas clashing with Dana's pink Playboy bedspread. We used to draw an imaginary border line down the middle of this room, between our beds, all the way to the window, and then promise we would never cross it. An attempt at personal space and a farce of pretending to respect each other's stuff. We plundered each other's territory daily. Stole, hid, broke, lied. Lied extravagantly. Dana once denied taking my jeans while *wearing* my jeans, and then she left the house in them. Wiggling her bum while I chased her in my towel and bare feet. I want to scream in impotence even all these years later and my eyes are prickled with angry tears while my heart beats really fast and this isn't useful preparation for seeing her.

It's *Christmas*. I try and make myself have an appropriate emotion. I send loving thoughts towards the back of Ian's head. It's not his fault I hate him.

Chris'd asked how I was spending the day, that was the text: 'What you doin tomorrow?' A question, starting a chat. I replied, making it sound better than it is, like seeing my family was a good thing. Didn't mention James. What I did bring up, and I'm proud of myself for this, is Ian. Said I had brought my 'new boyfriend' to meet my mum. That makes it sound fresh and exciting, I think, makes me seem unavailable. Chris replied straight away that he was 'really happy for me' and I replied, 'I'm always happiest when I'm single tho', with a shruggy emoji. I haven't actually been single since I was fourteen but I don't like being the kind of person that needs to be with someone to be complete or fulfilled. I really admire it when I read about celebrities who say they're content alone because I think that sounds sophisticated and I hope I can say it one day. I think that will be a sign of healing.

Ian has turned over and is blinking his eyes, looking at me. I decide to smile, no teeth, just half-moon lips and soft eyes. He smiles back and we are silent and gazing at each other and maybe there is true understanding here, a communion—

'Happy Christmas.'

He ruined it. I cross the historical boundary to join him in Dana's old bed. It's warm under the covers and really smells of him, his eggy smoke smell with a hint of Mum's lavender bubble bath. Ian hugs me from behind and I'm looking back to whence I came. Literally my past. The thin bed I did my homework on and cried myself to sleep in. Got up resentfully every day and went to school from. The bed I terribly lost my virginity in. All these life events that feel like they happened to someone else and I just have access to the memories. But it wasn't me; I wasn't her. I'm a chrysalis. I'm waiting. We saw this on a nature programme – I'd always thought a caterpillar grew wings on either side and became the middle bit of the butterfly, but it doesn't. It turns into jelly. The caterpillar goes into its chrysalis and completely breaks down, back into all the ingredients, the primordial goo of a butterfly. It is blobby nothingness and then it restructures and builds back up from scratch. And all that counts as life: the caterpillar is still alive even though it is utterly destroyed and disappeared and gone, which is amazing.

Looking at that bed – *my* bed, technically, although I didn't buy it, I was just someone's daughter so they provided furnishings – but looking at the bed, what I remember clearest is listening to my CD Walkman, boyband albums full of the purest love and promises, and I'd get so fizzed up I wouldn't be able to sleep. That feels like a me I recognise. I would run out the batteries and the boys' voices would deepen and skip and I'd lie there frantically planning how to be worthy of their lyrics.

I've accidentally rubbed my butt into Ian's groin. It was reflexive. I wasn't even thinking about him and didn't notice I'd done it until he pulled his body away from mine.

'You're on your period,' he whispers in my ear, and his breath is old and dead on my face.

He's so pleased to have an excuse. Ian hoards reasons to reject me. He can't because he's hungry and he can't after he's eaten because he's too full. He's either tired or wired or in any kind of mood. He's thinking about work, or a film he saw, or he wants to talk to me or he wants time alone. Once he said he'd just had a wank in the shower and that was the worst, I think. I was right there in the bedroom and he'd gone off to lock the door and do it without me. Also he sometimes complains 'The neighbours are in', which is another terrible excuse – they're all terrible excuses because he won't admit the obvious, which is that he doesn't want to have sex.

What he has recently conceded, this was only a couple of weeks ago, was that I 'make it worse' if I seem like I 'want it'. He made out like he was helping me, giving me a tip on how to handle the situation. Distilled down, after I'd pushed him to clarify, Ian said that he finds my initiating sex a turn-off. Any sign from me that I want to touch him, or be touched – very off-putting, apparently. And this is the bind we are now in – that I'm in, I don't think *he* cares. He's created the perfect situation for himself. If I want sex I have to wait for him to initiate it, which he never will because he doesn't want it.

We're lying still, breathing. Our bodies separated by a couple of inches of space, the muscles in my back taut with maintaining this tiny meaningful distance apart from him.

I am supposed to be grateful and accept the shape of our relationship. I don't know what love is, but it's not this. It's not being treated like a horny binbag of rotting leaves. I asked him once why he won't even kiss me. I wasn't shouting and freaking out, by the way, I was being calm and listening and hoping I could make it better. He said he doesn't like kissing in case it might turn me on.

I sigh, another accident, but this time Ian ignores it. Now I'm concentrating on breathing normally. I inhale and exhale with studious focus and contemplate the fact that it's Christmas Day. All this mundanity is occurring on Christmas morning . . .

I once heard a man on a podcast saying this time of year is bittersweet for adults because they try to recreate the magic of their childhoods and are disappointed when they fail. But surely what's more likely is that most people have never felt *any* magic and it's an appalling discovery to find out you were supposed to. So once a year, every year, here it is again, regressive season. Have a drink and be trapped and stare into the abyss of the truth that no one in your family understands you.

My mum likes Ian, of course she does. Last night she said, 'He's the best boyfriend you've ever had, he's really the one for you.' Then Ian gave her a hug like she'd said something lovely and I carried on watching TV because niceness doesn't count when she's pissed. Also Ian shouldn't be too glad to receive her compliments – earlier in the evening she'd described Vladimir Putin as 'charismatic'.

I wonder if the butterfly has the caterpillar's memories? That would be interesting to know. Can they remember, are they scared by the change? It must be very weird to transform from one creature to another when you've never done it before. Like giving birth to yourself – but while dying. These are very profound thoughts I'm having. I can't wait to text them to Chris. Of course, when the scientists or botanists or whatever cut open the chrysalises to see what's going on inside, they kill the butterflies. Not on purpose, but that's what having a look inside does. So yes, now humans understand the process, but at what cost?

I'm sure this relates to the Jesus monkeys we were talking about yesterday but the connection eludes me.

'Will you ask my mum what happened to her cats?'

Ian hadn't noticed they aren't here but she's more likely to talk to him about it. I don't think she's killed them or anything, but worryingly I can picture it. Her. With a sack by the riverside. And now I've imagined it, I feel unsettled like it's slightly possible.

I didn't know sex was important to me. If you'd asked me two years ago, while I was still with James, I would have said sex was a brief and unlikeable jumble. Not horrible exactly, but a thing you have to put up with and then feel relieved when it's done. Like an injection or swallowing a vitamin. When it's over you know you've done the right thing. But now I have the opposite. I feel relieved when we start having sex – there's a brief respite. A restoration of normality. But soon the wait until it happens again has begun. Days and weeks of trying to work out what I can do. Be thinner. Need nothing from him, seem free and cheerful and non-initiating, but I always crack eventually and cry and say, 'What is the *point* of us being together?' Which doesn't make him sorry, and it doesn't make him understand.

He always says something along the lines of 'But we had sex so recently', the insinuation being that I'm a nympho and his non-existent sex drive is a figment of my imagination.

I first asked him about it when we'd been together for about six months. We'd gone to a hotel for the weekend because his mum gave us a voucher. The website had shown a swimming pool and a local pub with a big fire and it was supposed to be nice. But the breakfast cost £17 so we had to get one delivered to the room and share it, and in the evening we walked to a garage up the road to get sandwiches which we ate standing on the hotel lawn. That wouldn't have mattered if we'd been getting on. The room had a big clean bed and a bath in the corner and Ian wouldn't come near me. He got up and moved somewhere else when I sat too close to him. When I ran the bath he went and sat in reception to 'give me some privacy'. I tried to kiss him on the Saturday night and he told me he was constipated from all the toast and sandwiches.

On Sunday morning I googled 'what to do when your boyfriend is frigid' and spent too long on a Reddit thread that made me despise straight people. Then that night as we walked along to the garage I was so gentle in asking, because at this point I was still desperate for it to work out. Did he have a low sex drive? Or was it me, had I done something wrong and was there anything I could do to improve things?

See, that's not too much, is it, that's not emasculating; it's working towards a solution. It's caring. We could've got to know each other better. But he was so defensive. Talking about how intense I constantly am and why can't we just be organic and 'go with the flow' and 'when the moment's right it'll happen'. After we'd got our dinner (he chose a baguette, really Freudian-ly) Ian said that all his other girlfriends had been really satisfied and thought he had too high a sex drive if anything so it *was* my problem.

And I always think, what if we hadn't already moved in together – would we have broken up then? On the hotel lawn, eating dinner from a carrier bag. Driven back and said goodbye and then been free. But I'd already moved all my stuff into his basement flat near Ilford, partly because we loved each other so quickly but also because it made financial sense because I had no money. And whenever I promise myself I'll break up with him and be on my own, a spreadsheet of numbers with minuses next to them starts rolling through my mind and I think 'HOW?'

A new glimmer of possibility twinkles at me: the golf club. I should find out how much they pay there. Whether it's more than the pub and if they need anyone, maybe even a managerial something? Would that be weird with Ella or might she help me because she feels bad . . . or maybe she'll leave and get a job somewhere else because of Chris? On the back of this shiny new idea an even better one occurs to me. I should get injured at The Slipper. Break something really important like my head or spine on a slippy floor. Or I could trip over the glass wash door when it's been left open and smash my face and nose. I could get reconstructive surgery with some of the payout money. I could get a smaller nose and bigger boobs then become a stripper; they earn loads. And if I had a new face, massive tits and couldn't eat except through a tube or something, I'd look great.

I sit up with my back against the headboard but Ian stays lying down so his face is looking at my thigh. I wonder what he's thinking about. Is he plotting his own escape?

He did fancy me at the beginning, or at least he wasn't repulsed by me. I was on my period the first time we ever did it and he didn't care, it was fine. It was all over his sheets and duvet and when he realised, in the morning, he staggered around like he'd been stabbed and was bleeding

out. He told me to call an ambulance and we really laughed
and I thought he was special. Especially because we'd met
at scaring while putting fake blood and gore on every day
– this post-coital crime scene seemed apt. And when I
walked home I felt grateful that I'd met him. That I had
got the job in the first place and that I'd found him there. I
had been so low after Australia and then breaking up with
James and bang, there was Ian, handy and available. I liked
myself around him. That's what I remember thinking on
the walk home: I was so grateful he liked me because he
made *me* like me.

The audition for scaring was quite funny. It wasn't really
an audition, more of a workshop, but I really really needed
the money because of owing Dana and my credit card bills
and needing to find somewhere to live and blah blah blah.
And the first bit was humiliating. We had to walk around
in a circle, there was about thirty of us, and we were all
walking in the same direction around the outside of the
room, and the man – I didn't know who he was at the
time but assumed he was a boss or someone – he called
out different characters for us to become, like 'Zombie!'
and we all had to start being zombies. If you didn't know
how, you could just look across at what other people were
doing. Arms out in front, dragging a leg, dribbling – stuff
like that. We did loads: vampire, werewolf, mummy. And
you just had to throw yourself into it and make noises or
even get on the floor and howl and crawl if you wanted
to stand out. It all made me want to die – not acting, but
actual death. I had so much fear, not because any of the
other applicants were actually scary but because I realised
I wouldn't get the job. I was so uptight and half-hearted

about it. I didn't even want to be good at yelling and limp-
ing, but I needed the work so much and this was £13 an
hour. That's more than double what I get at The Slipper,
by the way. If I ever needed proof that my life has gone
backwards.

I can hear someone clashing pans below us in the kitchen. The longer we stay up in here, the less Christmas
there'll be to survive.

After the circle bit, the man who was running things and
two other men, they all sat on chairs at one end of the room,
but with their backs to us. One of the men was Ian, but I
didn't know that yet. All the rest of us were down the other
end and we were told to come forward three at a time and
be as scary as we could be, and if we were scary enough the
men would turn around to face us and that meant we'd got
the job. And god this was when it got really bad. Audition-
ees were screeching and shrieking, throwing themselves all
over the place. The three men on chairs were hardly ever
turning round. I was waiting near the end, wondering how
to get out of the room without even trying. This was so
pointless. Only two of us had got a job so far, out of about
twenty. And now people started trying different things, like
being silent and staring menacingly or whispering things
we couldn't hear into the chair men's ears, and this seemed
to be working better and a couple more guys got jobs. And
then a girl sat down cross-legged in the middle of the room.
I thought she was refusing to do it and I thought 'Good for
her', actually. But then, while the people either side of her
were slithering or pretending to be ogres or whatever, she
announced in a very matter-of-fact voice: 'I was ten when
my uncle started molesting me.'

Ian softly nudges me in the ribs.

'What you thinking about?'

I feel like I've won. It's a small victory, a little thing like a blinking competition or a thumb war, but it's mine.

'*You*, actually.'

It's nice not to have to make something up. I don't think people should ever ask what other people are thinking because you are just forcing them to lie to you. If they'd wanted you to know what was on their mind they'd have said it out loud already.

'Remember the scaring audition and Katya said her uncle abused her?'

Ian laughs and grabs my foot that's nearest to him and wiggles it.

'Wasn't it her dad?!'

'I can't believe you turned round.'

'It was the only way to stop her!'

All of the chair men had turned around immediately and Katya had jumped up and celebrated, thinking she'd got the job three times over and done really well. Then she'd left the room to fill out forms with the others and the rest of us were left looking at our feet or taking sips from our water bottles, thinking 'What just happened?'

'That was how you got the job. You should thank her really.'

Ian is tickling my foot now, which is annoying. I pull it away and elbow him a bit. He climbs in front of me and gets out of bed.

'I need a piss.'

I stay where I am and close my eyes.

That was the thing, she'd made it even worse. It was

already too much, grown adults pretending to be monsters in a bright dance studio at two in the afternoon. But now the rules had been broken. And by bringing up child abuse, which is like, it's not a thing you can bring up at any time without absolutely everyone feeling a lot of feelings, whether it's happened to them or not. And I was thinking 'Surely they will stop the audition now. Or is one of the chair men going to ask if we're okay and make a joke to ease the tension?' But on their chairs they were looking at each other like 'What was that?' with eyebrows raised. Then the man who was running it simply called up the next group. And they snarled and yelled but it seemed so dumb and like going through the motions and no one got a job, they all left. And then it was my group, the last three people remaining. And we had to come forward and I didn't have any ideas at all. All I could think was how bullshit this whole day had been and I'd spent all the money on my Oyster getting here. But I stepped forward with the others and then something took over me, and I—

I don't know what it is, actually, it's not the first time it's happened, but I wasn't in control anymore, someone else was piloting. Like in *Quantum Leap* where the guy leaps in and takes over to fulfil some important purpose and I'm just trapped inside me watching him achieve it.

Whatever the reason or higher power (or lower power), my legs walked forward with the others and they were doing their creatures around me, but I didn't change my posture or make any noises. When I got behind the chairs I sat cross-legged, purposefully, like Katya had. Exactly *where* she did. And then – and I don't know how I did this because I can't even do a Liverpudlian accent, I can't do any accents – but I did one, I did a perfect impression of Katya; it just came out of me and I said exactly what she had said, word for word.

And then there was a pause. Everyone stopped. And in my own voice I said, 'Scariest thing I ever saw', and after a second of more pause the chair men laughed. And the other scaring applicants all laughed. Which was – well, it was just a relief. And the main boss, Anthony is his name, I know now, he shook my hand and told me I'd got the job, and all the other people in my group got the job too because it was too much to get anyone to be a zombie or vampire after all we'd been through. Then everyone went for a drink to celebrate in the pub opposite the station, except me because I didn't have any money and said I had to get home.

Someone had saved me and I don't know where it came from but I remember feeling brilliant about it on the tube back and writing in my diary that I thought my life had started.

It occurs to me now that if it had been a *Quantum Leap*-style situation, which I believe is unlikely, but if it was – what was the reason? What was so importantly vital that it needed to happen? It can't just have been about my finances. Was I supposed to meet Ian? Is he my destiny and we are meant to be together? I did use to think that for a while. Can someone be your destiny for a bit and then afterwards not be? Or maybe they can be a stepping stone to more destiny – but it all needs to be lined up?

As I wonder about the cosmic inevitability of myself and Ian I can hear him in the bathroom. There is a metallic clanging, which is how I know he's using Mum's fancy bronze toilet brush. I suppose that's considerate of him and a sign of good manners. It's also revolting and I don't want to know he's having to do it. But I also don't want to see his shit on the side of the toilet.

See this is why you can't love anyone you live with. Because of their digestive system.

I wonder if that's why Dad left us.

FAQs Dana and James's Wedding

So, we are going big with this and I'm sure lots of you will have questions but I'm sure you'll understand we have a lot on our plates and will not be able to answer any queries so hopefully everything you need to know is here. I must stress — PLEASE do not text me asking me things like what to wear or what we want for a present because I will know you have not read this FAQ sheet. I do not have time to deal with extra admin because I have only a year to organise a major event and will not be able to have even one day off!

The things we do for love!

Love Dana and James

Q) What shall I do for a present?

We would really appreciate your 'presence' at our wedding as your main present, but also we are collecting cash gifts on PayPal for our dream honeymoon which is driving across the US of A and seeing the sights. The link is on the invitation, or below, or you can do us a BACS if you find that easier. Or cash on the day if you're an old fogie haha.

Q) What is the dress code?

The main thing is that everyone feels comfortable and like they can have a good time. Within this, if you are coming to the day bit at the church, we would advise pale colours and silky fabrics, lots of hats and long gloves, think Hollywood glamour, Marilyn Monroe, Christina Aguilera, that kind of thing. For the evening 'do' the theme is Burlesque (the film with Cher and Christina Aguilera) but classy. So basques and figure-hugging clothing, but trousers or skirts on the bottom. And heels — the higher the better. PLEASE do not wear anything from Debenhams because I know all the clothes from there and it will remind me of being at work.

Q) Can I bring my children?

There is no one to look after children at the hotel and so we agree it would be much easier if people just organised childcare for the weekend at their homes. This is better all round as it means you can really relax and let your hair down without worrying about nappies or feeding! Also there is a big lake on the grounds and we wouldn't want any little ones to fall in and ruin the day!!!

Q) I am a vegan/allergic to peanuts/low-carb diet, will I be catered for?

Due to so many guests coming along, this will be an issue to speak to the caterers about on the day. I am sure they will be able to fix you something, but if not maybe bring a packed lunch just in case as the hotel is too far from Chelmsford to be reached by Deliveroo.

Q) My partner was not invited, can I have a plus-one?

We had a long hard think about this and have invited everyone we LOVE to our wedding. Sometimes we really LOVE someone, but not their partner, and so we invited them by themselves. We see this as a really good opportunity for you to make new friends among our social group and you will end up with new friends for life. As it is our special day, I want everyone I love to be in one place and I don't want to have to be polite to people I don't get on with, just because they are someone's boyfriend or wife. Of course if you know someone who has not been invited but they would still wish to be part of our magical day, please give them the PayPal link and we would be most grateful for their contribution. <3

I'm watching Dana make James an omelette sandwich. They've just come from breakfast, a betrothal breakfast or whatever, and the first thing James announces as he walks in is that he's starving. My mum was apologetic about it, fussing around and getting things from the fridge, like his greed is her fault. And now Dana is waiting on him like a flirty butler. 'Do you need a cushion on that chair, babe, do you need a top-up, babe?'

James is sitting opposite me drinking Buck's Fizz from a mug because he said he didn't want a 'nancy glass', meaning the very regular glasses Ian and I are drinking from. Although I notice Ian has stopped now. He took one pointed sip to prove he didn't care how James judged his masculinity but hasn't touched it since so obviously does. Mum's on the phone upstairs somewhere, so it's just us siblings and our current and ex-boyfriends in the kitchen.

There's a mental condition I once read about where people say their husbands or wives have been replaced by impostors. I can't remember what it's called but they wake up one day and say, 'Oh yeah, you look like my partner but you are definitely NOT them. You do all the same stuff and sound the same – but your essence is changed, I can tell.' Then they ask for a divorce or whatever and instead get put in the mental asylum. I think I have a version of that with James. He looks the same and does mostly the same stuff, but his essence must've changed because he's not him anymore. Not my him.

It was the only proper holiday I'd ever had abroad when we went to Lanzarote. At first I felt shy when we went out to bars because they were loud and full of tourists dancing 'Gangnam Style' or singing along to the Crazy Frog. But then I'd have one drink and feel fine. That's because they just pour the vodka in over there, they don't measure it in little thimblefuls. They pour it in so when you ask for a vodka and Fanta Lemon it's not lemon-coloured, it's almost clear. And it's not nice to taste either, but suddenly you're having a fantastic time and a deep conversation and then dancing like a pony with everyone else. It was on that holiday I got so drunk I told James about my ambitions. About acting and the biographer and being someone one day. And James told me I should go for it and he believed in me and now he's marrying my sister so . . .

I've been civil, by the way. Said hello and happy Christmas to both of them. Dana hugged me and I let her. She hasn't seen the Christmas twigs yet and I'll admit I am looking forward to her reaction. She's talking so much it's like having the radio on, a chirpy monologue about her work and friends and Stephanie's engagement ring. Dana didn't want an engagement ring because she thinks her hands are ugly, which is lucky because James hasn't bought her one.

'—and it's the only time people from different departments actually get to socialise, and it is nice to know the people who work there, I mean it's such a big place and I walk through Furnishings every day if I'm going to the toilet or to get a panini and I want to know who I'm waving at and saying "Morning" to, and a book club is the perfect

meeting place because it's not just sitting around drinking
and talking—'

'Well, it is.'

James doesn't seem too keen on the Debenhams Book
Club.

'Yes of course it *is*, babe, but talking about books and
literature. Which is much better.'

'Why is talking about books superior to, say, talking
about a TV programme? Or a computer game or football
match?'

Ian throws this down like that's not his exact snobby
opinion. James responds by shaking his hand across the
table. Men are pathetic how they bond by being mean. I'm
watching Dana's back as she butters toast; I can't tell from
her body language if she's bothered.

'The one we're reading this month won *the Turner Prize*!'

She's not listening to anyone, not even herself. She's
bragging about a book winning a prize for paintings and
pauses only for the massive fart of the ketchup.

'Sometimes I don't like the stories in the books at all.
AT ALL. Sometimes they are about awful things happening – horrific.'

Ian is shaking his head at me. We will slag her off together later; this is why I needed him here.

'I have to skip pages—'

Dana puts the food in front of James. It stinks. I don't
like eggs at the best of times, and this is very much the
opposite of best.

'—but once we all talk about it and other people say
what they think I usually like the book a lot more, sometimes I realise I really enjoyed it—'

In Lanzarote, James told me his dream was to set up his own car-dealership franchise, which 1) is what my dad does – Oedipus much? And 2) he's actually done that since. He's achieved his ambitions and I wish he didn't know about mine.

'—and I wouldn't get that with a football match, we couldn't discuss it and analyse it and then I'm persuaded, *Yeah actually we didn't lose to Man U, did we?*'

She's putting on a dumdum voice even though she *is* the dumdum.

'Dana . . .'

Ian presses his leg into mine under the table but I'm not starting anything, I'm genuinely worried she's had a brain aneurysm or had her drink spiked.

'. . . are you alright?'

Dana plonks herself onto James's lap with the performative aplomb of Liza Minnelli finishing a song.

'I'm the happiest I've ever been.'

Dana smiles at me while James scowls over her shoulder because she's blocking his access to his second breakfast.

'I really want this Christmas to be nice – it's the only one I'll ever have as a fiancée.'

Why do we need to divide time like that, into festivals and birthdays and moments? Time is already divided into practical and usable chunks and, really, none is more special or finite than the others. Goodbye, precious minute, I'll never get you back, you're gone forever, bye-bye, sorry you had to smell of eggs. I like the idea of the past being gone, even this moment – the present – instantly consigned to the past. There was something Ian said once about all our cells dying and being replaced that made me feel so floaty and calm. How every microscopic element of us changes and reboots and so we are not even ourselves anymore after a few years: we've grown into a brand-new person.

James pats the chair next to him for Dana and she moves obediently. Then for a few moments we are watching him eat. His mouth twisting and clenching like a toothed anus. I can't believe I ever touched him or let him pump away behind me.

'What is that thing with all your cells being renewed so you become a completely different person?'

James starts answering, even though his mouth is full of food and I was patently not asking him. Ian doesn't care; his eyes are cast longingly towards his homosexual drink. I keep my face blank but I refuse to absorb anything James is saying. I've zoned him out. I am doing my own mental maths.

I want to know how much time has to pass until James did not touch my current body but an old one. A different me that has flaked off and disintegrated down the plughole. The caterpillar me, un-existed except for some recollections. It's only been three-ish years since Dana told him and he dumped me; I don't know if that's enough.

'What did you two have for breakfast?'

Is Dana making boring small talk or trying to be a bitch? I wave my nancy glass of orange and prosecco in answer as Mum sweeps back in. She's wearing a red sweater that says 'I'm a Ho Ho Ho' across the front with a denim miniskirt and knee-length boots. Her hair is tonged and there is badly applied contouring along her cheekbones.

'Ready for church?' is out of my mouth before I've even decided to say it. But no one laughs, even though it was objectively really funny. Mum ignores me and squeezes Ian's shoulder on her way to the fridge.

'You look lovely, Pippa.'

James is sucking up as usual.

'Where's Ron?'

Dana's face is so innocent, like she really doesn't know.

'I thought he'd be here?'

'That was him on the phone . . .'

Mum is pointing behind her, giving Ron's non-presence a geographical location.

'We did gifts on the twenty-third.'

Mum starts washing up the bowl and pan Dana used while telling us what Ron got her: gym shorts and a membership for the new SoulCycle in Chelmsford.

'Leave that, Pippa, I'll do it,' James offers, exactly as Mum is finishing.

'Ah, that's thoughtful, what did you get him?'

Dana is such a suck-up.

Mum got Ron a TK Maxx voucher so he can get some new shirts for work. Vouchers are so depressing. But I guess she couldn't give him a proper present, that exists, in case his wife asks where he got it.

'And where is he?'

Dana's face doesn't betray any maliciousness, so yet again I have to question her intelligence.

Mum throws the tea towel into the washing machine.

'He's with his other family.'

'Oh Mum, I'm sorry, I thought he'd sorted all that out.'

Dana gets up to hug Mum. They hug for as long as it takes me to down my drink and then James pushes his chair back and joins them, hugging their hug, resting his tilted head on my mother's, and they all have their eyes closed and I don't know where to look.

Ian nudges me as if I should say or do something, but what?

PUPIL	SUBJECT	TEACHER
Sophie Collins	Religious Education	Mr Donaldson

Class interaction: 2/10

Sophie is clearly bright and has the ability to succeed, however she often uses her gift with words to be disruptive or steer the class off-topic. Sophie has a questioning mind, but too often these questions do not relate to our syllabus, which is not created to 'give her life meaning' as she so eloquently put it, but to get her a pass at GCSE. Sophie is particularly blistering about Christianity and it is difficult to maintain the 'safe space' of the classroom when she is in one of her moods. For instance she recently alleged that Mary Mother of Christ was an 'underaged victim' of God and claimed that Jesus's conception had not involved 'consent'.

I would appreciate some parental input if you have any idea what I can do to improve the situation.

Written work: 7/10

Sophie seems to engage much better with written work (perhaps because there is no one to show off to) and managed to meet most of this year's deadlines (which is an improvement on last year). My main concern with Sophie's essays are that they contain elements of, shall we say, the fantastical. Sophie writes of visiting India this year and having lived on an ashram, yet when I checked with Sophie's form tutor they too doubted this was the case.

It is vital that Sophie learns the difference between 'stories' and reality if she is to flourish in her studies. And indeed, in her life.

Overall: 5/10

Sophie is by no means a hopeless pupil, and when she puts her mind to a task there is clearly no stopping her. Her main strength is her interest in other cultures alien to our own, and she seems to have a strong sense of principles and morality alongside a healthy dose of cynicism.

There has been an improvement since last year's shenanigans, and I have found no menstrual products in my desk or cupboard.

We're doing presents round the twigs. Mum got me a Filo-fax. I want to cry because it's leather and expensive and I didn't know Filofaxes still existed. As I opened it she said, 'You used to love mine when you were a little girl' and I feel so ungrateful. I couldn't bear how she looked at me for reassurance like she'd done a good job. I swallowed the crying to save her feelings and now it's turned into nausea for some reason. The Filofax is in my cross-legged lap, so wrong and so precious.

Dana didn't comment on Mum's deconstructed Christmas tree so she must have been round and seen it already. James called the twigs 'classy' and my mother responded by blushing and doing jazz hands. Baffling.

I had to sit here and watch Dana and James swapping their gifts. They made a big show about how they're saving money for the wedding and only doing small things – then unwrapped the biggest parcels under the twigs. They've got each other monogrammed bathrobes from the spa hotel James proposed at and they've put them on over their clothes, giggling. I'm pretty sure Dana bought both of them because James looked surprised at their reveal. Ian has avoided my eye throughout.

Here's some background: James is the tightest person I've ever met. There was this thing in *Sherlock* where he can look at a room and see all the clues and information written next to ornaments and furniture; James does something like that but with what things cost. He is constantly pricing everything that's available and provided so he knows how much he's saved or made. When we were together and he went out with friends, he'd be tallying all night. He loved coming home and bragging how he'd only bought one round so was £30 up. 'Up', he called it, when he'd literally been sponging off people he was supposed to like. It's so unattractive. And he'll be doing it here too: four-egg omelette, grated cheese and two slices of bread = £2.50 up.

Mum is drinking prosecco directly from the bottle and James is letting her top up his mug without a flicker. Three gulps of prosecco = £1.65 up. And now Dana is folding their wrapping paper and telling Mum she'll be reusing it, so it's obviously rubbed off on her.

I just got such an <u>appalling</u> mental picture of James rubbing off on my sister that I've reluctantly let Mum refill my glass with her unhygienic backwash. I need to numb my brain and for time to pass. Need to get through today and tomorrow, get a job at the golf club then get my face and tits done.

It's because James is so obsessed with money that the credit card thing bothered him so much. He called my mum as soon as the first bill arrived. He shouldn't have been opening my mail, as actually that's illegal. Mum mentioned that I'd borrowed money from Dana too. I know all this now because I had to do detective work afterwards, piecing together how my life had been destroyed. So James called Dana and then like a little busybody she went through my stuff at Mum's and opened all the post and James brought round the letter from his flat and they laid it all out on the floor and added together what I owed like little psychopaths. And this was their foreplay, apparently – sad. Dana acting the big I am and telling James she would research his 'legal position'. I mean, they could have googled it but they went to the Citizens Advice Bureau like a couple of dweebs.

I keep trying to catch Ian's eye but he still won't look at me. I want a moment of acknowledgement recognising how bizarre and hard this is but he's playing along with everyone else. He's not touched or hugged me once. He's being polite but I can feel his separateness. I can feel his *neutrality* and he's not *allowed* to be neutral. It's not like he doesn't understand; he knows all about James. The first proper conversation we ever had was when I told him about it during after-work drinks. That was when we bonded – because he was sympathetic. And now he's kneeling in fluffy pyjamas, pretending this is all completely normal.

My rejected eyes fall to my lap and the brown Filofax. Mum's was blue, and I didn't love it, not like she thinks. It was talismanic, if that's the right word? It was always with her, always valued and precious. What I loved, because she was always checking it, was that I could put notes or pictures in there. I could hide them in pockets or sleeves or under a paperclip and wait for her to find them. My favourite was when she discovered something at an inappropriate time, like in a work meeting. I loved hearing how everyone had laughed when she'd pulled out what she thought was a business card but had in fact given an important client my glittery drawing of a goat. It was like I'd been there; it made me omnipresent. Even though she was always at work, the people at work knew about me.

My other favourite was when Mum slid a completed 'quiz' across the table to me. My quizzes were always: 'Do you still like me? Do you still love me? Am I a good girl?' And no matter how naughty I'd been, Mum always ticked all the 'Yes' boxes before she gave it back.

It must be menstrual hormones because I feel like I've been run over by this memory. Like my skin is struggling to hold all my insides in. I stroke the Filofax slowly with a flat palm.

I can't help but hold Mum responsible for Dana and James. She didn't warn me that they were off spying on my finances and reading the small print together. All the time, by the way, James was sending me those terse little emails, so he was lying to *me* too. I wasn't in the wrong. Or not yet. Except about the credit cards. And after I saw Chris I called Mum because it was morning in England. She had me on speakerphone but she didn't tell me Dana was there until I heard her. I told Mum I'd met someone amazing then I heard this 'What about James? What about the ramifications of your actions blah blah blah.' Because Dana's really moralistic and a bit of a baby about things like that. I was annoyed she was having a go at me and hung up, but what I didn't expect, though, is that she would tell him.

Ian's passed me my presents wrapped in a Waterstones carrier bag. It's three books. A novel with shrubbery on the front, a biography of Nietzsche and a collection of essays by a male comedian. They're all books he's already read and recommended to me. I was feeling disappointed until I saw James roll his eyes, then I decided to be really grateful. I may have gone a bit over the top pretending to be excited and not knowing which one to start first. Dana picked up the novel and I prickled as she read the blurb on the back. It's about someone who undergoes 'a journey of self-discovery' by tending their grandparents' garden. I was waiting for her to make fun of it but she started on about her book club and how she'd recommend it to them. Ian has told us several times that the author is a black woman, and I don't know what I'm supposed to reply to that. But now Dana is saying, 'It's so *important* to read black writers', which is something she must have heard at Debenhams. James is contrary as usual – 'Why?' – and that's made Mum laugh hysterically. Ian stares at me meaningfully but doesn't do or say anything else. Then he looks down at his hands and shakes his head with disbelief and I know he's storing this away for a debrief with one of his intellectual friends. He's on safari here, a superiority safari. I have changed my mind. I won't read any of the books he's bought me. I'll take them to the charity shop first week in January. That's the appropriate place for a Nietzsche biography, tucked between Jeremy Clarkson and Nigella Lawson and costing a pound.

Thankfully Dana and I don't get each other presents; we haven't for years. They used to cause too many arguments. What we would do is buy something nasty, and then act really innocent and 'I had no idea' when it got opened. So an easy one is to buy a dress that's two sizes too small. And it should be really nice and look good when the person first holds it up so they think 'Oh this year she's got me a proper present.' But then when they try it on it's tiny and humiliating. And that's when you should say something like 'Oh no, you must've put on weight.' That's what I

did the year Dana turned eighteen. It was an expensive
dress from Karen Millen – it had lace and flowers on it and
would have been good for first dates or being a wedding
guest. And while she was spewing about it and going mental I stayed very calm and apologetic and said to Mum, 'I
thought she *was* a size six, how should I know, she seems
so thin.'

I'm enjoying thinking about it now. I know it reflects
poorly on me but it was revenge. The year before, Dana
had wrapped up and gifted me the make-up bag she'd
stolen off me a month earlier. She'd denied taking it but
I knew she had it because she kept wearing my yellow
eye shadow and pink-glitter blusher. And when she gave
it back everything in the bag either was broken or had
run out and that was <u>all</u> my make-up, I didn't have anything else. And when I was trying to explain to Mum what
an awful thing Dana had done, she took *her* side and was
laughing, saying it was a 'funny prank' and 'That's what
Christmas is all about, Sophie.'

My legs are falling asleep from sitting on the carpet so
I get up onto the sofa, even though I hate the smell of the
white leather. Mum used to be poor but now she has quite
a lot of money, and while she still lives in the same house
she's treated herself to fancier things. Like this squelchy
couch, loads of candles no one is allowed to burn and several jug vases from Oliver Bonas. She also has a wine fridge
just for wine. And a glass coffee table and creamy cushions.
This room used to have lino with an unconvincing wooden
floorboard design, which was always cold and tacky but
very practical to wipe clean. We used to slide on our socks
and pretend to ice-skate on it. When Dana knocked her

tooth out being Hulk Hogan it wasn't even a drama, apart from the tooth. It's unrecognisable now, like a family never lived here. We've been erased.

Ian follows and sits next to me. I haven't given him his present yet. I don't think I can in front of the others. From up here I have an unobscured view of Dana tickling James's neck hair, puke.

I don't know the exact details of them getting together and I don't want to. I know about the Citizens Advice and dobbing me in and that when I came home he didn't want to speak to me again. A couple of months later Cousin Beryl said she'd seen them in Costa Coffee and I thought it must've been a coincidence, but it wasn't. Dana admitted it. She told me they made each other happy, as if that's an excuse for anything.

When I was little I had this fantasy about a mix-up at the hospital that meant Mum'd brought home the wrong baby. I awaited the joyful day when the doorbell would ring and it would be someone from Social Services holding the hand of a different little girl. One who was darker like me, and quite sombre. They would say, 'We are so sorry, Mrs Collins, there was a fire alarm while you were giving birth and in the ensuing melee all the babies went back in the wrong cots.' And my mum might be like 'I didn't hear a fire alarm' and Social Services would tell her she'd been off her face on painkillers and couldn't remember properly. And then the social worker would push the new little girl into our house and pull the fake Dana out. They would say, 'This one needs to go to her real family that live in Basildon. They are all fishmongers.' I hated fish at the time so I believed going to Basildon for a life of fishmongery was a fitting punishment for Dana's crimes. And all she'd done at that point was be preferable to me.

Pins and needles attack my feet as they come back to life. I wriggle my toes and wonder where the cats are and if they feel rejected.

She's still preferable to me.

I didn't plan to say goodbye to Fake Dana or even wave out of the window as she was driven away. I'd simply shrug at Mum and say, 'Told you so' or, 'I tried to warn you.' And the new Dana would be my best friend and confidante and somehow, I'm not sure of the logistics of this, we would be twins. Exactly the same age and understanding absolutely everything about each other without needing to explain.

Mum hated it when I said Dana was an impostor or that I missed my twin. She told my form tutor Mrs Smith that I was 'addicted to lying'. That's when I learned you shouldn't say everything out loud; most of it's safer inside. But I knew I was a twin – I knew because I could feel it and I missed her. That might be where my sadness initially came from, actually, my original grief. This would've been when I was about nine, just after Dad left.

By the time I was twelve or thirteen I gave up on the fantasy. Even if there had been a mix-up at the hospital, we'd all been with the wrong families so long that Social Services would probably leave us as we were and think 'no harm done'. My consoling make-believe was replaced with something new: a fear. A morbid worry that I would kill Dana, accidentally on purpose, and end up in prison. As she became more enraging my paranoia grew. What if I happened to be holding a knife one day? And Dana said or did something nasty and SNAP. Like the *Quantum Leap* thing, but in a bad way. No one would believe it wasn't me because I'd be holding the knife and had done it. So I resolved never to hold sharp knives, never to chop or slice, just in case. But I still had dreams where I did it with my hands, strangling her, and then (in the dream) I'd calm down and realise what I'd done and be sorry but it'd be too late. One thing that made me feel better recently, not that I have those dreams very often anymore, but I heard on a true crime podcast that you have to strangle someone for ages and ages for them to die. Like nine or ten minutes even, and I would never do it for that long, it'd be like a minute maximum. But it's scary because I've felt the feelings. When she wiggled down the road with her arse in my jeans I would have killed her if I'd had a gun or a car to run her over with. I'm so glad I didn't because I don't want to go to prison. School was bad enough; I couldn't cope with prison bullying.

'Are you two going to have kids?'

Ian tenses next to me and for a moment I think Mum is asking us, but she's kneeling in front of Dana and James and pointing the prosecco bottle between them. They're still wearing their robes and they look to each other before answering. I don't know exactly what the look means, but they're clearly uncomfortable. They'll have talked about it before, surely; you have to talk about it. I should warn them about the wire monkeys.

James's voice is playful but firm when he responds, 'Pippa, that's private.'

That won't work. On a normal person, yes, but not our mother.

'There's no privacy in this family!'

Mum's laughing at her own wittiness. It makes her seem insane and the sad thing is I think she's having a nice time. Now I'm sad that—

'James wants to wait a bit.'

Dana has deflected by saying it's down to James: clever move. I try not to think about the fact he got me pregnant. Try and fail. It *was* his fault. He always said condoms were tight on him and made it uncomfortable and it was often too much of a palaver to get him to keep one on. I made the mistake of sharing that detail with Ian when I told him about the abortion. I thought I was talking to him about a miserable event in my life but all he heard was that James had a big dick. Ian commandeered my hurt and renamed it as his. It became about respective penis sizes and subsequent worries of comparison.

Mum's preaching to James about how she was young when she had her children.

'I was much, *much* younger than you and I never regretted it.'

Her words are becoming sing-song as she's holding on to them too long, stretching them out because she enjoys them so much. Youuunnnnnger, neeeeeever. Dana and I catch each other's eye. We've heard this speech before, a lot. All through our twenties, in fact. I got it on my voicemail when I was briefly and unintentionally knocked up. Dana got it almost daily when she was breaking up with Dane and Mum was advising her to get up the duff first because 'at least then you'll have a baby'. Dane had hit Dana's head against a wall during a row and Mum was still advising impregnation, which gives you an idea of her warped priorities.

The outrageous thing about hearing this sermon again and again is Mum's complete memory failure. She *did* regret it – she regretted it so much. She used to sit on the end of one or another of our beds crying and telling us how she never should have had us. That she had no life and it was all our fault. That no man would want her because of us. It's why she resented Dad so much – because he could leave and she couldn't. Although she nearly did, with Charlie.

'Where have the cats gone, Pippa?'

Bless Ian, trying to change the subject. James nods at him gratefully.

'We can't have kids yet because I'm not ready to give up smoking!' Dana announces chirpily, which ends the inter-rogation. Now she's standing up and patting herself down for a lighter. She walks towards the stairs but addresses me over her shoulder. 'Want one?'

I do but I shake my head. Ian would complain and call me Fag Ash Lil.

'They've gone, Ron's allergic.'

With that bombshell, Mum is up and down the stairs too, muttering about putting the potatoes on. She hasn't opened the present I got her; it's still leaning against the twig pot. It's a new chopping board. I thought she could use it for dinner but she's not even picked it up. It's the only present I bought this year.

For a split second I'm frozen. My fear response kicks in thinking I've been left up here alone with James. But then Ian starts talking and I remember he's here as well. My cheeks get flushed and hot and I try to breathe enough air in.

'Shall we play Trivial Pursuit?'

James is surprisingly keen and leans over to root through the cupboard under the TV. Ian offers to head to the kitchen for more drinks. They seem very matey, which I consider a huge betrayal on Ian's part.

'I'll go.'

I want to get out of this room and never come back.

They shout what they want at my back as I'm leaving. Beers. Because they're men, I suppose. Because men must only drink beer with other men. Passing some macho bonding test by denying themselves any of the nice drinks.

The Express MediClinic
45 Tottenham Court Road
London
W1T 2EA

November 20—

Dear Sophie Collins,

Thank you for your recent phone call and email. It was lovely
to hear you enjoyed working here and would like to return.
We are afraid there are no vacancies on reception at present.
Good luck with your search and we will, as requested, keep
your details on file.

Hayley Hooper, HR, Express MediClinic

No one's thrown pieces or swept the board off the table or anything like that. So far all tension has been very mature and restrained – passive-aggressive, bubbling up when someone is asked to repeat a question or someone else has taken too long to answer. Dana suggested we should team up as couples or, as if that wouldn't have been bad enough, 'boys versus girls'. Before I could say anything both James and Ian insisted it'd be better if we all played separately. James said we would 'get more goes that way' while Ian lamely suggested it would stop my mother feeling left out. I thought it was because neither of them wanted to be stuck with Dana but now we've started it's become clear there's something else going on. Some unspoken Who Is The Best Test they're playing out with primary-coloured plastic triangles.

Dana is oblivious to it. She's been giggling, giving illegal hints and being generally annoying. She over-celebrates when she gets an answer right by punching the air or putting her top over her head like a footballer – even when the question was easy. When she guesses a wrong answer she says something clichéd like 'Well, you learn something new every day' or 'Won't forget that for next time.' Her cheeks are flushed with the Baileys she's been drinking. She's very alive, I'll give her that.

James also seems to be enjoying himself, especially since he started winning. For the first few rounds he was

getting frustrated. Twice he claimed that he knew everyone else's answers but was getting harder questions on his
turn. Then, once he got his second cheese, he chilled out
and he's being cocky now, taking his time. Nodding when
someone else gets their answer correct like 'Yeah, I knew
that too.' He's got green, purple and pink so far; I've got a
pink too and Dana has an orange. Ian is the only one still
going round with an empty disc. He's got loads of his questions right but keeps failing on the cheese ones. He hasn't
tried to make any excuses, just silently sipping from his
can, staring at the board with venom radiating from him.

It would've been simpler if they'd just gone out to the
garden for a fight. I think Ian would prefer to be punched
in the face by James than be beaten at general knowledge;
it would hurt him less. He's gone to his dark place. Lips
tight together, forehead slightly sweaty. Ian is objectively
cleverer than James, he's read a lot more books and been
to university, but Trivial Pursuit has questions about things
like stick insects and Lady Gaga, and Ian's lit and drama
course at Durham couldn't cover everything. When I saw
how seriously he was taking it I thought it was about me,
for my benefit, for my honour. But as it's gone on I've realised it goes deeper than that: he's playing for his penis.

There's an enforced reprieve now for Christmas dinner.
Mum is serving directly onto our plates, pale roast potatoes, green beans, sweetcorn and some broccoli that's been
microwaved in the bag and made the whole house smell
of farts. I feel sorry looking at it, sorry for all of us. Ian is
lying about how nice it smells while Mum starts slicing
the Quorn roll with its clear sheath still on. There's some
passing of knives and forks and pouring of gravy and I'm

alert, waiting for James to make some pro-meat comment. He won't be able to let this moment pass.

'Are you a "vegetarian" as well?'

James has fingered bunny ears around the word and directed his question to Ian. The question is loaded with something, underlined. Meat is like beer and Quorn is like nancy glasses.

'No. No way.'

James nods approvingly and I suddenly feel like a supporting character in someone else's thing. I'm at the same table but not involved in the action. Playing along, I take a big mouthful of food and chew. Ian watches me, his own fork dangling surprised in the air. My unimportant character happens to be comfortable eating; she swallows and goes back for more. Mum is watching me too.

'So nice . . .'

I'm concentrating on the physical actions as if a director has given them to me. But as I taste the next bite of food I am suddenly ravenous. I breathe to slow myself down before the next bite. Oh my gosh I am so hungry. I chew and eat and I deserve it. I am in a trance of mashing foods together with my fork and then raising them and pronging them between my lips and starting again. Wow. All I can hear is my own jaws and all I can feel is my satisfaction. I am a wolf, I am a lion. Or a badger or a truffle pig. I am all five senses and a salivating orifice.

It's not until I slow down and try to catch the last few bits of sweetcorn that I hear what the others are talking about.

'They were my babies, *are* my babies, but if Ron was going to move in then they couldn't be here and that's just the way it is.'

The poor cats.

'You mustn't think I'm heartless or did it easily – my heart is *bro-ken*.'

Sing-song on that last word again. Ian and James are still eating but Dana has put her cutlery down and is concentrating on Mum. My stomach gurgles loudly but no one reacts. I look at Ian but he's got his head cocked, listening thoughtfully.

'While they were here he had an excuse. He couldn't leave Tania cos he had nowhere to go. Couldn't move in, could he? Because of the cats. He was so allergic – couldn't go more than an hour or two without coughing or getting hair on his suit trousers.'

'Could he not take tablets or whatever?'

Dana's question is reasonable but Mum's gone on the offensive.

'No one liked the fucking cats anyway, you all made fun of me when I got them.'

We didn't make fun of her. We worried that she wouldn't look after them properly and she's proved us completely correct by shipping them off to— I don't even know where they are.

'Where are they?'

'Why, you going to take them?'

Mum starts clearing serving dishes even though people haven't finished. I tell myself this is a soap opera. That the mum character is conveying her emotional turmoil by being noisy with the bowls and plates. Then the mum character starts a monologue about how no one understands how hard it is to be in love with a man who has . . . She searches for the word.

'. . . *commitments*. And all I can do is wait and wait and accept the crumbs from his table. And I'm not allowed to text or call – can you IMAGINE what it's like not to be able to text or call your *boyfriend?*'

Mum slaps her hand on the worktop and I forget for a second and think what good acting she's doing. Or actually it's very over the top, but good for a soap opera. Probably because she's watched so many.

Dana tells her to come back and sit down and starts doing her soothing, manipulative thing. She's going on again about the Debenhams Book Club and some book she thinks Mum would like. Mum doesn't take to the change of topic straight away.

'The cats are at the bloody PDSA, if you must know. Safe and looked after. I *do* know what I'm doing, *I'm* the parent here, I wiped all your bums—'

The fourth wall has been broken. I'm visited by a montage of absurdist scenes, my mother changing the nappies of an adult James and Ian. I don't know why she thinks historical poop-cleaning means she's earned the right to never be questioned.

Dana tries again describing this book and now Ian is feigning interest. I wonder if he will make us go back to Trivial Pursuit or pretend to forget it was happening. Can he accept being in unofficial last place if the game is abandoned or will he risk losing officially by going back to it?

'So it's about how, because she's a therapist this woman, so she speaks to loads of people from all different relationships, and obviously a really common thing is infidelity. And so she calls it, like, reframing, if you reframe it as a normal thing. Or rather the expectation of monogamy is not normal – or yes, it's normal, but not natural, and that's why it doesn't work.'

James is nodding in agreement and even dares a glance at me.

'She has a podcast as well, Mum, where you can listen to the couples talking. And there's really interesting stuff about staying together after cheating. Which is what happened to Toni from Customer Services, right – when she forgave her husband she says she lost loads of friends. They all kept on judging her or making comments saying she should leave him. The book was her recommendation, actually. And Toni says people were looking at her like she was weak, but it's proof of how strong they are together and how strong *she* is, like Hillary Clinton.'

Dana continues, moving on to describe a podcast where a celebrity interviews interesting 'normal' people about their life experiences. And she's talking about an episode with a couple who had 'survived infidelity'. It sounds familiar, and I realise I've heard it too but I don't say anything. I didn't believe it, the forgiveness. It was clear that what she really wanted, the wife, was for it not to have happened. And the nearest she could get to that was to stay with him and pretend it didn't matter, that was the closest she could get to undoing it. The wife used the phrase 'back to the way things were' over and over. That's not processing, is it? It's denial. Dana's going on like there's something holy in reconciliation but Mum disagrees, obviously.

'Well, if Ron's wife forgives him, what does that make me?'

'A cat lady with no cats,' I think but don't say.

'Sometimes infidelity is a mistake, but sometimes it's love. It's the beginning,' Mum continues.

Chris's face pops into my head and as I wonder what he might be doing today, James looks directly at me, like he can hear my thoughts from across the table, and says, 'Women do it more than men anyway. But they usually get away with it and don't get caught.'

We all look at him. It must say in the stage directions 'Everyone looks at James expectantly' or 'James has every-one's attention with this bombshell.'

Mum LOVES this. She's slapped the table, saying she agrees women *do* do it more than men, that women can be 'conniving' and can't be trusted. Dana is nodding dutifully like she's learning something. James is waving his mug around while he warms to his topic.

'Yeah, so women are much better liars because of their verbal dexterity, their brains are wired by evolution for getting away with lying—'

Mum is giving him a round of applause now.

'*That's* feminism.'

My mum doesn't know what feminism means.

'There was an article about it on the internet.'

James has namedropped 'the internet' like it's a peer-reviewed journal.

'Can you send that to me? It sounds really interesting.'

Something unspoken passes between Ian and James and it enrages me. Now Ian's giving James his email address. My stomach gurgles again and I feel like Mum as I get up with my plate and head for the sink; there's nothing else to do with my anger except stomp a couple of feet away and loudly tidy up. I run the tap on my plate and the sweetcorn survivors

slide down into the sink. I'm trying not to think about what
I ate and where it is in me. What it looks like now.

'You really hurt me, you know.'

I stay very still. I hope very, *very* hard that James isn't
talking to me. That someone else will reply. I look out of
the window in front of me and I see my reflection. Pale
and ugly, holding a plate. Bottom teeth biting up into top
lip like a terrier. There is no movement behind me. Maybe
if I turn round they'll all be gone. Like the *Mary Celeste*. A
table abandoned – a mystery, they'll say. But I'll know it's
because I wished so hard to never see any of them again
that God finally took pity on me.

'You've never even apologised.'

There is no God.

Ian clears his throat like he's about to say something,
but nothing comes. I turn the tap off. How am I the bad
man here? He's marrying my little sister.

I decide to count to ten in Italian.

Uno. Due. Tre. Quattro. Then whatever the Italian for
five is. Then the Italian for six.

'I hate being here on my own, doing all this on my own.'

Ah. I knew if there was a long enough gap my mum
would make it all about her again. I am exceptionally
grateful. Dana and I have heard versions of this speech on
a multitude of 'special' occasions. I don't turn round but
place my plate in the plastic drying rack.

'I'm the spare wheel, the third one. You're all in couples
together and I'm the skivvy making dinner and cleaning
up after everyone . . .'

I come back to the table for more plates. My character
is a good daughter, she is doing what she can.

'I'll wash up, Mum.'

My head feels tired. I think I'm hung-over already.

As I take Ian and Mum's plates to the bin to scrape, I listen to James reassuring her.

'You're not alone, Pips, you're with your family.'

'Yeah.'

Ian's input is unconvincing but bless him for having a go. Dana's quiet; I'm not going to bother either.

'And this time next year Ron will be with you.'

I don't know if James has even met Ron but when I glance over my shoulder Mum is holding James's hand gratefully. I want to switch this programme off, it's too annoying.

At least my character's tense moment is over.

'Has he said that?'

They must've met, then. James probably goes to that same dumb gym.

'He's clearly besotted with you.'

James probably thinks he's being so kind and caring, such a good future son-in-law. He probably wants an award for saving Christmas. He hasn't yet learned that it's a black hole. You chuck all your words at it and it doesn't make a difference. It doesn't make her feel better – sometimes she won't even remember. I'm struck now by the similarity with Ian.

The soap opera has gone, I've lost it, it wasn't believable.

I've finished washing up the plates and Ian comes over to look for a tea towel. I pass him a faded spotty one and he picks up a fork to dry. This act of domesticity triggers Mum again.

'Are *you two* going to have children?'

Shit. I smile at Ian in apology as I pass him a dinner plate, but he doesn't smile back.

'You don't have to be married or anything.'

She must be desperate for grandkids.

I don't know what to say. I never know what the truth is. I don't know—

'We haven't decided yet.'

Ian has answered for both of us. He was a bit pointed. There's no talking for a few moments, just the clatter of cutlery and the squeak of the tea towel.

Mum gestures around the room.

'Aaaaall this is about the birth of a baby—'

I have no idea what she's talking about – what baby? Then I realise she means Christmas itself. I want to go to bed.

'—and I'm redoing my will and need to know how to divide everything up. I've been having these pains in my kidney . . .'

As Mum begins to plan her death out loud we each instinctively jump into action. I open the fridge and start calling out the names of desserts that aren't in there.

'Tiramisu? Pavlova? Banana split and custard?'

Dana makes a big fuss of choosing some music on her phone.

'Tunes – we need tunes.'

James suggests opening some brandy he got given by his colleagues then runs upstairs to retrieve it. Liquor will make the situation worse in the long run but may give us a few minutes' reprieve.

Well averted by the busy business and movement, Mum gets up – 'There's only ice cream' – and opens the freezer.

I feel mature and accomplished: we've got through it. We have avoided a crisis and saved the day. But Mum's found a blue rectangle in the freezer drawer and is waving it around shrieking, 'I forgot the Yorkshire puddings!'

Dana, Ian and I are all telling her that we didn't miss them, don't even like them. James comes back with his bottle and suggests we eat them with leftovers later (Yorkshire pudding = 30p up). But it's too late: Mum is weeping dramatically. Her back against the fridge, face in her hands. The tinkling intro to Mariah Carey's 'All I Want for Christmas Is You' fills the room and Mum sobs over the first line, 'You kept *judging* me and *picking on me* and made me forget the Yorkshire puddings . . .'

As I watch her, not knowing what to do for the best, I realise the answer is that I don't think I'd be very good. I don't have what it takes to be a parent.

Right so I've been reading the 'debate' if you can call it that
and I think you all need to put your own precious emotions
and sensitivities aside and use your BRAIN and MIND on
this. The way I see it there are two sides to the 'free will is an
illusion' argument that people take umbrage with – and that
is good and evil. If there is no free will, there is no good, and
your little bleeding hearts cannot bear that because all your
films and songs and f**king Clinton Cards have tricked you
into believing that it is only human goodness that makes life
worth living. Sorry, but 'goodness' is no more worthy than
'badness', and it is mostly subjective anyway (see my post
on the Good Vs Evil thread from earlier this year for further
elucidation). More upsetting to many of you (and there is no
room for UPSET in a debate IMHO) is the fact that if there
is no free will, then it is unfair to punish those who commit
'evil' deeds (again subjective). But think about it, if you were
Hitler, or Myra Hindley or Harold Shipman, if you WERE
them. And you had their exact DNA/genes and their exact
life experiences – socialisation/education/family life etc then
YOU would behave as they did. You would commit those
same deeds. There is no magic bit of your consciousness that
could exist separately to your body and mind and override
what you consider to be evil, in fact your whole perception
of what was evil would be the same as Hitler/Myra Hindley/
Harold Shipman and you'd find their behaviour and actions
REASONABLE because they would be yours.

I think this is the easiest way to explain the absence of free will to any of you who are new to the concept and struggling with this altered understanding of yourself and humanity. We are the same as any other animal. Dolphins are rapists and penguins are necrophiliacs and we don't put them in prison do we???!!!

Hope this helps. Ian

We've left them to it. Trivial Pursuit is now into its third hour and even Dana wasn't giggling or learning something new every day anymore so we issued a joint resignation and escaped. Now we're shivering outside the back door smoking her tailors and sharing a mug of Baileys. We've been getting on, that's what's unusual. She's not annoying me, she's just sweet and talking about herself and seems to be as affected by Mum as I am. Although neither of us has said anything specific.

Mum was upset after dinner. She drank a lot of the brandy, remembered the wrongs perpetrated by several historical lovers (culminating with my father) then went quiet. At sixish she went to the loo and never came back. I went to look and she's in her bedroom with the door shut, locking us all out. I heard the end of *EastEnders* switch to *Coronation Street* so I know she's still awake. She's resentful we're here. As if we've descended and invaded her space against her will. Every year this happens, and every year I swear I won't put myself through it again.

Will that closed bedroom door haunt me at her funeral? Will I wish I'd knocked on it, pulled it off its hinges and shown the woman more compassion? What will I think about as they roll her coffin into the furnace – the Filofax? The cats sitting in cages at the PDSA over Christmas?

Je suis Mum's cats.

At least Ian is having a nice time. He's made quite the

general knowledge comeback. It was five cheeses to four when Dana and I came outside. James's been blaming it on booze, saying he's too drunk to remember things. He slapped his head a couple of times like 'Come on, brain, you should get this' but he blatantly wouldn't have known the head of the UN or the capital of Peru even when sober. The mistake James is making is that all his fussing is fuelling Ian. It's building him up like Marshmallow Man in *Ghostbusters*, making him grow. His eyes are twinkling and his skin is mottled and sweaty and it's awful. A few times he's given James the correct answer without looking at the back of the card – which should be against the rules. And he's pretending to feel bad when James's wrong answer is close, like 'Oooh, ouch, almost – it's nineteen _seventy_-five. Thought you had that one.'

Part of me can't help feeling our conversation hasn't helped him. James. I was hoping, what with Mum having her meltdown, that it was done, that he wouldn't bring it up again. But he caught me on the stairs and—

'You don't want to be a bridesmaid, do you?'

Dana's question surprises me. I take a puff and look across Mum's crap little garden instead of at her face.

'Ever?'

'Mum says you have to do it, or that I have to ask you at least, give you the option.'

'But *you* don't want me to be?' I check with disbelief.

'I was thinking by next year it won't be as weird, we'll all be used to it?'

Her inflection makes it a question. *Will* it stop being weird – is that how it works? Time passes and we simply forget that she met her fiancé through me when he was my boyfriend for two years? That he once sat at our kitchen table for an incredibly similar Christmas dinner holding *my* hand while Mum had her breakdown.

I take a deep breath. Cough some cold smoky clouds from my mouth before inhaling again.

I love smoking. It's so real. It pins me to the world like – like a *pin*. Like when you send your location on an iPhone: POP, 'Here I am', here I stand. Smoking. Alive and inhabiting this precise exact moment. I never even notice my breath if I can't see it. Never acknowledge its magic. And now it's floating above Mum's crazy paving and over next door's garden then up towards the moon. I love the moon. It's skinny tonight and looks lonely. I wish we had twin moons so they could have each other. I mention this to Dana and she agrees and passes me the Baileys mug. Then she says they'd be like sky boobs and we both laugh for ages until eventually we are laughing at how much we're laughing. We'd be a really good advert for smoking.

'We thought if you talked about what happened, then everyone can move on properly.'

They've talked about talking to me. They've planned this. The little lecture I got on the stairs was so they could move on.

I exhale some more smoke moonwards and realise I don't care very much. I relax into the abyss of not caring because it is very, very nice. I nod at Dana like 'Yeah'. Like 'Well done' and 'I agree' as she imagines a utopian future where we all exist and are somehow coexisting.

Is that possible?

If Dana really actually stays with James forever there will logically come a point where the beginning and what came before it won't matter. With enough time all life dries out and becomes history. Just events and statistics that can be coldly contemplated. Like in 2012, one hundred years after the *Titanic* sank, they decided to make it into a theme park. This was in Japan, I think, or China. That's one hundred years between a massive tragedy, hundreds of people drowned in freezing black waters, becoming a fun ride to ride. My icky break-up is obviously nowhere near as disastrous as mass death at sea. Even with the abortion and the threesome – probably about five years max until it's theme-park-suitable.

So maybe Dana's right: it will stop being weird. And my next boyfriend won't feel the need to beat James at a board game because I probably won't tell him that bit of the past. I'll ignore it and it will get dusty and James will become only Dana's and they will have no bearing or impact on my life. They'll have children and I will play with them and I won't wonder what my one would have looked like. I will have let go. I'm enjoying this idea so much, this rewriting and reforming and— I start telling Dana about the chrysalis stage and becoming goo. For some reason she doesn't believe me and is asking too many questions about how and why. Our phones are in the living room so I can't google it and now I'm doubting it's definitely true. My tipsy brain tries to remember the name of the programme I saw it on, when—

'I don't want to be a bridesmaid.'

My mouth has lurched forward with an honesty that I do not possess.

I heard it but I don't believe that was *me*. But like, god bless Irish cream liqueur or the baby Jesus's birthday because for whatever reason Dana is fine. She says, 'I get it' and doesn't seem pissed off or disappointed. It wasn't a test I failed. She doesn't seem relieved either, which might've hurt my feelings.

My shoulders drop and I've got the tingles of new blood flowing into the muscles at the top of my back; it feels lovely and I suppress the urge to yawn. Unravelling nicely, I attempt some flippancy.

'I can't wear a bridesmaid dress anyway. I'd look like Dad in drag.'

Dana laughs while inhaling then has a bent-over cough.

I look mostly like Mum, except when I put make-up on I look more like Dad for some reason.

'Did he text you?'

I brought him up by accident and suddenly his absence is massive and if he's contacted Dana and not me I'll—

'Not yet.'

Ha ha Dana has hope.

'But I think they're a day behind in Australia.'

My silly little sister.

'They're a day ahead, bub. It's Boxing Day there now.'

My shoulders rise again. I feel bad about trampling on her optimism but it was stupid. What's that Einstein quote about expecting different results from the same person? I shouldn't feel bad – I'm here, aren't I, I'm not the parent who didn't even text. Or the one who locked themselves in their bedroom half of Christmas. Talking like this, it's become clear that *we* are the main parts. This has all been about us, the sisters. I hadn't realised. I tell my mouth not to share these thoughts and Dana offers me another cigarette.

'I'm smoking all your fags. I'll buy you a new pack tomorrow.'

Dana smiles and shakes her head like 'You don't have to' – probably because we both know I won't. I take the pack off her to look at the warning picture; I couldn't work out what it was upside down. It's some kind of diseased womb. Dana laughs at my disgusted disbelief.

'"Smoking Kills Your Unborn Child" . . . Ha ha, would have saved me a fortune.'

I mean. I *was* trying to be funny but I guess if it was your fiancé who got me pregnant you wouldn't laugh, because Dana doesn't. Also technically it didn't cost me anything because I borrowed the money from James's dad's girl-friend Stephanie. And I still haven't paid her back. It's on the finance breakdown repayment schedule that Dana worked out for me while she was stealing my boyfriend.

I look at Dana and she is looking at me and I don't want to ruin this moment. This could be the beautiful ending, the denouement after years of tension and misunderstand-ing. We are the next generation and we have managed to rise from our family's ashes pure and unscathed.

'I don't want to be anyone's bridesmaid. But I do want it not to be horrible anymore. He is just yours and we all forget anything that happened before.'

She didn't steal him. I didn't lose him. I just lost, and it's my own fault.

There's a yelp of celebration from inside the house and it seems to support and congratulate me for my mature and evolved sentiment. Dana and I listen and I think we'll probably have to go back inside if the game has finished but—

'I love drinking.'

—she's still talking. And she's refilling our mug with a bottle I hadn't seen her put in her big green coat.

'Your pockets are massive.'

We laugh for ages and ages and our breath is everywhere around us. I tell her I love drinking too. Because I do.

'Does that mean I'm an alcoholic?'

Dana holds the cup up to my mouth to give me first swig of the refill. This physical gesture is nostalgic and while I swallow the gloop, wishing it was more thirst-quenching, Dana says something outrageous.

'If _she's_ not, you're not.'

Dana nodded towards the house when she said 'she'. It was very pointed. We have never discussed this.

'How do we know she's not?'

We laugh again. That's an in-joke, you wouldn't get it. One of Mum's things when she's drunk is to go on and on about how she's not an alcoholic.

'_I just get drunk really fast, it's not like I drink a bottle of whisky a day . . ._'

Dana is doing a good impression of her, holding the mug hand out to the side like an unsteady teapot waving his spout. Mum's always had this definition of alcoholism that involves hard spirits; Sauvignon Blanc is exempt.

'She gets drunk really fast . . .'

Dana takes a puff and exhales.

'. . . because she _drinks_ really fast.'

Dana holds her hand up for a high-five. This is very unlike her. I hit her waiting palm but I'm not comfortable joining in. I look up to Mum's window in case she's watching us but it's dark except for the blue flickers of

the reflected TV. What if she's watching *us* on her screen
– from secret cameras? I shake my head to stop me thinking it.

Mum does drink really fast. She's in a rush to get to the
worst bit of drinking, the being-off-your-face bit. She skips
the social bits – the chatting, laughing or feeling mellow.
Even when we're here she drinks alone. But never hiding
it. Aunty Pat is the exact opposite. Or rather, she is exactly
the same but in the opposite way. She claims to be teetotal but hides mugs of vodka in the kitchen cupboards
and swigs while pretending to peruse the breakfast cereal.
And if you're out she'll bribe a barman or waiter to spike
her drinks so that she can order pious Diet Cokes all night
and drive home completely pissed. They're both drinking
to forget the same childhood but even they don't drink
together. It's a solo activity, not a team sport.

'Like Ian and James and Trivial Pursuit!'

Dana's confused.

'Sorry.'

'What?'

My astute observation doesn't make any sense unless
you're in my head. We're both quiet now and I don't know
what Dana is thinking about – probably how dumb I am.

I'm about to sigh but I stop myself. She'll ask me what's
wrong.

I'm reliving the confrontation with James on the stairs.
I was shocked at him standing so close to me; I couldn't
take it in at first. He was talking and . . . he was calm, not
angry. It was like an apology to begin with – saying he
knew he hadn't been a perfect boyfriend and maybe he
had a lot of growing up to do back then. He wasn't looking

at me, he was looking up and to the side. Above my head. I watched his lips and his stubble as he went on about how Dana's the only person who knows what he went through so she understands. He told me he loved me and I nearly fell down the stairs, then I realised he meant in the past, that he loved me then. Which is weird because I don't feel like he did – I can't believe it.

'It's not even about *what* she drinks, it's about how she behaves.'

Dana's still thinking about Mum. That's good.

I didn't interrupt him – I couldn't think of anything. I just wanted him to get to the end. But then I got worried. He was saying how he never thought he'd ever meet anyone else after he'd been 'hurt so badly' and I thought 'Shit, what if he tries to hug me? What if he wants to hug at the end and I'm stuck on this stair and can't avoid it?' I think I'll evaporate if he ever touches me, I think I'll boil to death inside my skin.

Dana is exhaling smoke to the sky, her neck stretched up like a werewolf howling. When did she get so rebellious? It's my turn to talk now, so that we can bond over what we've seen and lived through. But I can't.

Anyway, he didn't want a hug. He wanted to tell me that because Dana was the only person who had been there, who knew what he'd 'been put through' – that's how he knew she was the only woman he could ever be with. And then he stomped off back downstairs. Like it was me who'd stopped him and been taking up his time – like *he* was relieved to get away from *me*.

Dana is looking at me, waiting. I decide to stick up for Mum, for balance.

'She talks about her drinking because she's paranoid we're judging her for it.'

There. If Mum was listening behind the hedge or has bugged the lawn I won't be in trouble. Or if this is a documentary about sisters trying to become friends, I'm the good sister, the thoughtful eldest one leading by example.

Dana looks back towards the house – I've disappointed her. Or maybe she's checking Mum isn't peeking out of the back door, ready to pounce?

Dana nudges me with her elbow.

'So you had a good chat with J? Cleared the air?'

What can I do?

I nod.

I'm not doing enough. She needs something from me and all I can do is look across the garden and wish this wasn't happening.

'Where've you gone?'

I change the subject.

'Do you remember when she was gonna leave us and go to Spain with that guy?'

Dana remembers. We've never talked about this either. She'd have been about seven or eight. I tell her that's what the cats remind me of and she agrees. Except we were the cats that time, standing between Mum and true love. The unwanted element her boyfriend was allergic to.

'What was his name again?'

'Charlie.'

Dana is hazy on the details so I remind her about Mum coming into our room. Telling us she'd only be gone a year or so. It was kind of like she was asking our permission. She did ask our permission, I think, she wanted us to say we were okay with it, that we'd be fine if she left. I was thinking about this earlier but then I forgot. I want to ask Dana about next door's dog.

'But at least she stayed – in the end.'

Because Charlie dumped her. That's what's worse. It wasn't her choice. And her heart was broken and it was our fault and she cried all the time.

'That's when she started with the wine and the dancing around and—'

'Ohhhhhh.'

Dana hadn't put two and two together. Hadn't realised there was a genesis. And now we've run out of Baileys and my throat is sore from smoking so I shake my head when Dana offers me her second-to-last one. She taps hers on the packet and puts it back inside too. Now I've started talking about this, I can't stop. My words spill out as I admit that the worst thing about Mum drunk isn't the crying or rages, it's the irrational 'love' that comes out of nowhere and doesn't feel real. When she wants to stroke my hair and call me 'precious' and 'beautiful' and . . . Dana is nodding and listening. But I shouldn't be saying any of this, I can't put it back—

'I keep imagining her funeral, but I don't feel anything, I'll just be numb and not crying and then society will hang me in the town square in France—'

I've gone too far.

Dana is looking up at the moon.

I'm drunk. I am the hypocrite who is drunk and maybe *I* don't realise how mad and out of control I seem . . . Maybe everyone hates me when I'm like this, they just don't tell me to my face. I sound like her anyway, talking about funerals and imagining her dead.

Je suis Mummy.

Dana turns and steps towards the house without looking at me and I realise this is over. Whatever this could have been, I've done it wrong. I've been too disjointed and negative and my brain is too slippy now for me to regain control. My thoughts are overlapping and out of the dog park, yapping all at once and pulling in opposite directions.

Dana opens the back door carefully and puts our cup in the empty sink. One of us should rinse it or it'll be another thing for Mum to shout about tomorrow, but Dana keeps moving.

It's so quiet. I wonder what Ian and James are doing and, more worryingly, what they've been talking about.

As we tiptoe through the kitchen Dana whispers to me, 'I want us to be normal sisters.'

And she's walking in front so she can't see me. But in case she can feel it I nod in agreement. I am agreeing that that's a reasonable thing to want – not that it's possible.

How could it be when neither of us knows what it means?

QuickQuid

20 December 20—

Dear Sophie Collins,

Further to your recent short-term loan application for £500 we are writing to advise you that we cannot extend credit to you at this time.

After reviewing your supporting documents and paperwork we have found that you are classed as a risky investment due to insufficient income and a low credit score.

There are many ways you can improve your credit score before applying for any future lending to avoid disappointment.

Wishing you all the best this Christmas season,

Klover

Vicky Clover at QuickQuid

I went to sleep without speaking to Ian – he and James have embarked on some kind of bromance. They agreed to call Trivial Pursuit a draw, fine, but they then turned that truce into a kind of party. Ian made toasted Brie sandwiches in the Breville while James downloaded an old Cliff Richard Christmas album, which they both sang along to. Then they started shouting about God, not arguing, but too-loud talking about what they believe and don't believe. It was ridiculous. James decided to convert from atheist to agnostic and expected us all to be excited. Dana and I were just sitting there trying to concentrate on *Shrek 2*.

When it got past midnight I told Ian to turn the music down and he got all petulant like I was embarrassing him. I was only worried about the neighbours and wanted to go to bed. There's only so many times any sensible person can be expected to sit through the lyric 'children singing Christian rhyme' without being suicidal. So Ian, James and Dana decided to go out for a drive together. I don't know whose car they took or where they went or who was driving but they were all over the limit and I'm furious. Partly about the dangerous driving but mostly about Ian's lack of loyalty.

I came up and tried to fall asleep but anger was pumping through me where my blood should be. So I was still rigidly awake when Ian came into the room, and he was wobbling around taking his shoes off and telling me that I had no right to be pissed off, that he was just 'making the best of a bad situation' and trying to enjoy his Christmas. Why is it HIS Christmas? Why does everyone always think it's theirs?

I had fitful anxious dreams where whatever I was trying to do, I couldn't. Boxes wouldn't shut and cardigans wouldn't do up and I couldn't move – I would swing my limbs but couldn't go anywhere. Then I fell in a stream and I couldn't get out and the water was getting faster and deeper. I knew I was dreaming and kept telling myself not to fight against it, to relax and float, but I couldn't float. I kept sinking and trying not to inhale the water and drown because Melissa Cable told me at school that if you die in your sleep then you actually die. Then I fell off a cliff and woke up.

That's where I am now, in my old bed, awake, looking across at Ian's sleeping back in Dana's bed, déjà vu from yesterday. My abdomen and upper thighs are aching with period pain which'll get worse if I don't take tablets soon. I break down the beginning of my day into manageable chunks to persuade myself to start moving. Get ibuprofen from bag. Go to bathroom for sink water. Swallow. Change tampon. Brush teeth if I can be bothered.

I'm still in the same position but I have a things-to-do list.

The pain gets worse with a hangover, and the bleeding gets heavier. Which is unfair.

Knock knock at the bedroom door. I stay quiet because I don't want anyone to come in. Mum shouts cheerfully from the other side: 'Ron's here!' Then I hear her steps retreating downstairs. Ron is in the building and Mum sounds so happily carefree, like nothing that happened yesterday happened. I'm wondering how she isn't hung-over when Ian turns around, looks at me and croaks, 'I wonder if Ron's here?'

I imprison the laugh my body yearns to respond with. He can't pretend he's on my side now.

'You have no idea how worried I was. I thought I was going to spend my Boxing Day identifying your mangled-up body.'

My Boxing Day? It seems I can claim ownership of a swathe of time just like everybody else.

Ian is contrite now, delicate and breakable. Even from a couple of feet away I can smell the tangy acid of booze emanating from his mouth and sweat pores. He's pulled the duvet all round him like a fat worm with a little man face, his hair all sticking up. I remember when I used to fancy him crazily and now he's like a film I'm watching but not enjoying very much. People say you fall out of love, but it's not as simple and one-directional as a fall. That would be brutal and easy and whoosh, down you go. This is like – potholing. We are potholing out of love in damp darkness with no clear way out and increasing claustrophobia every day.

Bloody hell – I'm really chuffed with that analogy and can't wait to tell Chris. I've written a list of things to talk to him about in the notes on my phone even though I don't know if I'll see him again. Or when. I didn't text him all day yesterday and it's nourishing me somehow. Like savings in the bank.

I suppose I should break up with Ian really, either way.

'I didn't want to tell you in front of your folks yesterday, but I wrote sweet messages in the books.'

His face. While calling himself 'sweet'. He really likes himself, which is so annoying.

I worry for a second – I gave those books to the charity shop. He'll be furious.

No, I only thought about doing that, they're in my bag. Phew.

Ian's looking at me, so I crawl to the other end of the bed and get my rucksack. At the top is the Filofax; I put it on the duvet next to me. Resisting the urge to check my mother hasn't written me a note too. What would she have said? 'Sort your life out'? That message was implied.

As I get the paperbacks out onto the bed, I remember that my present to Ian is still in the front pocket. I unzip it and throw him a flat square covered in cartoon Rudolfs. It's such a shit present. I tried to borrow money but it got rejected. I don't watch him open it, I can't. I put the Nietzsche book on my lap and leaf through the front pages until I find Ian's writing. I can't focus on what it says because I'm so aware he's holding what I made.

'Sorry. I know it's rubbish but—'

'Did you handwrite all of these?'

I nod. I enjoyed it, actually; it was relaxing and numbing, like wrapping cutlery. I only copied out poems by poets Ian has mentioned he admires, like Rilke or e. e. cummings or John Donne. And poems are free on the internet, they don't seem to be in copyright or anything, you can just write them out. Or print them if you have a printer. Ian adjusts the duvet around himself and says thanks. I don't know what else to say about it. I don't need to explain to him that I don't have any money, so I look down at his thin, front-leaning scrawl on the title page of the Nietzsche biography:

Dear Sophie, your 'beautiful mind' will love this x x x

If anyone who wasn't me saw this they would think it was such a kind compliment. If you were browsing in the charity shop and happened upon this message you'd imagine a very nice relationship. Someone thinks Sophie's mind is amazing, you would presume. How lucky to be Sophie and so appreciated. You might even be jealous of me. You might wish your boyfriend took more notice of your mind and its beauty. That's what I would probably think if I wasn't me and this was someone else's book. When, actually, if you found this book in the RSPCA or the Mencap then you shouldn't be jealous. Sophie clearly didn't want it anymore; the inscription was no longer precious. Maybe it's an old reminder of an ex who cheated on her, or an uncle who molested her? Or she's dead and someone's donated all her stuff. Either way, not lucky.

My eyes water at the idea of fictional molested Sophie's death. What a waste of her brilliant brain. When I glance up, Ian is smug-smiling because he thinks I'm affected by his clever message. Duh.

It's an in-joke, you see. Not a ha-ha joke that's actually funny, but a reminder of the thread that winds through us and back to the beginning. That's what being a couple is, I think, an identity overlap, because so many things happen when only the two of you are there. Or it's not identity overlap – it's story. You are bonded by shared chapters until one or other of you decides the narrative has finished.

I don't know if it's hormonal or a hangover or the conversation with Dana but I am really philosophical today. Maybe it was all those unsatisfying dreams? Maybe being unhappy ripens your brain for good thoughts?

Ian is gulping from a glass of water that I didn't know he'd brought up. I gesture for him to pass it to me and poke two Nurofen out of their shallow holes and down my throat. While I drink, Ian holds his hand out to take the water back and I get the urge to throw it across no man's land. I pass it nicely and see he has a wet chin. I look back down at the inscription instead of saying something barbed like 'Drink much?'

So the story is, the first time we went out, it wasn't a date, it was after-work drinks with a few scarers, but it became a kind of date because Ian bought me a red wine and only spoke to me all night. I don't normally drink red wine, and this one was very heavy and bloodlike when I'd have preferred a something and Coke with ice. At first I stayed talking to Ian at the bar out of politeness because he'd paid for the drink and was sort of my boss. He was teasing me, saying I was silly to be scared of the other scarers even though I knew them and had seen them putting on their make-up and getting ready. I admitted I was frightened of the dark in the tunnels, and had he even considered that a <u>real</u> murderer might sneak in to kill me? It would be the perfect opportunity. He could be holding a bloody meat cleaver, coming to get me, and no one would stop him – he could walk right in.

Ian was laughing very loudly, I felt embarrassed of how much – people were looking at us. So I suggested we go and sit in the beer garden. There was only a bench free so we had to sit side by side with our backs to the pub wall, looking outwards at other people drinking. It was still sunny even though it was nearly eight o'clock and it was like an advert for how perfect London can seem in the summer. Men were smiling and wearing sunglasses and women were drinking pints and those green London parakeets kept flying over squawking. Ian was too hot in his jumper; it was a navy one like a fisherman would wear, but he couldn't take it off because he'd spilled fake blood down his T-shirt and didn't want to get arrested and we laughed about that. And, sitting next to him, I saw he had writing down his jeans. Numbers, actually, a sum, like long division. And I poked his leg and said something like 'Been doing your tax return, beautiful mind?' Because of that film where the mad man does maths in inappropriate places. And Ian laughed really really loud again, for ages. And for months afterwards he would remember sometimes and quote me and laugh again. Until it got used up as a joke and wasn't funny at all anymore, but it was still a nice reminder of – what? Good times, I suppose. Hope.

Mum's shouting downstairs, calling us down as if Ron is Father Christmas himself.

'Come on guys, HE'S HERE!'

I stand up, shake off my pyjama bottoms and put my jeans on. I'm going to bleed into my pants if I don't go to the bathroom soon. As I'm dressing I notice the tension in the silence around me and Ian. We've been ignoring each other for too many minutes while having our separate thoughts. I don't mean to ask him but it's already out of my mouth.

'What are you thinking about?'

He shrugs and lies.

'Breakfast.'

Fine. I walk out of the bedroom to the bathroom and lock the door without looking back at him. I check the corners for cockroaches, turn on all the taps and sit on the toilet.

The thing it should say on wine bottles, like those warnings on fag packets, is that the first glass is the best glass. That's the one that has all the nice fuzzy buzz and potential in it. All subsequent glasses get progressively worse, until the fourth or fifth one which has paranoia inside. With Ian in the beer garden, I sipped that furry dehydrating red and it metamorphosed into something velvety and special. I looked across the courtyard at tables of chatting flirting London people and told Ian I knew I was bad at being a zombie but I needed the job because of my finances. I told him about the break-up and how stuck I was (the simple version). Then Ian told me he'd had a similar situation. That he'd broken up with her a year ago, and afterwards she'd quit scaring (she'd been a zombie too). Then he poked me in the leg, even though I had nothing written on my jeans, and said something like how he always met girls at work. Which I ignored. Because at this point, even with all the happiness floating around, Ian was just my supervisor who I was only sitting with because he bought me a drink.

I change my tampon, flush the toilet and avoid looking in the mirror that runs along the far wall. I should go back to the bedroom, or to the kitchen, but I don't want to. I run the taps of the bath and then sit down on the floor, listening to the gushing water. I haven't even put the plug in, I can't be bothered to wash. I just need a minute.

I made the red wine last ages and by the end of it I was in love with the planty taste. I was having a nice time – I enjoyed having Ian's focus and attention and it was easy. So I got up to get us a second round. It was payday, I could've got it, but probably because I'd told Ian how skint I was he made a big fuss about wanting to buy more drinks. And while that meant I had to agree to 'same again', as I sat waiting for him to come back I did feel . . . glad. About this job and this sunny evening and these nice people. After the horror of James and the embarrassment of Chris, I was in a new life now. It was starting. I would have friends but no entanglements, no men or starving myself and caring what I looked like. I was even thinking I should maybe write my debts on my jeans so they were always there, then I would see them gradually diminish as I paid them off. Something really good would happen when I was solvent – there would be a final reward. Although I couldn't imagine what that might possibly be and I still can't.

There are footsteps outside the bathroom. Ha ha, Ian needs a piss. I decide not to open the door, but he doesn't even knock. He waits outside for half a minute then gives up. He'll have to go downstairs and be observed by our big family photograph. I hear his creaking ankles as he descends and I wonder how James will greet him today, if they'll continue where they left off or if it was a one-night friendship-stand? All awkward and frosty in the light of day. I turn the taps up higher so I don't have to listen.

I don't know why I ended up telling him. Maybe because I wasn't trying to impress him, or maybe because

I was talking out towards the beer garden and didn't have to watch his face for a reaction. I told him what had happened with James and Sasha.

I'd never told anyone about it before because I still didn't understand what I was telling. What had happened was, after we'd been together for a few months, James told me Sasha was coming out with us. Sasha was his ex who I knew was a beautiful glamour model because James never stopped going on about it. They were still friends and I tried not to be jealous about it because that's feminism. I'd complained at work and Connie said having a partner who's friends with their ex is a good sign because it means they'll want to stay friends with you too. HA – ridiculous to even imagine now.

So we'd gone to Brighton. It'd been like a montage of a good night out on a TV programme: loud music and not being able to hear what was being said and licking salt off each other's hands before tequila shots. But what they never show on TV is that no one can do shots without getting incredibly ill. I mean, those actors will be taking shots of water, which is fine – hydrating, actually. But when it's actual tequila and sambuca and Jägermeister and you've had three or four it is a very disgusting kind of drunk. All terror and spinning. Either being sick or trying not to be sick, and – and I was the latter. But Sasha was so amazing and we were getting on so well. She kept getting me up to dance with her and touching me on the shoulders and she had this glitter body lotion on that made her shine.

And James said we were too late to get back to London so we should get a room, so we walked to a Travelodge along the seafront. It was all fine at this point. We were arm in arm, helping each other walk and shout-singing that song that goes 'der-na der-na der-na-na-na' before becoming shouting about being MAD and YOUNG and in LOVE. And Brighton has absolutely massive seagulls and they made Sasha scream and then we'd all laugh. And I guess when I realised, I— But I didn't for ages. Even when I saw the room only had one double bed, I didn't understand.

I was sitting on it, taking my shoes off and trying not to focus too hard on anything because the room was so spinny, and Sasha sat next to me with her hand on my leg and started kissing my neck. And I still didn't realise. I was panicking, thinking 'Oh no, she thinks I'm a lesbian.' I always worry people can tell I'm a lesbian and that I'll be the last to know. They called me a lesbian at school so I've doubted myself ever since. Maybe I'm really repressed and that's why I don't have any gay feelings? I hardly have any straight feelings either, so something's up.

I didn't know what to do. I felt so embarrassed and awkward and I thought James would say something to stop her, so I looked round for him but he was watching us. Watching like he liked it. And *that's* when I understood.

I told all of this to Ian at the pub. With the sun on my face I felt drowsy and far away from what'd happened.

I'd excused myself to the toilet and drunk loads of sink water with my hand like a scoop. And when I'd come back they'd both been in their pants and tried to touch me and drag me to them, and they chuckled and flirted like they were irresistible. Sasha tried to undress me and James tried to go down on me and I wriggled away. Not saying anything, just rolling out of reach when I could and pulling my top down and my trousers up when I had the chance, and eventually they stopped bothering and then we all went awkwardly, diagonally, to sleep.

When I finished the story I turned to look at Ian for the first time since I'd started. His cheeks were pink because of the sun and his warm jumper and maybe embarrassment? And then I blushed. After sending all my words outwards and across the pub garden, turning towards Ian I was surprised by this unexpected intimacy. He didn't ask any questions or make any flippant jokes. He didn't say anything fake like 'I'm so sorry that happened to you' and he didn't touch me. What he said was 'No one should ever make you do anything you don't want to.' Ian's eyes were calm and his words were so reasonable. I felt much better and so grateful and I think I confused that relief with being in love.

Reprieve for Chelmsford's Suspected Serial Attacker

A suspected perpetrator was released on Tuesday due to legal loopholes.

Chelmsford Police announced today that they have had to release the suspect, who cannot be named, and suspend all charges after it was proved that the arrest involved 'procedural issues'.

There has been much outrage on the Chelmsford Police Facebook page, with many asking for the alleged offender to be named and shamed.

Duty solicitor Ron Cubitt had DNA evidence thrown out of consideration as his client was not properly briefed when he gave his sample and had not received legal counsel at the time.

A spokesman for the Chelmsford Police has stated that the CPS do not consider that they have enough evidence to go forward with a prosecution.

Duty solicitor Ron Cubitt was contacted for comment and claimed, 'Local police need to be aware of the very laws they are there to enforce if they ever want to catch this wicked criminal.'

As we pull off the driveway and onto the empty street, Ian puts his hand on my arm and squeezes. I look straight ahead and concentrate on my posture. I'm not even sure what just happened. I'm confused.

When I came downstairs there was a tense atmosphere but I wasn't worried – I assumed it was to do with Ron being there. I'd missed breakfast because I'd stayed in the bathroom so long. I only came out because my phone needed charging. I'd been googling to see whether women are more likely to commit murder when they're on their period and that'd sucked me down a wormhole of cases where female killers used PMT as a defence. It's really interesting. Cos on the one hand you don't want to reinforce the stereotype that women go batshit on their periods, but on the other hand, if I ever *do* kill someone, it will definitely be on day one or two of bleeding and I'd want that taken into consideration. Thinking about that had cheered me up and made me laugh at myself a bit. So I was calmer and thinking 'Oh I can manage a few more hours with my family' and also 'I'm over the worst this month so everyone is safe.' Stupid cow. Then I'd spent twenty minutes or so reading about whether PMT is a mental illness, which led me to a menstrual question-and-answer page. The top one was: 'If I die with my tampon in, will they take it out before they bury me?' and I was intrigued to know the answer. People also asked whether your period carries on after you've died or while you're in a coma, eventualities I hadn't previously considered. By now my phone was on 5% so I flicked water on my face like I was in a cosmetics advert and went down to the kitchen.

They were all in there. Dana, James, Ian and Ron sitting round the table and Mum standing by the sink with her arms folded. No one acknowledged me and the only seat was next to James so I stayed standing in the doorway. Mum sounded annoyed, saying, 'It's over a year away', then Ron was shrugging defensively, saying he'd 'see what he could do' while I tried to work out what they were talking about. Ron looked awful. He's shaved his last remaining head hairs off finally, which is an improvement, but he also appears to have tripled his sunbed minutes so his head is very conker-y. He was wearing a leather waist-coat over a white T-shirt while Mum was wrapped in an entirely leather outfit: wrap dress, headband and yester-day's boots underneath. She squeaked when she moved, which meant I couldn't focus on what was going on – I'm too easily distracted. I wonder if I'm autistic? Or is that the other one – attention one?

Sitting in the car now, it's gappy and cloudy in my mem-ory even though it was only a few minutes ago. James was eating toast with his mouth open. I remember noticing that because it was awful and I'd thought 'Yes, another 40p for the ledger, eh, James.' I was glad, though, because it stopped me being hungry. I wanted a black coffee, but what was going on? Dana was the only one talking. About her hen do, I'm pretty sure. I decide to ask Ian, 'How'd the thing with Ron start?'

'What thing?'

'Before I came down?'

'Dana tried to give him a wedding invitation and he refused to take it.'

'Dana did?'

I think back and this time my memory puts a white oblong card on the table in front of Ron – it wasn't there before. But surely Ron would have been on Mum's invitation and wouldn't need his own? Like how my invitation says 'Sophie plus one' on it. Doesn't it? Maybe I *haven't* got a plus-one and they expect me to sit through their nuptials alone. If they don't give me a plus-one I'm going to have sex with one of James's relatives and I don't care who it is or how disgusting they are.

'I wonder if Mum asked her to?'

'Definitely that.'

We are nearly at the motorway and the car is warming up and there is a spreading, lightening relief in my body as we put distance between us and them. Even with the lump in my throat.

Dana was spraying out words like a cliché fountain. It all sounded absolutely dreadful. About how she wanted a make-up artist to do all her hens' make-up so they looked like drag queens, how they would go to a karaoke bar and everyone would be given a song to sing (decided by Dana) and then they'd have a Chinese up the Shard and watch the sun go down before going to Tiger Tiger for dancing. I was looking at her and trying to keep my face polite, fighting the eyeroll waiting in my brain. I was trying to stay in a compassionate headspace and not be judgemental when she met my eye, but it was like she didn't recognise me or something; her eyes were hard and she said, '<u>You</u> can't come.' Which was difficult to react to because I didn't want to go and thought it sounded absolutely horrific. I thought she was joking about how I wouldn't have *wanted* to go—

'They're arseholes. I know they're your family but they are.'

Ian's being supportive now so I nod at him like 'Thank you for being supportive' when what I want to do is shout 'Where was that attitude yesterday, you little toad?'

I think again about the blankness in Dana's eyes a few minutes ago. Maybe that's what a quantum leap looks like from the outside. There was someone else in her, someone who had no fondness for me whatsoever. Or maybe some kind of shape-shifter? Either way, it was a person or being or *force* that didn't know what Dana and I'd talked about last night because it announced 'You can't be a bridesmaid' like it was new information.

Ian's concentrating too much on not talking – he's like me when I'm doing an impression of a normal person. Hang on, he's acting guilty.

'Did you know what was going to happen? And you didn't warn me?'

Ian keeps his eyes on the road. We are coming up to a drive-through sex shop that used to be a Little Chef. I'd point it out to him if I didn't think he was a shit boyfriend and a coward.

'I heard them as I walked in, but they stopped talking when they saw me.'

Ian shrugs and I want to hurt him. I want to tell him how much I hate the wiry hair on his shoulders and his concave little chest. I want to tell him all his worst fears about his penis are true.

'And I couldn't turn round and come and tell you, could I?'

'Why?'

'Because they'd know it was me who told.'

I wonder if this cowardice is connected to penis size? If one begets the other.

I squeeze my lips together and watch the Little Cleft whizz past my window. They've incorporated the original sign and logo really well, a neon flashing bra over the chef's apron.

Ian is sighing like I'm the one being annoying.

There used to be an old man who stood outside the sex shop and protested it. He had cardboard signs and painted slogans. When he first appeared, people laughed and beeped at him from their cars – what a silly billy, trying to stop people who want to buy a dildo on their way home from work. But he didn't give up, he stood there all day in all weathers, and eventually everyone felt sorry for him. He should've been indoors in the warm, enjoying what was left of his life. The local paper wrote about him and his protest and people rooted for him and his beliefs and morality. Even though it was the least successful protest of all time, as the sex shop said the old man actually helped drum up business with all his signs and informative articles. Thanks to him, everyone knew precisely what they sold and exactly where they were on the dual carriageway.

My phone rings. I can't help but be hopeful as I get it out of my pocket but it's number withheld.

'Is that them?'

Stupid Ian is hopeful too.

'They're not going to call me to apologise,' I snap at him, then silence my phone. It's still vibrating as I put it back in my coat.

'Maybe they hid the number so you'd answer?'

I'm not going to reply because he's being too bloody foolish. I look back out of the window instead and wonder why anyone would buy a house next to the motorway. To be confronted daily with grey railings and ugly road out of every window. How could anyone enjoy their decadent breakfast of marmalade on toast when they live in a cloud of exhaust fumes? Even the grass along the path is flat and unliving.

Ian's question continues to hang dumbly.

I never answer withheld numbers because I've been in debt too long. Even just holding the phone and seeing it happen sends all my blood and breathing off and away. Like I'm being chased while trapped and, well, I suppose that is exactly what's happening. Clever body. Also, Mum wouldn't know how to withhold her number, even if she had had a change of heart. Which she wouldn't have. She said she never wanted to see me again.

I need to find out what Ian overheard but I'm ignoring him and can't ask.

The way Dana spoke to me, as if last night hadn't happened . . . Maybe she was drunker than I realised – maybe she *is* an alcoholic and all her memory cells have been destroyed by milky liqueurs? Or maybe that's when she was incarnated (is that the right word) by the body-snatcher. That's why she seemed sweet and nice last night then this morning she was herself again, dead-eyed and vicious. She told me I was 'banned' from her wedding and I don't even know what I've done.

My phone starts vibrating again in my pocket. Am I stupid to look at it? In case it *is* Mum and there was a mix-up and whatever they thought I did—

'Answer your phone.'

'Don't tell me what to do.'

I half-pull it out of my pocket to look at the screen.

'It's still unknown number.'

'Answer it.'

'No.'

I would hope that call-centre debt collectors don't work on Boxing Day, but maybe they do. Perhaps they get paid double because it's extra-surprising and they catch people off guard. The poor debtor is relaxing on a relative's sofa enjoying a leftovers sandwich and answers their mobile without thinking and then the operator is like BANG, 'YOU owe us FOUR THOUSAND POUNDS and we need to work out HOW you're going to PAY IT BACK, NOW!!!!' Those phone calls are excruciating because they aren't bothered if you cry and they aren't nice or caring. The debt collectors are just reading off a sheet in the call centre. Probably laminated. And they don't deviate from the questions. It's always 'How much will you be paying this month?' And 'Do you have a debit card to make a payment now?' The last time I answered, which must have been about four months ago, she made me go through all my incomings and outgoings and she had my bank statements on her computer. She was like 'Hmm, you spend a lot in The Slipper – is that a public tavern?' and I was like 'No, I work there and they make you pay for food, I only get a discount' and the woman said, 'Can't you take a packed lunch?' Which was when I cried and she continued not to give a shit.

My phone does a small chirrupy vibrate to let me know I have a voicemail.

'Who've you been texting recently? You're always on your phone.'

Me and Ian have never actually had a row. We don't shout or fight, we sulk and simmer.

'Nadia at work is pregnant and deciding whether to keep it.'

That shuts him up. I can tell he's thinking horrible things about me, probably about how I'm an abortion expert and should be on commission. I'm riding this mini-rush of pride about how good I am at lying, like whoosh, out the words come without me even having to think. Then I'm hit by a crash of shame, remembering my reality-show montage and how hated I would be by the general public. On *Love Island* they even show the person's texts so the whole audience would know that it's Chris I've been messaging.

I take my phone and wave the screen in his face.

'But those calls are from the <u>bank</u>, which is why I didn't answer.'

Ian is still looking at the road ahead of us. There are more cars now, lots of people escaping their relations.

Sometimes the calls aren't even from real people but automated robots who say exactly the same things. They give you instructions like 'Press one if you can pay in full today, press two to pay your monthly minimum.' There is no option for people who can't afford to pay and want to be left alone. The robots are at least easier to hang up on because I don't worry about hurting their feelings or ruining their day. The people always sound so forcibly cheerful and I know they're pretending because I used to work in a call centre and it is really *really* bad. Actually, that was my worst-ever job. You have a headset on and you don't even get to choose when to phone someone, it just beeps and comes straight through – like *you're* a robot. And the managers can listen to you at any time from their headsets and then come over and bollock you because you deviated from the 'script' or gave up too quickly. They call it a script so the out-of-work actors can tell themselves they're playing the 'role' of a call-centre operative. All my jobs have been for out-of-work actors. I really thought becoming an actor would be easier than this because I'm good at pretending and lying. But it's actually impossible – I can only get the non-acting bits of acting. Like never getting on the property ladder or having a holiday. And still earning the same at thirty-two as I did at eighteen.

I open the window a tiny crack for some air and breathe deeply and remind myself of the plan. Golf club, personal injury suit, plastic surgery. I remind myself not to eat today. We stop at a red light and an elderly couple make their way slowly across the crossing in front of us. They're smartly dressed like they've been to church or a drinks reception but they seem to be heading for the big B&Q in the retail park. I'm about to wonder how long they've known each other and when they last had sex when Ian presses the button on his side and rudely closes my window – the window I've just opened because I feel sick. He doesn't look at me or say anything and I don't let a muscle of me react. This is classic us. So passive-aggressive it's boring. Sometimes I hear about violent men and I think at least with them there would be peaks and troughs, some break in the monotonous tension.

I don't mean that. I'm scared of violence and hate pain. I'm just trying to make myself feel lucky to have a boyfriend who doesn't hit me but blaaaah. It's just more sadness coming in at me sideways. I'm sad for the shit other people have to put up with. And I'm sad for old couples and I'm sad for sex shop protests that don't work and I'm sad for all the people who work in call centres.

Ian accelerates forward at the green light and I watch the old couple getting smaller in the wing mirror. There are cars on either side of us. Everyone looks miserable. No one is singing along with their radio or honking and mouthing 'Happy Christmas.' Just tense faces staring ahead. I continue to ignore Ian.

My mind rewinds itself to examine exactly what Mum said. Ron got up and put his arm around her at some point, but not at first. She started by accusing me of talking about her. I thought it was what I'd said in the garden – she must've heard me say I wouldn't cry at her funeral. No way I could deny it so I just stood there. Maybe that was when Ron got up with his arm? Supportive, exactly what you'd want from your married lover. Mum was still talking, going on, at this point still quite calmly, about child abuse. And monkeys. That's when I looked at Dana, Ian and James sitting at the table. I thought she'd gone mad – I needed their faces to confirm it. But Ian was so pale and worried and I realised . . . Yes, that's when I realised. It was the experiment – the starving babies and their wire mothers.

'I don't understand how she knew what you'd told me about those monkeys? We were in the car.'

Ian gulps and – this is it. It must be. This meaningful pause. Is he about to tell me the truth? Secret cameras, child me was right? I watch the muscles in Ian's jaw clench and unclench. Is he battling with his conscience? Deciding that he can't continue with this cruelty, with everyone in the world knowing apart from me? Another swallow. Come on, tell me, my mum can see and hear me at all times because I'm being watched.

Ian's still silent so I open the glovebox to check if there's a camera or recorder in there. I imagine how my face would look from that perspective, and my expression: surprised but also 'I knew it' and then looking relieved that all the lying and paranoia is over. Ian is about to tell me how she does it and I'll always be grateful to him.

I close the glovebox and check under the flap thing on the roof, the thing with the little mirror. There's nothing under there but my own square reflection. I look blotchy, and my lips are very dry. I remember I haven't even brushed my teeth yet and flip the flap back.

Mum whispered when she told me to go. Or to get out. Words to that effect. And then the shouting started. That I thought she was a bad mother. This wasn't me shouting, it was her – shouting at me what she thinks I think. She called me ungrateful, said she's done everything for me, given me everything, ruined her life for me.

Maybe that's when Ron got up and moved over? Because she was hysterical now.

She threw a bottle of washing-up liquid at me but it missed and flew out into the hallway. I didn't look to see

where it landed; I was staying very still. The peanut inside
the M&M, coated and separate, away from the action. Or
if I had to describe it properly, what happens to me in
these situations, it's like the sleep mode a laptop has. Light
blinking but not actually on. Using minimum battery and
not present in any functioning way.

I close and open my eyes a few times to remind myself
I'm awake now. This makes my eyes start watering and
the grey motorway gets blurrier each time it reappears.
I'm feeling sorry for myself and yearn for something com-
forting. Not a hug, I hate hugs, they're too confining and
imprisoning. A pat. I want to be patted like a dog and slink
off to a soft basket. Oh next door's dog again, her black-
and-white face and kindly brown eyes and—

Sorry sorry sorry.

Mum shook her fist at me, like in a cartoon or something.
Repeated that I should 'get out'. And when I turned to go
upstairs, no, it was after Ron'd told me 'I guess you'd better
leave', that's when I turned and Mum yelled behind me:
'Just because you're unhappy doesn't mean it's MY fault.'

Well, touché.

But I didn't think of that at the time. I walked upstairs
on heavy lumpen limbs and refused to meet the eye of any
family photographs on the way. I got my bag and put my
shoes and coat on. I made the beds and I left the Filofax
there on the Playboy duvet.

Ian swallows again and I turn my head to him. I want
him to put his hand on my leg or to squeeze my hand –
but why? I hate him.

I take out my mobile and look at the voicemail notifi-
cation. It says two minutes twenty-two seconds. Must've

been a robot who didn't realise it was communicating
with another robot. Or maybe it did. Maybe they flirted
and had a—

'It's my fault.'

Ian's finally talking.

'Of course it's not.'

I pat Ian's shoulder because I think he's referring to
my debts, that he should've paid them off or something.
That's such an unbearably kind gesture and actually I
would marry him if he did that. I think that might make
me a kind of mail-order bride, though, and that's immoral.
Or maybe it's fine because I'm white?

'It is – I was telling James. When you were outside. We'd
finished quizzing and were just chinwagging . . .'

Quizzing? *Chinwagging?*

'. . . having a giggle.'

Surely he didn't talk like this at the beginning or I would
never have taken my clothes off.

'He was telling me about that polygamy article and
some stuff about male sexuality and, well, we're quite
alike, y'know . . .'

My stomach churns corrosively with yesterday's carbs
and today's painkillers.

'. . . and I was telling him what *I've* been researching
and reading recently and so – we were talking about my
interest in ape experiments—'

'Monkeys.'

As I say it I hear what Ian is trying to tell me. He carries
on, about how he thought he could trust James and feels
let down. Ha. Ha. Ha. Ha. Ha. Ha. Ha.

Ha.

When my parents got divorced I could tell I was supposed to be upset, so I faked it. Especially around my dad, so he wouldn't realise we were all glad he'd left – not because we didn't like him, but because now the shouting would stop (little did I know). Once, I asked my dad why he didn't want custody – why he didn't fight for us? Or at least me. And I cried a little bit so he'd think I was bereft and inconsolable and everything. And my dad responded by telling me that I might not even be real. That *he* might not be real. That I could be in a jar, or rather my brain could be. And scientists, they could attach wires and electrodes to the brain and make me believe I was seeing and hearing and experiencing and feeling all kinds of things – except they weren't really happening. My dad said I could be an experiment. He said, 'The people in the lab want to see how you'll react and so they test you.' What he was getting at was that life might seem hard but you can make yourself feel better by telling yourself 'I'm just a brain in a lab covered in wires and they want to see how I will cope.' I know it sounds crazy but this used to calm me down. A deep breath and the mantra 'Nothing is happening, it's just a simulation that looks and sounds and feels real.' You're not really being punched behind the bike sheds, your boyfriend isn't really initiating a threesome in a Travelodge, your mum isn't really disowning you on Boxing Day.

So, if Ian telling James and James telling Dana and Dana telling Mum is a <u>test</u> . . . how should I react? What am I being judged on? This is where God could help me. If God's the experimenter at least you're being told all the time how much he loves ya and is rooting for you. Much kinder than a guy in a white coat going 'Oh look, she's crying, we broke her – write that down. The findings of our experiment are that being lonely and misunderstood is not nice for a human being, how INTERESTING.'

Maybe they are pushing me to break up with Ian?

I hear the tick-tock of the signalling light as Ian turns the car and, oh, he's pulled in to the McDonald's Drive-Thru. It's a do-over. Everything could have been so different. Ian folds his arms over the steering wheel and rests his head on them. I try not to imagine the bone of his skull underneath his hair.

Ian exhales a deep sigh and I inhale resolution: I'll never marry him. He is a very very bad boyfriend. Or maybe I will murder him and say it was my PMT? I can't be put in prison if I'm a brain in a—

'You haven't had any breakfast.'

Ian's head is still on his arms and his speaking is all muffled.

'I don't want anything.'

He sits upright and takes the keys out of the ignition.

'Well, *I* haven't had any breakfast.'

He gets out and slams the door like I'm in the wrong. And he's taken the keys. I watch his stupid body walk away.

How does this happen? I stayed with James too long and now I've stayed with Ian too long and why? Why can I not finish, what am I scared of? Losing the shared story or realising there *is* no story? There's a sane part of me that knows I'm more miserable staying than if I left.

When we left Mum's earlier they were all chatting again in the kitchen. They did not shout goodbye. I could hear Ron asking James who his best man was going to be, and

James saying how he was 'breaking with tradition' and going with a 'best woman'. His good friend Sasha.

In the story of Dana and James, I am a blip. A hiccup of history that brought them together. I am a small detail of no consequence once my purpose was served. I'm not even the most important brain in the jar.

I open the car door and walk towards where I can see Ian queueing through the window.

Soph —

Sorry to be sitting here by myself like some sort of creep. I wanted to continue our conversation but that bloke at the bar kept joining in. Who is he? You have to put up with him all the time? You're a saint, I couldn't do it. Isn't serving people the worst? I literally feel it killing my soul. Anyway, I'm gonna chill here until you close and then maybe we could go for a walk or something. I feel like you have a really interesting take on everything, and it does me good to have a good friend to talk to. As I said, I really fell into this depression over Christmas, and I don't think I should be alone.

I know you can't check your phone at work or I would have text you.

Also why don't they have music in here, it's so quiet I can hear my pen on this napkin!

Chris X

P.S. This is quite old-fashioned isn't it? I feel like Charles Dickens or Oliver Cromwell.

'SoOOoooo . . .'

She's making that tiny word go up and down and all over the place like a rollercoaster.

'. . . lucky I *didn't* have a sambuca! Like *you* told me to!'

Nadia elbows me a couple of times and giggles like a loon. That's not what I told her at all, but I smile and nod like she's right. Anyone watching would think we were really good friends and that feels nice. Maybe Kermit has seen us on the cameras in the office and thought 'They're getting along well.' We are. It's like sunshine in here today even though it's spitting outside and has been dark since 4 p.m.

I'm having déjà vu times two because Chris is here. Or rather, he's there, about seven feet away behind me. I can probably see his reflection if I— Yes, there he is between the big vodka and the Taboo. Sitting at one of the two-person tables writing something on a napkin. He's really concentrating. I'm going to take him a drink as soon as Nadia stops talking to me and then hopefully I'll see what he's scribbling. I focus my eyes back on her face and nod some more like a nonplussed person would. Someone with simple thoughts and no ex-lovers in the room. Nadia has decided to keep the baby. She seems really glad and I wonder what I should feel. A new person is going to exist and I'm waiting for an emotion related to that. Pete is plonked on his usual stool, listening like a nosy parker, and when I look across at him his eyes are wet and bulbous like he's going to cry. Maybe I'm a non-violent psychopath? One of the ones who don't kill etc but also don't give a shit about any other person.

'. . . which is why I'm going to recommend you for promotion—'

Hang on what why?

'—then you can cover my maternity leave!'

She is lovely, Nadia. This is incredibly thoughtful of her. It's a week into January and I was supposed to have drastically changed my life by now. That's how I know I'm not a psychopath: I'm not successful enough. There was a book, Ian was into it but also thought he could write a better one, and the book said there were lots of psychopaths who don't murder anyone but they also don't empathise AT. ALL. Which makes them really good at jobs and being in charge – they're all politicians or bosses. Which isn't me. All I've achieved so far this year is a fringe, and it looks really dreadful because I cut it myself. A step backwards really, at least for my face. If there's anything I've learned in my thirties, it's don't cut your hair while crying. There should be special scissors that assess your self-esteem before opening their sharp legs—

Wow.

For a second my mood buoys because of how good my invention is, then sinks as I realise that smart scissors would be really expensive and only save the hairs of rich people. I wouldn't be able to afford my own creation. They probably wouldn't even want me on the advert for them because of my fringe.

I once watched a make-up tutorial where the woman

said you have to really love your lips when you put lipstick on, like say to yourself (in your head presumably if you're on the bus or something), 'Oooh, what lovely perfect lips I have, what a nice shape' etc. And then your lipstick will go on better. You'll do a better job. I've never tried that because I have very thin lips, the top one barely covers my teeth and can look quite snarly, so I'd never believe myself pretending to like them. Anyway, I think the opposite is true as well. You shouldn't cut your hair while telling yourself you're an ugly cow. But I couldn't afford to go to the proper hairdressers and pay them to tell me.

Nadia is pretending to work now, humming while cutting up a lemon into little slices. We won't need them, it's dead in here. Everyone is skint or doing Dry January. Our only real customer is Pete, who's currently dabbing his eyes with the sleeves of his shirt. How much do the police get paid? I bet it's a lot cos he must spend forty quid a night in here. Depressingly, that's about what I earn for a shift. We could cut out the middleman and I could buy beers from Tesco and charge him to harass and bore me at my flat. I wonder if I could be a sex worker and have sex with people but only for a lot of money, like £200?

I look at Pete and he looks back at me and I hope he can't read minds. That would be such a lucky skill in the police. I tell him I don't want to fuck him with my eyes just in case. He still looks upset and drippy but I won't ask why. Maybe Nadia's news reminded him that he used to be a baby and now he is old and gross. He has loose skin under his eyes the shape of sideways crisps. I bet he would haggle over the price, I bet he would be like 'That was only worth eighty quid' and you'd have to argue with him. I wonder if you can be a sex worker who only works in pitch-black and never looks at the man? Because that would make it easier. I could tell the clients that it was a kinky thing, sensual, rather than because I found them repulsive.

I turn round to check if Chris is still here. He is. He looks up at me from his writing and I wave. It's like on the buses but closer and stiller and I've got a fringe. Chris is wearing a duffel coat; it's a mustardy colour and looks new. Maybe he got it for Christmas? I can ask him about that, but what worries me is that it's still done up, like he could leave at any moment. I want to take him a drink because then he'll have to stay and drink it. I pick up a pint glass from the shelf near my legs and look for a tea towel. I'm holding one! Silly. I use it to wipe the glass even though it's not wet. I'm pretending it is. Stage one complete: I am holding a glass.

I go over the six New Year's resolutions that I'm – I don't know what the word is – maintaining? Resolving? Or seven, if you include not cutting my own hair again. New Year's I was working here, which was fine because I didn't want to go out anywhere and we got paid double. There was something brutal about kicking people out at 11.20, though, especially as the only people left were Pete and Lisa and Rav. Groups only came in to preload cos it's cheap – they'd all left by about half ten, presumably moving on to places with music and atmosphere. Pete then spent fifteen minutes making up limericks and shouting them in my direction before (thankfully) a heavy cloud descended on him and he stared into space from his stool. Lisa I see once or twice a week – usually at odd times like

Saturday morning or Monday afternoon because she's a part-time nurse/part-time pizza delivery person and has to fit her drinking in where she can. She told me she'd booked New Year's off so she could 'let her hair down'. She kept going on about 'self-care' but didn't really specify what she meant and after we closed I had to clean up her vomit from the floor of the girls' toilets. Rav is my favourite regular, an extremely polite gentleman. His family think he's teetotal for his religion so he sticks to clear spirits and has water chasers. He doesn't want to chat; even on special occasions there's no small talk, just 'Greetings, Abi', drink order, then he sips away while doing crosswords on his iPad. Head Office won't let us have lock-ins like at other pubs, we'd all get fired, so I had to force all three of them to leave and spend the last half-hour of the year alone. You'd hope really pathetic people would become friends and cheer each other up – but they never acknowledge one another. They didn't even say 'Happy New Year' before they went swaying off in different directions, nearly getting run over. That's why my first resolution is to be nicer to regulars. Because they can't even be civil to—

'I'll get a round in.'

Pete gestures with his glass to Nadia's genital region.

'To celebrate.'

Blimey. Pete has never stood anyone else a drink in the whole time I've worked here.

'Oh that's *very* kind of you.'

Even when he brought his wife in once he only ordered for himself and she sat next to him eating a sandwich in clingfilm she'd brought from home. Pete tries to pass me his glass but it's policy never to reuse them. I've told him that several hundred times – it's in case people's mouth germs get on the beer spouts. I have to use the one I've been holding and wiping, back to stage zero.

'Usual, please.'

His sour tone makes it clear he wanted Nadia to pour it. Pete still hasn't forgiven me for not being called Abi. Now he doesn't use any name when addressing me, just speaks in my direction, which I prefer. I pour him his pint and think I will use the 'one for me' for Chris. But when I put the ale down in front of him he passes me a fiver and starts slurping away. It turns out the celebratory round was for Pete only. I give Nadia a deadpan look and she turns away to laugh at her lemons. Maybe she'll ask me to be godmother? My fourth resolution is to be more part of the community.

'Does the dad know?'

'My dad? Or the bubba's?'

I shrug because I don't know if I've asked a rude question. But she hasn't mentioned a boyfriend or—

'Neither.'

She puts down the knife and folds her arms and leans against the back bar like a sassy friend in a movie.

'I didn't want to say anything until I knew what I was going to do.'

Nadia looks at Pete now. He is looking back at her, wet-eyed again. I can't tell if she's furious at his blatant earwigging or telling him he is the father. I *can* imagine them having sex, as long as she's on top and he's lying there, mouth-open ASTONISHED that it is happening. Fat men look thinner lying down because their belly tucks around the sides underneath them.

We are all silent now, standing in a triangle. It can't be my turn to talk – I'm no part of this.

I'm feeling the heavy itch of a secret, but unfortunately my third New Year's resolution is to gossip less. This is the first time I've been tested. It's good that I'm noticing the urge. I want to text Ian or run upstairs to Kermit and blurt it out. No, this is good, this is hot stuff and I'm still standing here and haven't told anyone. Resolution number two is not to lie. Five is to learn how to make myself orgasm. Six is to have my own opinions and not just agree with whoever I'm talking to. I came up with them on the way home from work that night. I think they'll help me like myself.

It was a good walk. Time was turning itself inside out and people were in the streets yelling and singing and there were loud low fireworks from back gardens and it felt good to be separate from it all. I felt powerful to be outside it and not included. The moon was nearly full and I looked at that lonesome soul and thought about how that's the real time, not calendars and clocks. I really am going to do something this year, I'm certain. I have to.

I pick up a new pint glass to pretend to dry. Pete's gone for a piss and Nadia is reunited with her lemons so I dare myself to start pouring a beer but I need to get used to holding the glass first. This is a crime, after all. I got sacked from my last pub because I was caught giving free drinks and the whole experience was humiliating. That was my cousin Beryl's fault – she just walked away without paying and I got the blame. It's the memory of that, being marched to the office and having to watch myself back on the CCTV. Being forced to give back my laminated staff pass, Stephen the manager calling me a thief, urgh, it's the memory of this that's slowing me down.

Ian was out all night on New Year's Eve with people from scaring. I wasn't invited because no one likes me anymore because I left without saying goodbye. I quit and didn't work my notice and they said things to Ian like 'I thought we were friends' and 'What's her problem?' The stupid thing is that I left because I wanted to break up with Ian. I thought if he wasn't my boss then it would be easier but I still didn't. And now it's eight months later and I'm still living with him, just in an even worse job. Although working here is how I saw Chris again and now he's sitting over there. How are you supposed to know when something is meant to be or whether it is just *being*?

I think it was Ian doing revenge. He didn't text me to let me know he wasn't coming home and I didn't call asking where he was because I knew that's what he wanted. I tried to imagine him having sex with someone else but I couldn't make myself care. I even imagined it was in our flat on the chintzy chair or the navy bath mat, but it was like watching David Attenborough. No jealousy, proof that we are dead at the root, like a tooth that doesn't even ache anymore. But apart from that we've been getting on okay. Bobbing around each other. Oh, he did tell me I needed therapy and should go to the doctor – I wasn't even crying at the time, I was calm and sitting on the toilet.

The other reason I quit scaring was because Dana was stealing some of my earnings. I hated the thought of her spending <u>my</u> wages on cinema tickets for James or snacks for him to eat. He'd be enjoying being paid for and having treats while I was eating subterranean sandwiches that always tasted like face paint and fake blood. But now I earn much less and still owe Dana nearly a hundred so I don't know who really got punished. Yes I do, <u>me</u>. So I don't need therapy, I can work this out by myself.

Pete's clambering back on his stool and I smile at him for my resolutions. He looks behind him to see who I'm smiling at. I try to smile more warmly but my top lip is stuck to my teeth.

I haven't heard from Dana or Mum. I did get an email from Dad; it was really nice and friendly so maybe he could sense that I'm being ostracised too, ha ha. He hasn't replied to my reply yet, though.

Nadia is gesturing with her head.

'What?'

She's – she's doing a thing. It's like a pony trying to throw off a crown or something— Oh.

Chris was at the bar behind me. He must've crept up. When I turn to see him he hands me a napkin that he's folded into a little square.

'Is it okay if I wait over there?'

'Yeah. Your Guinness is settling – I'll bring it over.'

Technically I've just broken resolution two. I don't know how that happened – all the words slid out and created a fictional drink. Chris nods and turns away, so I quickly step over to the Guinness pump to stop my eyes trailing after him. I can feel Nadia and Pete; their attention is heavy on my body. I must be convincingly ordinary now. I pull the oversize Guinness lever towards me and it squirts into the glass. I still have the tea towel around it. Something moves in my peripheral vision – it's Chris, sitting at his table and gesturing with *his* head. Why is everyone acting like ponies?

I flip the lever back and see the glass is nearly full so I pour a bit down the sink before placing it on the little Guinness waiting plinth. Chris is pointing now. Oh, at the napkin. It's on the bar. I reach to pick it up and Pete raises his eyebrows at me.

'That the boyfriend?'

'Mind your beeswax, Pete.'

I really like Pregnant Nadia. Pete is laughing because she told him off and now I'm laughing and it feels like a bubbling freedom escaping me.

What funny thing can I say when I give Chris the drink?

I don't know why I chose Guinness but it's the only drink people buy and then walk away and have to come back and get later. I pour the last third. It's such a shame Guinness doesn't taste how it looks or it would be really nice. If I was doing the advert now I'd turn to the camera and say something poetically descriptive like 'Guinness: it's liquid night-time' and then I'd drink a sip without wincing. I once did an advert audition for pâté and they made me lick it off a spoon and said 'Show how nice it tastes' but I couldn't because it didn't. Carla from scaring told me the girl who booked the job was a vegetarian and only mimed licking it.

Right, there's a full pint now, sitting under the tap. Stage two complete. This would be so much easier if we were busy but January is pub apocalypse. There's only about three people in The Pilgrim and they've got a log fire – we can't compete with that. The only advantage we have is that we are cleaner, or at least, our bar and drip trays smell more chemically.

I had no premonition or expectation of this, of Chris coming here again. He stopped texting me after Christmas, which seemed inevitable. I presumed he was busy having fun and had forgotten that I even existed. I checked my phone a lot, out of habit, just in case etc, but I know better than to message him first. So I didn't. But I read over our old messages a lot. And I stocked up and stored things in my head in case he did get back in touch. Clever ideas or interesting facts. I read the books that Ian got me, well, tried to, they were really boring. So while I didn't text Chris I did sort of live my life for him. I was doing things to maintain his interest and impress him, as if he was observing me.

There was a text on New Year's Eve at about 2.30 a.m. but I was already in bed. I didn't see it until the morning and I'll admit something happened when I saw his name. Not a stomach flip or anything, but a tightening. A shallow breath. When I opened it all it said was 'HNY' so of course I wondered what he'd been doing. Who had Chris been with that he was too busy to write those three words out in full? Also, did he actually think of me, separately, as an individual – or did he send that message to everyone in his contacts?

Because it was so confusing and Ian still wasn't home, I wrote about it in my diary. The truth of it and how I couldn't stop thinking about Chris. And that honesty felt brilliant, like instead of sitting outside myself watching judgementally I WAS myself. Then I got worried about Ian snooping and reading it so I ripped that page out and hid it inside the dust jacket of a Margaret Atwood book on my shelf. Then I worried what if Ian changed his mind about reading women and found it? So I tore the page into small pieces and flushed them down the toilet.

I can't help but worry about what'd happen if Ian read my diary so I usually write it in a cryptic way so he wouldn't get annoyed. So like – after I read all the messages he wrote in my Christmas books I put in my diary that I loved them and outlined why. Except all the reasons were the exact opposite of what I really felt. For example I wrote that I felt really understood by him, when in fact they made me sure he has no idea who I am AT ALL. And the oppositeness, that's how I'll know what I really meant when I read back, but Ian wouldn't. He'd think it was nice and I am happy. The only problem with this encoding is that if I'm not around to explain it to my biographer then they might assume everything I say is true. And they'll write some chapter about how Ian and I had a great love affair or how he was 'The One' and then future people won't understand me any more than Ian does.

It's probably because of Dad's affairs that I'm so cautious. Never leave a paper trail. I wonder how Ron is with that? You have to be so careful with receipts and phone bills and it's a lot to think about. One of Dad's girlfriends, Belinda, she left some stuff in our house. Tampax in the bathroom cupboard. Lipstick blotted on tissues in the bin. And then when that was too subtle a whole running bag with smelly gym kit under Mum and Dad's bed. Belinda must've wanted Mum to find out and Mum was fuming about the audacity of it. I bet Belinda told herself she had a nice lip shape when she was putting her make-up on – to be taking such time and care over it in her lover/boss's family bathroom. Maybe that's why Mum doesn't feel bad about Ron: she's justified it. Retaliation to the universe, or balance or something.

When I think about it too much now I recognise that the biographer thing is, well, I would *never* say it out loud or tell anyone. You can't tell people you will one day be very important unless there is some proof or sign of it already. And I am not there yet. I don't even know what it is I'm going to do that'll be so remarkable and special. It started when I came up to secondary from junior school. Suddenly I was very wrong at things, very wrong at being alive. Whatever I said, everyone thought I was weird. I didn't know how to do an impression of a normal person yet. I was so visible everywhere I went, every corridor, in the lunch line, even hiding in the nurse's room pretending to have period pain. They saw me and laughed because I was holding something stupid or wearing something wrong or reading Enid Blyton still. But whenever it happened, which was constantly, I felt the – like Matilda – a strong beam of powerful energy. Except it couldn't move things, it was an energy of assuredness that I was going to be important. They couldn't see it now, but they would one day, and then they would know. My happy ending solidified every day and became more and more definite even though I had no idea of the specifics. I would be like those people on *X Factor* and *Britain's Got Talent* who say, 'I always knew I'd be a singer' and you watch and go 'Oh wow, it was destiny – they were so sure.' I knew knew knew too. Except not with singing, unless people start to think a different kind of singing sounds nice.

Whenever people do interviews like in the *Evening Standard*, actresses and models and designers and stuff, they'll pose in their big outfit and the headline will say 'I always knew I'd be a star'. Special people are aware of how special they are first and then the world agrees and they're proved right later. After school I thought that acting could be my thing, because it's about pretending to be someone else. That seemed to be the key. Everything that's so shit about me wouldn't be in the characters – I could escape it and have none of myself left and that would make me probably the best actor in the entire world.

From: MERCPERTH@AOL.COM
To: sscollins@gmail.com
Subject: RE: Happy Xmas luv Dad

Hola my Chica, excuse me sending from work email I had
your address saved here lol, wanted to 'reach out' and send
you Christmas Greetings and say happy new year. Know
you're too old for presents now and that your old dad always
gets the wrong Thing anyway hang on
The email has gone weird and now all the writing is on the sode
hang in
No I can't fix it hope it's not too distracting
ANYWAY THINKING OF YOU AS ALWAYS
ALWAYS TELLING PEOPLE ABOUT YOU
AND YOUR SISTER
HOPE YOU CAN VISIT AT SOME POINT BUT
KNOW YOU'RE SCARED OF SPIders and that the buses
doesn't pay much. I always tell people you oknw all the facts
about London and you;ll have to take me on a tour next time
I'm in London. Belinda sends her love, she;s been working on
the garden and we have a parrot feeder. Heaven!
Couldm't find Dana's email so tell her I say hello or to get in
touch if she's calmed down now about her birthday
Lots of luv
Dad xx

I've moved the pint of Guinness twice: once onto the back bar, then onto a beer mat on the front bar directly in front of Chris. I wanted him to come over and get it, that would be the most natural thing to happen, that's what people do when they've paid and walked away – they walk back. That would have been the least conspicuous thing. The <u>most</u> conspicuous thing is for me to keep moving it like I have been. We don't do table service, is the problem – it's actually very against the rules. In training they are super-strict about it, telling us we are NOT insured to be carrying drinks around so we mustn't do it. 'Even if the customer has no arms' was Kermit's joke but it wasn't a joke because it's true. They'd have to ask another customer to help them or drink at the bar. I could pass them a straw, but that's it. The rules are very clear. If I were to carry a drink to someone's table and I fell and glassed myself in the face, on my head be it. Or face. I was thinking about this recently but I can't remember why.

I've seen someone get glassed and it was horrifically horrible. Some lads were in mid-week – Siobhan said she thought they were on coke because they were so loud and shouty. They were playing on the *Who Wants to Be a Millionaire?* quiz machine. We don't have it anymore because no one ever played it and the tune was obnoxious. Also it was false advertising because it only went up to £40. But these lads were on it and then these other lads, much quieter, they said they wanted a go. I didn't notice at the time, I thought they all knew each other. They played a round together, I'm not sure if it was a competition between them or an alliance, but one of them pressed the wrong button and lost the winnings and then it kicked off. Mostly punching. But one of the quiet ones held his beer bottle by the neck and smashed it off a pillar and then pushed it onto another man's head. And it wasn't like gushing blood but a spray that you couldn't really see, but I was covered with it afterwards. My white work shirt had millions of the tiniest red dots all over the front. And Pete didn't help. He did nothing except make jokes about how I had to 'take my top off for evidence'. We had to call 999 and Pete walked out before the other police arrived. By then all the lads had gone too, all we had left was a video of what happened.

I'm trying to use mind control to get Chris to look up and realise I've made him a drink and come and get it. I stare at him but he's reading. I can't see what the book is. It's insane that—

'You like him?'

Nadia's voice in my ear; she's looking over my shoulder. She smells clean and natural like a fresh spring bush. I bet she uses an expensive shampoo. I turn to her and I don't know how to answer but my eyes tell her enough because—

'Got it.'

But I don't know what she's got. She winks at me and I resist the urge to copy. I can't do one eye without the other, it's more of a blink.

When I opened Chris's text, alone in bed on New Year's

Day, I replied immediately, except I wrote 'Happy New Year' out in full and put a celebrating emoji at the end. Then I waited in heightened tension for him to text again at any moment. Which he didn't. So my expectation lessened over the last few days until I assumed I'd never hear from him ever again. I was alright about it, at peace. This wasn't like when he stood me up in Australia and I was sunburned and hung-over and *humiliated*. I only had to live the rest of my life without him in it – and I can do that.

But it *is* crazy because yesterday I was feeling proud of myself because I remembered that parable – I think it's a parable. It's about monkeys who get their hands stuck in vases. What happens is the hunters put sweets in these vases or jars, and the monkey wants a delicious treat so he puts his hand inside. But once the monkey's hand is gripped around the sweets it is too big to come out again so the monkey is stuck and the hunter comes back and gets him. And so the parable ends with this very wise statement which is: If you want to be free, all you have to do is let go. Because if the monkey let go of the sweets he could escape. And I realised that's like Chris. If I let go, admit I'll never have him, know him – that there is nothing even to gain from chasing him – then I can be free.

But it's like the universe was listening because, what, twenty? Thirty minutes ago he walks through the pub doors and right up to me. He was moody but I didn't notice because of his new coat. He didn't even make an excuse about why he was here or walking past. Then he spoke to me grumpily like I'd done something wrong. Asked about a voicemail, asked me why I hadn't replied. Nadia was standing next to me listening. And I said I didn't know, and that I hadn't got any voicemails. Which I haven't. And I kept thinking it was a prank and he would crack and laugh any second. Then Pete came in and I had to serve him and Nadia tried to serve Chris but he told her he would wait for me. And I was listening to their conversation even though Pete started telling me about some people whose house burned down and they think the dad did it for the insurance but it got out of control and he killed his whole family by mistake.

What is the monkey supposed to do if he lets the sweets go but the sweets seem to sense that release and jump into his palm and beg to be gripped, what then?

When Nadia came to say hello to Pete I stepped back to Chris, who was looking down at his hands on the bar. I wanted to give him a compliment on his long fingers and his turquoise ring but he started talking. Saying how he'd been sad and low and that he'd told me all about it on that voicemail. And that he'd been disappointed I hadn't replied, because he might have done something stupid and hurt himself. But I haven't had ANY voicemails. I have no idea how that's happened, unless – what if Ian found it and deleted it?

Then Chris wanted to know if I had read the Camus yet (he pronounced it properly) but he didn't wait for me to answer, he told me he thought he was like the main character. That's when Nadia came back over and Chris asked for a napkin and sat at his table and I really seriously wish there was a way of knowing some of the future because if I'd anticipated this, that he would pop in and be my friend and *need* me, then all that stuff after Australia would've been so much easier. That sick terrible regret that – well – I wouldn't have needed to carry it around inside me making my life worse. Why can't memory go forwards as well as backwards? So we can see what happens later and now won't be so hard. You'd have all these assurances: you *will* get married, that job *is* round the corner, someone *will* die and leave you thirty grand inheritance and you can pay off all your debts and go on a sunny cruise.

I decide to be confident about the future even if I can't see it. Off I go. Nadia is getting glasses out of the dishwasher, one by one.

'I'll collect some empties on the way back,' I tell her, and pick up the black pint from the bar and carry it with me as I lift up the hatch to come around the front. I'm heading straight for Chris as if this is—

'He hasn't paid for that.'

Pete hasn't turned around. He's looking at me from the mirror behind the bar, like a hairdresser. I'm right behind his sloping back because I automatically stopped walking when he spoke. Something is telling me to throw the drink at his greasy-haired head. It would smash his skull and flatten him onto the bar. Nadia would scream and I'd be fired and the police would come to take the CCTV footage. My hand wanted to do it, just for a moment: I felt the electrics of the possibility of it in my fingers. Is that the bacteria? They were considering the pros and cons, weighing up the consequences.

I don't want Nadia's baby to hate me.

I put the Guinness down on the bar and take a walk for empties. There aren't any, there's barely anyone here, I'm just walking about like a twat. When I'm near the toilets, Chris pushes his chair back and goes to the bar. Nadia passes him the drink and he gives her some coins. Oh god, he realised. He heard and he's saved me. Pete is watching and glowering and I am flooded with success. If this was a computer game the gold coins would be spinning and I'd be eating and swallowing them all, ching ching ching ching bonanza! Chris is drinking now and I'm high on winning. I walk back to the bar like I've achieved everything I meant to. I'm imagining what character would be purposeful like this, swinging their arms. A lawyer? Tom Cruise as a lawyer who almost killed someone with a pint glass, but in the end he didn't need to and he won the case anyway. So I'm muscular and compact with big white teeth as I return to the hatch and tell Nadia charmingly, 'I'll take care of the glass wash, you're pregnant!'

It's so odd to use that word in a positive context.

Tom Cruise wears off as I take over moving damp glasses one by one from the washer to their rubber-matted shelves. He wouldn't do this. Even in *Cocktail* he only did the flipping and mixing bits – never the clean-up or anti-bac spraying.

My fantasy is that I'd be 'discovered' in an everyday setting. That's what happens to some actors. They are waiting at a bus stop or shopping at Westfield and a director sees them and goes, 'That's it, they're the one I need.' And then when the film comes out the actor says in interviews, 'Yes, I was only at the shops or waiting for public transport but I always knew I was going to be a star.' If a director came in here and he was looking for a barmaid, but she was the kind of barmaid who didn't belong here – she was, she had a long face. And the wrong name badge?

No director will ever be looking for what I'd provide,

so how could it be me? Even my fantasies have given up hope.

I do wonder – I don't know how to find out. But are there people who believe they're special, who *know* they'll be a singer or a star, except the world doesn't agree and it *doesn't* happen? When would they realise, like how old would they be? Is it only on your deathbed you'd go, 'Oh wait, I guess I didn't "make it" after all – I just wanted it.' They never interview those people in the *Evening Standard* or *Hello!* magazine so I can't find out. There's never a woman in a normal-sized outfit with no make-up on next to a headline: 'Didn't Happen for Susan'. If I knew that other people felt like I do and are as *sure* as I am and then achieved nothing, then – well, at least I would know that's a possibility.

I'm crouching down, sliding a couple of small wine glasses into their home, when I hear Nadia and Pete quietly chatting. They're focused on each other and I finally have a private moment to get the napkin out of my pocket and read it.

Jeez Louise.

Chris says he's going to wait for me, until I finish work.

I try to imagine what that'll be like. I'll walk outside and – then what? I can't picture it, there's just blank there. What will we talk about and what will my face do?

All this future I had no idea about. When I was watching him from my bus, when I was crying in the shower after Australia, when I was getting into bed by myself at 12.17 on New Year's Day.

I stand up to look for a wiping cloth and remind myself – I must be prepared. This could be a trick. But, I don't know if it was the Tom Cruise walking or getting on so nicely with Nadia, my body isn't worried. My pulse and bones are solid and trusting underneath me. I'm pleased with them, but remind myself that I mustn't start doing this. I mustn't forget.

The thing about school, towards the end, the problem I had. I blame myself, of course, because I fell for it more than once. I kept falling for it because I was so desperate for it to be true. How it worked was, one of the popular girls would start with a pleasant overture – always very subtle. Then she and other girls would build it up over time, days and weeks. It took longer the more they did it. The story would build and layer, piece by piece, until I'd believe that this time it was real. 'I noticed Jamie kept looking at you in maths', 'The boys had a sleepover and Abbas talked about you in his sleep', 'My brother Stephen saw our year photo and asked if you were seeing anyone?' They'd give me compliments that I didn't realise were lies. They used cosy friendliness to wheedle out my confessions. I'd feel safe enough to admit I hadn't kissed anyone yet, that I didn't believe anyone could like me, especially – well, especially anyone. Those girls were like the conmen on documentaries, grooming me, dripping hope into my ears until I'd fizz uncontrollably about some boy simply because I believed them that *he* liked *me*. It took a lot for me to trust enough, for me to get to the moment of – this makes me want to be sick – telling Abbas how I felt. God, or trying to kiss Jamie. With Stephen they put notes in my bag, poems and declarations nearly every day, until I wrote one back to him and – well, that was a very bad time. I didn't go into school for two weeks afterwards and wouldn't have ever gone back if Dana hadn't slapped Susannah who masterminded the whole thing.

It's useful to think about this and harden myself to whatever Chris is up to.

Although, what occurs to me now . . . I always liked boys who I thought liked me because I so much *wanted* someone to like me. And I liked Chris . . . so . . . did he like me? Is that what I was picking up on and he *has* liked me all along and—

'We don't both need to be here.'

It takes me a second to register where here is that we both are. Nadia's completely right, of course. I'm wiping a pristine back bar with a dirty cloth and she's sliced up about twenty-four lemons.

'I'm going to tell Kerm—'

She's already walked away. I turn to survey the pub. There's Chris on his table still reading. Pete on his stool at the bar. It was so sad when his wife came in, she was so suspicious of us all. Like we might be pestering him rather than the other way round.

Whoops, I accidentally meet his eye.

Behind me I hear the camera scanning the width of the room. The office door bleeps and after some stair-clomping Nadia is back and smiling.

'He says one of us can go.'

I'm not sure what is—

'I'm going to stay cos I need the money.'

Nadia pats her tummy, then winks at me again.

I need the money too but I have nowhere to pat meaningfully and also I don't want to stay I want to go so I'm going

DEBT COLLECT
──── UK ────

19 January 20—

Dear Miss Collins,

Having received no correspondence from yourself regarding our two recent letters we are writing to inform you of our next steps.

Your total debts to be repaid are comprised of
- £6,215.11 owed to Lloyds Bank PLC
- £2,225.41 owed to Meridian Companies and
- £4,900 owed to Barclays Bank Plc.

Total amount to be repaid at your earliest convenience is £13,340.52

If we receive no payment and you continue to ignore communications our next steps include contacting your employer, visiting your place of work and appraisal of assets at your home. We may also employ Civil Enforcement Agents to seize items of property and/or holdings.

Please call 0-800-916-8800 immediately to make your payment.

Thank you for your prompt attention to this important matter.

Sincerely

Fiona Schultz, Debt Collect UK

Chris has his hands in his coat pockets walking next to me. We are quiet at the moment. Cars are going past in the opposite direction, headlights blurred by a light drizzle. I have no idea where we're walking as we haven't discussed it, or anything except how unhappy he feels with his life in England and how much he hates 'Essex people' and how depressing winter is.

This is possibly the best thing that's ever happened to me.

I don't want to suggest we go inside somewhere in case that reminds him he wants to go home instead.

When people say 'It was like a dream' they mean it was THE BEST. They mean something was incredibly special and good, which is actually nothing like a dream. Or not a sleeping dream, anyway. What is truly, *actually* dreamlike is my current sense that someone, probably Chris, could turn into Buzz Aldrin or Saddam Hussein or Robbie Williams any second. Or that gravity might stop working or the whole street turn sideways and become a castle I can't escape from. Tonight is like a dream in that I'm watching it from somewhere else in my mind and not really living it. I definitely don't have any power over it; it's happening around me and I'm simply grateful that my legs aren't being sucked into the ground like in other recent dreams. My skin is numb to the scraping wet wind – I don't think I've breathed for at least an hour. Tonight has been two-dimensional ever since Chris arrived at the pub with his sad angelic face and new coat and handed me a napkin note.

This is the problem with telling yourself things aren't real all the time. If you're always reminding yourself you might be a brain in a jar or starring in a manipulated TV programme then, yes, that's a good coping mechanism, it helps when things are hard. But times like now that I *want* to be occurring don't touch me. I want to experience this properly – rough and sensory and absorbed into all of my pores – but I'm a kite floating behind it. It's as unreal as everything else. I've undermined all of life, dug so many holes underneath it that it's collapsed completely.

I'm about to bring up sinkholes and how cool they are when I realise Chris is still talking. He's critiquing his Australian girlfriend – he's saying he misses the dog more than her. It seems she used to try and control Chris through microaggressions and make him feel bad about himself because he didn't like doing housework. He couldn't 'see' it, apparently.

'Like the washing-up was a ghost?'

Chris is really laughing and I smile like I made a joke on purpose. More words jump out while my mouth is flexing and pleased with itself.

'We had a dog that lived next door to us.'

This is dangerous. This is dangerous for me.

'They kept it in the shed but I was allowed to walk it sometimes.'

Maybe this is why I've always been drawn to Chris. Maybe he is the only person I can tell about the dog who will understand.

'She was black and white and I took her to the park and round the lake and stuff. The man is dead now, he killed himself. I found out at Christmas.'

I shouldn't have put that bit in, it's irrelevant. Chris is looking at me like he feels sorry for me. Am I a drama queen? Do I live for drama and attention?

'She was fine when she was with me. But at night in the shed she would cry and cry and whine and bark. And the man from the house, Aiden, the dead one, he would go out and—'

Chris is really listening to me.

'—he would . . .'

'He hurt her?'

I nod.

'He kicked and hit her and I could hear him.'

'I'm glad he's dead.'

'There was nothing I could do. I couldn't rescue her – I wanted to ask to buy her but my dad said no.'

Chris reaches out and squeezes my arm. I was right, he is the only person that would ever understand this.

'One day another neighbour called the RSPCA and they came and got the dog. They came round and told us all of the things the man had been doing to her. He'd—'

'Shut up – I don't want to hear any more.'

'Sorry.'

'It's making me angry.'

I want to apologise again but I hold it in. Chris is looking ahead of him now. I didn't want to make him angry.

Chris has gone quiet again and I don't know what to do. We continue walking but a disjointed silence has descended and I feel ashamed, like I've been told off. His jaw is clenched and he's put his hands back in his pockets. We've fallen out of sync because Chris has sped up; his body slants forward slightly, leaning into the rain and his next step. I presume he's thinking of an excuse to get away from me. I am getting my face ready to look fine about hearing it.

As our silence becomes more and more uncompanionable my brain whispers a highly confrontational question:

What did I want, then?

There is a red double-decker bus coming towards us. At night the yellow light from inside buses is so beautiful. All the passengers look like portrait paintings in a gallery, hanging up in their adjacent windows. Why didn't I tell Chris something whimsical like that instead of—

What did I want, then?

Nothing, I don't know.

I didn't even get to the important bit of the story, the whole point of it, which is that I don't think my heart will ever heal. How can it? I can't apologise to the dog and explain myself. Tell her that I was a child and didn't have any autonomy or authority or even my own shed to hide her in. Every time we went to the park I could have taken off her lead and let her go free. She could have found a new life or maybe even survived feral in a cave. I often thought about it. But I was scared of Aiden and of getting in trouble so I led her back to her prison and torment but it wasn't because I didn't care. I loved her very much and I was very sorry but I had no idea how to help.

I wish Chris would say something.

After the RSPCA had been round, it wasn't my imagination anymore, making sense of the sounds from their shed. I knew exactly what had hurt her, what the man had done. And I have to know that forever and just carry on.

If I'm a brain in a jar at least that never really happened to the dog. Or maybe that *was* the test and I failed?

What do I <u>want</u>, then?

What do I *mean*, what do I want? With Chris I don't allow myself to want anything. This is reconnaissance. I am finding out what is on offer. You don't just walk into a building demanding to buy shoes, you have to work out if it's a shoe shop first. Only then can you start lusting after heels and boots and plotting how to get them. Yes. That's the perfect analogy. First, what shop is Chris? Then second, how do I become a customer?

Ha ha, I guess Ian was right: I have been completely infiltrated by capitalism.

The other really important bit of the story is that my mum doesn't remember anything about the RSPCA or the dog and Dana says it didn't happen. So what am I supposed to do with that? Am I the schizo insane one, or— How can they not remember? But also, why would they lie?

What if I am actually mental, though? And that's why reality seems slippy so much of the time. In the book *Catch-22* the catch is that you can only leave the army if you get psychological discharge, which you have to ask for by explaining that you're mad. But wanting to leave the army is very sensible so they don't give psychological discharge to anyone who asks, so – no, I don't think this does relate to my predicament. My situation is that I seem sane from the outside so no one notices or tells me I should go to an asylum. It's only in my head, the madness. And there's no way of knowing if all this is going on in everyone else's head too without exposing myself, and I'd rather be insane and on the loose than locked up in a hospital.

Maybe Ian knows. That's why he said I should get therapy, because then the therapist will tell me I'm bananas. If this was the olden days he could just have me put in an asylum whether I was mad or not. That's how people got broken up with back in Jane Austen times. I always assume Ian wants us to stay together; it would be so funny if he wanted to be free too. If he was worried about how *I* would cope.

I need to rein my thoughts in. Chris and I are still walking as if we're going somewhere. The longer this silence between us goes on, the worse it seems. Like we've both forgotten how to speak or a sea-witch has put a curse on us and stolen our voices. Or, more realistically, like we are both still hearing the last things I said and thinking what a knob I am. I cough and force myself to start a new topic of conversation.

'Have you read *Catch-22*?'

Okay, that was a good question. Chris's whole demeanour has changed: he's immediately slowed his pace and is moving his hands about while he tells me who Jean-Paul Sartre is. I'm not going to presume anything about the intelligence of the people he usually hangs around with (Red Mouth, his girlfriend etc) but Chris is assuming . . . I mean, he hasn't asked . . . Now he's telling me about the existentialists, fully confident that this is the first I've heard of them. Which is fine. But it's funny because I've already been told all this stuff by an earlier man who presumed I knew nothing: Ian.

They'd probably get on.

'Do you write Reddit posts, in the philosophy discussion bits?'

'No.'

Chris shakes his head then carries on telling me about writers in rollnecks enjoying cigarettes and conversation outside Parisian cafés.

I wonder how Chris would've behaved around James. If the world was jumbled and reordered and *Chris* was the boyfriend who came over for Christmas, would *he* have made friends and betrayed me? I imagine James, Chris and Ian, heads together, elbows on the table, doing a pub quiz at The Pilgrim. They wouldn't be a good team because they don't have a wide enough range of interests. They'd be good at books and films then wouldn't even bother to name Rihanna songs. They'd be pleased not to know the names of any of the Kardashian offspring – even though it lost them points.

'They had an open relationship.'

That's the main thing I know about the existentialists so I've proffered it.

'Sartre and de Beauvoir.'

Chris is nodding now. I'm remembering James and his article. I hope Chris doesn't think I'm volunteering to be polyamorous with him. He taps me on the arm.

'It's called polyamory.'

I know. Is he flirting or . . .

'You can do that with intellectual relationships.'

Or . . . is he trying to impress me?

We are walking in the rain, on our way to nowhere, discussing French philosophers. If this isn't an intellectual relationship I don't know what is. I picture him upstairs with that girl, with the lips and the nice house. Why can't I recall her name? Samantha? Irish. I thought she was friendly but maybe she was manipulative. Maybe she used me to get to Chris and then used Chris to punish her Jewish fiancé?

'I always thought that Simone de Beauvoir would've been upset about it, though, his other women . . .' I say.

Ian told me about their relationship like it was something to aspire to. We were talking about soulmates back when I thought we were soulmates. I told him I liked the old idea – I think it was the ancient Greeks; they thought there was a place humans exist before we're born, and we're floating around or something, but we are also attached in pairs. So every person has two heads and eight limbs and we like it and feel fantastic and complete. But in order to be born we are broken in half – maybe to be able to fit inside our mothers? They don't really explain why. But it means that each of us is only 50% of ourselves and we have to find the person who is the other half and that's our soulmate. And as I was describing it to Ian he was pulling a shrivelled facial expression. He said something like 'That's not actually possible, though, is it?' Like I'd meant it literally. I obviously hadn't meant it actually happens – it's not in encyclopaedias, there's not a David Attenborough show about it. Sometimes it's nice to imagine those kinds of things when you're in love and feeling lucky.

Also it's not *that* much more far-fetched than science. Maybe it IS true and it's my other half I'm missing, not my twin . . . That longing and brokenness I felt. That I *feel*.

'. . . and of course Camus wasn't really a part of that, but he did agree with them about the war.'

I want to think more about who or what I should be seeking but Chris is clogging up my brain talking about French philosophers. Also water has seeped into the tops of my shoes and my toes are damp and squishy. I am trying to feel good and excited like when we left the pub but my mood has been a bit flushed down the toilet.

I thought what Ian described about Sartre and de Beauvoir was brilliant at first, because I still believed HE was brilliant. So much cleverer than me, which was very beneficial for my self-improvement. Ian explained how they had this electric meeting of minds. Caffeinated verbal sparring at pavement tables, sharing their ideas, reading each other's writing and encouraging each other to flourish. Who wouldn't want that? And when Ian said how they'd had an open relationship, with both having other love affairs – that part of it sounded aspirational too.

It was only later by myself that I got worried about Simone. I googled it and everyone said Sartre was a right philanderer and surely that would've made her insecure because it would've made *me* insecure. I could imagine her standing by a window or on a balcony looking down on the shapely buildings of Paris, wondering who her boyfriend was fucking. And she'd be worrying if it was because she was too fat or had a big nose. Because that's what I'd be doing. And I know Simone de Beauvoir is a separate person to me and a different person. But it's really difficult to imagine her not having all the exact same thoughts as I do. I would've put up with Sartre's behaviour because that was all that was on offer, BUT I would be playing a long game. I'd be hoping he would eventually realise I was the best girlfriend ever (because I'd been so accommodating and also because of the good feedback I gave him on his books and plays). So eventually he'd cancel all his dates with other ladies and just be in a normal relationship with me. He'd realise I had been enough all along; I would win.

'Have I offended you?'

Chris has stopped walking so I stop and step back to where he is standing. I am sick of walking, to be honest. I'm so cold.

'No.'

'I just think you're being a bit sexist.'

Am I?

Chris starts telling me why I'm sexist to assume that an open relationship only suits the male partner and is merely suffered by the female.

'—as if she doesn't have her own sexual needs, needs that couldn't be satisfied by a singular partner—'

I think he might have been talking about this for a while but I've been tuned out. I can't look directly at him so I look down at my hands. I should tell Dana her hands aren't ugly. She only thinks they are because I used to tell her so and buy her gloves on birthdays.

'—equally sexist to assume monogamy is an attractive state to women, or most, or any—'

I haven't been called sexist since Ian told me off about listening to serial killer podcasts. 'Why'd you like this stuff?' he was complaining, and I shouldn't even have to justify that. I don't ask him why he likes German new wave cinema or taking his ukulele to parties. Ian doesn't like the podcasts because they have women on them saying things like 'It's always the husband' and 'Every man is a potential killer, it's in their DNA.' That was what Ian took

offence to. He was adamant he didn't have any hypothet-
ical murderousness inside him and I told him I disagreed,
mainly because he was talking over my podcast and I kept
missing bits and having to go back. Ian's point was that he
is a really gentle guy with no 'innate weaponry built in'
but he was shouting at the time and punched the ward-
robe door, which did undermine him.

Before we left the pub I hid in the staff toilet and texted
Ian to say I was going out after work. I've been really good
tonight. I've changed. Maybe that's why I'm not enjoying
myself? I can't be due on my period because I just had it.
Although sometimes I do have another one straight afterwards and—

'Simone was probably into it even more than Jean-
Paul—'

Chris is still talking, and I'm glad. And I hope he's right;
it's far nicer to imagine that clever French woman having autonomy and a sexy time. I like how he's using their
first names now, like we know them. I picture them both
working on the buses, black rollnecks poking out under
the white shirt of the uniform. Scribbling clever ideas on
the lunch bus. They'd probably refuse to point out the
churches, though.

'—she was *French*.'

Chris said French like it was underlined. Like it meant
something more than coming from a country. He lightly
punches me on the arm so I look at him.

'She probably had hairy armpits!'

Chris is laughing now and I smile back at him.

I have hairy armpits. Not long intentional hair but
stubbly accidental spikes. Ian won't let me use his razor

anymore and my one got so rusty it was making me bleed when I used it. Then it looked like I had scabies on my legs and bikini line, which is as bad as being hairy but itchier.

We are standing looking at each other now. We stopped walking a few moments ago. We are not near anything except a phone box and some traffic lights. Something needs to happen. I use the thought of my armpits to give me momentum.

'I should get home.'

I'd like to give myself a round of applause. I'm so proud. Everyone at the bus stop should give me a standing ovation. Chris is peering at me very closely. I'm looking at the pavement and can't bring my eyes up because I'm scared he'll see all my thoughts in them. I don't want to look shy or like I care what he thinks so I pretend to be a painting. Inanimate and not bothered about being looked at. I am the *Mona Lisa* – not pretty, but resolute. I know who I am. I am someone who goes home before the night gets awful. Before I'm drunk and silly and wearing Chris's jumper and humiliating myself, before I'm drunk and silly in some Irish woman's fancy living room. Mona goes home and gets into bed while sort of smiling to herself about all the shame and self-hatred she's avoided. She has rewritten history, created her own ending, a better ending, she has peace—

'I want to talk to you more about that dog.'

What?

Chris turns away from me and starts walking towards a block of flats to our right.

TO: DanaCollins@yahoomail.com
CC: JamesT1984@hotmail.co.uk
BCC: list: luckyinvitees

Dear fans of lurve,

Apols for the mass email but don't worry this is great news. After a slight bombshell over the Christmas period as my Fiancé and I discovered that none of our parents were willing to pay for our wedding as we had naturally assumed. With this in mind we did all our sums and discovered that we can no longer afford the special event we had booked, even with the cash gifts we have already received from people who do understand what a special and once in a lifetime event this should be.

At first we thought unfortunately we would have to backtrack and maybe just do a small thing at a registry office which was soooooo depressing, but then we came up with the great idea of (drum roll purlease) a kickstarter!!!!!

So the wedding is still on the same date with same timings etc but now U can be a real part of it. Prizes, donation suggestion and links below.

Thanks so much and I can't wait to see you all in the Autumn, Get those diets and fake tans ready!!!!

Dana and James and true love 4Eva xxx

DONATION	WHAT YOU GET
£50	Your name on a buffet plate (you can use this plate to eat off too yummers!)
£100	you can pet/do a selfie with one of the alpacas we have hired for the day (if you don't know what an alpaca is google them they R so cute).
£250	a dance with either the Bride or Groom (watch your hands cheeky)
£500	you can sing a song of your choice in the karaoke
£1000	we will thank you personally in the speeches

P.S. if a lot of you buy dances or songs which we hope you do!!!! Then you will only get a section of the song to dance or sing, not whole thing, for obvious time reasons.

www.kickstarter.com/danasweddingofficial

'I'm not going to have sex with you—'

Chris has his back to me, hanging his nice coat up. The rack already has too many coats on it. I wonder how many people he lives with but I can't ask in case he asks who I live with. Is this lying, am I lying?

'—if you thought that's why I brought you back here—'

Most of them are girls' coats. One is long and purple with a hood. And there's a checked one that looks like Burberry or could be fake Burberry, I don't know the difference.

'—that's not what this is.'

Sorry what, pardon. I'm just hearing what he said about sex. Chris turns and is pointing back and forth between us at the 'this'. I nod.

'Duh.'

Really wish I hadn't said 'Duh' but I wasn't prepared for him to start talking about sex, even in the negative.

'I don't even really like sex!' Chris chuckles, and shrugs, and I have so many questions about why he had sex with that Irish girl, then? Also what product does he use on his hair because it's all up and curly still. I'm soaked but I don't think the rain has touched him.

I put my hands in my pockets and tell them to relax. And my toes and my bowels – they're all currently tense and gripping onto themselves.

Chris is walking away and I haven't taken my coat off – where would I put it? All the pegs are full. A door closes behind him and I'm alone in his hallway. There are three doors I can see, but they're all closed. Where has he gone? Is there a living room or have they turned it into a bedroom to make the rent cheaper? It looks so normal and smells like my aunty Linda's house. They must have a Glade fragrance plug-in. I'm listening out for other voices, for any sounds in the flat at all, but there's nothing, just a rumbling bus or truck passing outside. Chris pops his head out from the nearest doorway.

'Tea?'

This is mental. I am walking towards Chris, about to drink tea. In his flat.

His kitchen doesn't suit him. It's white and plasticky and has a big pile of washing-up. There's a window but it's one of those ones that only opens two inches at the bottom so that no one can throw themselves out. It's open to the max now, probably because someone's recently burned something. There's a charred frying pan on the stove and a smashed fire alarm on the table. I walk over to the window and look down. We're on the sixth floor so not dizzyingly high. There's a square patch of grass below and then a short line of parked cars and some flat-roofed garages. It's no Paris. Chris grabs my shoulder, which makes me jump. He's laughing but—

'Sorry.'

—I still apologise for my over-eager startle response. I hate it. I'm always being surprised and getting frightened when Ian walks in the room, even when I know he's in the house. Or sometimes if it's dark I'll jump at the shadow of the hoover or seeing the shape of a dressing gown or a coat, thinking it's a man – oh, his coat rack would kill me.

A whole pile of murderers by the door waiting to pounce.

My body is on high alert all the time, which apparently could be a past-life thing. My cousin Beryl told me your body remembers bits of what happened last time even if not who you were etc. I once sat next to a clairvoyant on a coach and even though I had my headphones in she told me I'd drowned in my last life. That someone had held my head under water. Then she said, 'I bet you hate swimming' and I agreed so she didn't feel like a bad psychic. I quite like swimming, though, and I'm not convinced about past lives. Why would you keep reusing the same people again and again, what benefit could there be? I'm probably jumpy because of the murder podcasts.

'Hungry?'

Chris is looking in the fridge. There are three different milks in there and two of them have names written on them in messy black pen.

'Are Sooz and Kirsty your flatmates?'

'No, I just like to name my milks.'

I laugh for as long as it takes him to get an avocado out of the vegetable-drawer bit. Then he gets a packet of bagels out from there too. I remember living in shared houses – that must be his section.

'And my avocados!'

Chris is holding the avocado aloft to show me the 'Sooz' written on it, so that can't be his section after all. I'm not going to ask who Sooz is in case Chris doubles down on his joke about christening foodstuffs. I don't want him to have a conversation with an avocado, but also, I don't know what I want. I really wish there was a pause button so I could take some deep breaths and get my head around this. Chris is gesturing for me to sit at the table, which has a round hole in the middle. I think it's a—

'It's supposed to be for gardens.'

Yes, it's a picnic-table kind of thing. The hole is where an umbrella would go. The chairs are wooden, though, and quite uncomfortable. There's a teapot in front of me with two Lipton tags hanging from its rim, and to my right a glass fruit bowl with several brown bananas in it. Someone has written 'Kirsty' on at least one of them in biro.

'I'm only staying here for a couple of weeks.'

'It's nice.'

'It's probably the reason I've been so depressed.'

'That could be the altitude?'

'Ha ha! Good one.'

Chris has put a bagel into the toaster and is leaning his back against the fridge with his arms folded. He looks like a model from the Next catalogue. I'll have some tea and then I will leave. But I don't know when that'll be because Chris hasn't put the kettle on yet. Will we have to use the dirty teapot? I put my hand on it to check the temperature but it's completely cold. I grip my fingers around the handle to remind Chris about the hot drink he offered but he's not looking at me or the teapot. He's looking straight ahead at the pinboard on the wall.

My eyes look where he's looking; there's only one sheet of A4 pinned onto the cork and it's a cleaning rota. Sooz, Kirsty and Sean have divided up the week into chores. I try to visualise Chris cleaning a toilet or hoovering but I can't. Also who is Sean – a previous tenant or a pseudonym? Imagine if Chris was a—

'I'm really bad at sex, that's the thing . . .'

Chris is rubbing the curly curls on the back of his head. I can see the inside of his wrist poking out of the end of his sweater.

'. . . and it ruins everything. Especially if I think I could be really good friends with someone.'

I freeze with cautiousness because I don't know what we're talking about. Australia?

Or that engaged girl?

I shouldn't have looked at his wrist. He must've noticed me eyeballing his vulnerable veiny skin and now he's telling me to back off. He knows I used to like him and he thinks I still do. I make sure my face is bland and blank like I don't fancy him and additionally don't care that he doesn't fancy me. I become *Mona Lisa* again, flat and made of paint.

'Like I think you and I could be good friends, I've always thought so.'

Has he?

'Come – I want to show you something.'

He stares at me for a second before moving, and all I can think about is that White Rabbit from *Alice in Wonderland*. Alice follows him because he's a rabbit and she's a child – all children like fluffy animals and chasing things. I am following Chris and it's got nothing to do with what I want to do, it's only because he told me. I'm behind him for a few steps in the short corridor of the flat, then he pushes open a pale-blue door and leads me into a small studenty bedroom. There's a pile of books on the floor next to a futon mattress. It smells of stale smoke and I can see two busy ashtrays on the carpet as well as a Granny Smith apple that's been misused as a bong. That's all there is. Oh, and a purple beanbag behind the door.

'You don't have a lot of stuff?'

'I don't like being anywhere for very long.'

I wish I was like that, but I really enjoy having lots of tops and trousers to choose from when I'm getting dressed. And I like having shoeboxes filled with cards people wrote me and photos of old school trips. I like having all my books on shelves so that I can look at them and remember everything I've read. And it's very important to have all my diaries with me and the folder of evidence for my biographer.

Chris tells me to take a seat and leaves the room. The White Rabbit wasn't this bossy. I have a choice between two soft furnishings and I choose the beanbag because even though we are not going to have sex, sitting on the bed is too suggestive – it's the kind of place someone would sit if they *did* want to have sex. I drag the bag into the room a bit so the door doesn't hit me when he comes back.

I stand next to a purple beanbag. I am in Chris's room. I am alive and I exist and one day I will die. But at the moment, this is happening. I need to think of some conversation topics for when he comes back so it isn't awkward that I'm very close to where he sleeps. Global warming. Everyone's got an opinion on that. And Princess Diana. I'll ask where he was when he found out she was dead.

I remember I was told to sit and so crouch down onto the beanbag. It sinks and I feel ridiculous. I have to clench several muscles to avoid slipping off; I'm tilted about thirty degrees to the right directly above one of the ashtrays. Something gleams in the carpet – it's crumbs of some kind, or maybe bulgur wheat? I am not going to stay long, I'll be off soon. I just don't know how to start the process of leaving. I try to sit upright but am sucked further into the bag as the polystyrene bits slide and rearrange themselves around me.

There's a knock at Chris's bedroom door and I panic and look uselessly for somewhere to hide as Chris re-enters. I'm so embarrassed to be seen fat and akimbo like this. Now my face is getting hot and god I bet I look like I'm blushing, blushing in his bedroom like an absolute weirdo. Chris is holding a tray in one hand and a very old heavy laptop in the other. I take the plate he passes me and, losing stability, sink down even further. My bottom is now fully on the floor. I could have just sat on the ground to start with – WHY DIDN'T I THINK OF THAT? Chris is plugging the laptop in, and takes a big bite of his bagel. He sits on the futon with his legs outstretched and opens the computer next to his legs. He's oblivious to me.

'You don't have a duvet?'

Chris is chewing and typing and doesn't look up.

'Is it in the wash?'

Chris shakes his head like it's normal to have only a sheet on your bed. His window is open to the maximum two inches and it's very chilly. I shiver and the beanbag's innards rattle but Chris is still looking at the computer. He doesn't even have socks on, his feet are naked and dangling towards me.

I remember Nadia telling me about a guy she'd gone on a date with. She'd met him at our pub and he'd been really slick and charming. He'd shaken her hand as he was leaving and passed her a rolled-up twenty-pound note with his phone number inside – that's the biggest tip anyone has ever got at The Slipper. Kermit once found a rolled-up tenner in the toilets but that was detritus, not gifted. I often pop my head into the gents when no one's looking in case it ever happens again. Whenever someone is acting cokey and loud in the bar I think 'Tonight could be the night' when I hold my breath to take a peep in there.

Anyway, the guy's bedroom was really cold. He told Nadia that the heating didn't work but when she left in the morning she saw his flatmate in the kitchen fiddling with the boiler and muttering. So Nadia says, 'Oh I think its broken', trying to be helpful, and the flatmate's like, 'No, luv, that's his tactic for getting birds into bed.' And Nadia left absolutely fuming because it had worked, she'd been so cold and got under the covers as it was the only way to warm up. She was planning to go ballistic at him when he asked to see her again but he never texted. I wonder if *he's* the dad? That would give her a good excuse to get back in contact with him.

Chris's room can't be cold for seduction because without a duvet the bed isn't even a warmer option. Plus he doesn't want to have sex with me, he's been very clear about that. So why do I keep thinking about having it with him? Maybe because I can see his long toes wriggling like little penises.

I can tell from the way Chris's arm is moving behind his screen that he's using the trackpad to scroll down a webpage. My bum is going to sleep on the floor and my feet are soggy and I wonder what he wants to show me and how it relates to next door's dog? I contemplate the food he's given me: two slices of avocado squashed onto half a bagel. There are herbs and chilli flakes on top and the imprints of a vigorous fork – he's gone to a lot of effort. I wouldn't usually eat in these circumstances but I'm worried Chris might know that girls don't eat in front of boys they like, so I have to eat to prove I don't like him. I'll devour this as sloppily as a wolf or a badger to prove I have no interest in him other than as friends. Unfortunately, as I lift it for a bite, my brain says the words 'sloppy green hoop' to me and I have to put it down again. I pick a bit of bread off the bottom part and put it in my mouth and pretend it's big enough to chew. Even as a wolf I'm a disordered eater. I've lived too long as an uptight woman to revert to feral freedom. Chris leans over from the futon and grabs the whole thing from my plate and folds it into his mouth all at once. There's a sliver of green slime on his lip as he smiles at me.

'It's just loading.'

I cough and choke into my hand while imagining a voiceover sarcastically narrating my ineptness during this simple endeavour: having a snack in a boy's bedroom. Chris proffers me his water glass and pats the bed next to him – I have to come and get it. I can't think of any other option but to go where I am beckoned. I am not a wolf, or even a badger. I am a domesticated creature who sits where I'm told. I'm the White Rabbit but a normal one; I don't have a watch and an appointment.

As I sip the warm tap water my nose is sucking up the fresh smell of Chris's aftershave and the warm Marmitey smell of his bedclothes. My head spins for a couple of seconds with oxygen starvation or—

'Watch this.'

Chris is focused on the YouTube page on his screen. He clicks and we sit side by side staring at a familiar sight. Two otters floating on a dark, rippling body of water. Occasionally they link up, attaching at the hands (paws?), then the gentle undulations of the water pull their little bodies in opposite directions and they lose their grip. Then after what feels interminable, too long, they find each other again and reattach. It's very sweet, obviously, but why are we watching it? This is incredibly confusing. Unless – is this connected to the conversation about soulmates and the Greeks? No, that was Ian, this is—

'It's otters holding hands.'

I look at Chris and he is wiping his eyes. He—

'Everything makes me so sad.'

He is crying. About some otters from over a decade ago. They are probably dead by now. Is this my segue into Princess Diana?

'Why are you showing me otters holding hands?'

'Have you seen it before?'

Chris seems surprised.

'Yeah, it was massive. Like that panda sneezing and—'

Chris shrugs and ruffles his own hair again.

'I quit the internet. I'm kind of anti it.'

Chris puts a hand into his jeans pocket and pulls out a really old Nokia. The kind that has Snake on it and only stores ten text messages. He throws it on the bed beside him and looks at it.

'I only want to live in the moment . . .'

Then he lifts his eyes up to me, looking like a sweet cartoon sheep.

'. . . even though it's exquisitely painful.'

Chris takes the water glass from my hand and puts it on the floor.

For a second I watch the sliver of green slime looming closer and then it's happening. This time I saw how.

www.reddit.com/truecrimefandom-bitchpodcasters

Right so I've read some of the earlier posts and I don't think that threatening to kill/maim/sexually assault any of these presenters is going to solve the problem. In many ways you are playing into their hands and proving their sexism RIGHT by behaving like the sociopathic Neanderthals they assume we all are.

My problem is with their logic (as usual lol). So if all men are 'murderers in waiting' (direct quote from one of the lasses on Murdsterbabble) then what should be noted and fucking CELEBRATED is that so few of us actually do it, it's probably less than 1% of men doing something that according to these women is written in our DNA!!! That's like if less than 1% of fish swam or dogs barked, that would defy the laws of nature. Further to that, even the busiest serial killer murders less than 1% of the people he meets yet these hysterical women act like it happens on a daily basis . . . glass half-empty much? Another thought I had was about how school teachers are no longer allowed to call kids 'bad' or 'naughty' because it makes them believe they ARE those things and behave worse. So these podcasters telling their male listeners they are all 'natural born killers' (direct quote from Blood is the New Black) is the reason murder rates are going through the roof – it's literally a self-fulfilling prophecy.

As for why women are so obsessed with this subject I've heard the theory (parroted by my current gf) that it's some kind of 'research' because men are so 'dangerous' and I'm sorry but that's BS. My theory is that it's another way for females to feel sorry for themselves/align themselves with the victim etc.

My main point would be that by giving murderers so much notoriety these podcasters are not only creating more of them, they are also giving them ideas and even encouraging them to be more creative in their brutality. This will be their own downfall as it's only a matter of time before a serial killer decides to take all these women out Dexter-style.

Ian

Turns out there are also crumbs in the bed – this dirty sheet would be a decent exfoliator. They're too big to be toast crumbs so maybe biscuit, or even granola? Maybe both. He must eat in bed a lot. I think about 'The Princess and the Pea' for a moment then remember I'm having sex and try to think about that.

I can still see the yellowy too-bright light of Chris's fluorescent bulb through my squeezed-shut eyelids. I wish I'd got up and turned it off at the beginning, but I was in my knickers by then and I didn't want him to see my bum and legs chundering across the room and change his mind.

I'm hoping Chris has his eyes shut too.

It's very loud – not on purpose, just in the absence of other noises. Our breath and slurping and rustlings are so humdrum they are undermining the sexiness of the sex.

I don't think I've ever been on a futon before, it's horrible. How could you sleep on it? It's like a big flat corpse. No springs, it makes any movement very clumsy and embarrassing – a close cousin of the beanbag. Why does Chris have such humiliating furniture? Perhaps he's always been appalled by human elegance and – my thoughts are rolling about again, I need to concentrate.

Chris's body is more rigid than I expected. Thin but weighty – like his futon, I suppose. His lips are quite solid as well. His kissing style is muscular, it's like his mouth is trying to push mine away, digging my head into the doughy bed.

I'm trying to keep my lips together but his tongue keeps jabbing through, shooting in like it's on important business then dashing out again. It's like a commuter popping back for his wallet before running back out to catch his train.

'What?'

I accidentally laughed a bit oh god.

'Nothing.'

It was the image of a tube train full of tongues with ties on.

His mouth is on my ear now THIS IS SO LOUD.

I think this is the most annoying thing about being an adult. Once everyone starts having sex all encounters are expected to be sex. There used to be a whole piano of sexual notes to hit, all in a different order. And people only played the ones they felt like that day. I used to like kissing for ages then rubbing up against each other with your jeans still on. I'd get so mad-horny and excited and the snogging would become frenzied and incredible. But it's like once you've reached the highest note on a piano that's all it's about anymore. A quick skim through the scales on the way up to bashing the last key repeatedly for ten minutes. The piano is not being properly played. I think Britney Spears or someone should do a song about this.

Like he's heard my thoughts, Chris lifts his skinny hips off me and slides out. I worry for a second that he's going to go down on me and I'll taste of wee and working in a pub – but thankfully he's using his hand. Am I taking too long? Have I annoyed him? He's poking his finger so deep inside me it's like he's trying to find my edges—

'ow'

I try to subtly pull away but he's on top of me and there's nowhere to go – the bed stubbornly presses me back towards him—

'ow'

He's becoming more enthusiastic, sausaging up and down, as if he's interpreted my yelps as exclamations. I clench and think about the poor geese who get their insides pulverised to make foie gras.

Ow.

I used to play this game where I'd pretend to be dead during sex to see how long it would take Ian to notice and check if I was okay. I gave up after a while because too often he didn't stop. He'd carry on and not care and then I'd cry when he was finished and then *he* would be angry with *me*. I shouldn't be thinking about Ian, I should be present and happy. But it strikes me now that maybe I am partly at fault for Ian not wanting to have sex anymore. Does that make it better, that we are both to blame? I think it does.

I'm not pretending I've died, but I am very silent and still right now.

I don't know why being under Chris is giving me such clarity about Ian but god, life is weird. Those times with Ian where his face in the dark became so Chris-like that my orgasms felt unfaithful, and now this. Someone should do a sci-fi which is like *Quantum Leap*, but with sex. So if you think about someone while doing it, then they'd arrive inside the person you're fucking. And they see through the eyes and – but what about when weird people occur to you like your parents and your mum's ex-boyfriends? It would be such a scary programme. Also no one has consented to the sex they're stuck having with you – that's a real issue. I don't think it would be commissioned.

James and Dana must think about me so much. I'd always be inside one or other of them, trapped and disgusted. This is probably the worst thought I've ever had but it has distracted me from—

Oh thank the lord Chris has pulled his finger out of me.

I'm about to be grateful until he springs down the bed and headbutts my groin. I pull my legs together and tug on his arm to bring him back. He resists me for a few moments. I watch his curly hair bouncing above my stomach and wish I knew how to stop sex without it being embarrassing. I try to pull him back on top of me so this will finish, but he misunderstands again and kneels either side of my head, posting his penis into my mouth.

Urgh.

I open my eyes for a brief second and watch from this alien POV. His balls and pubes and stomach curving above me with his grimacing face up in the distance. I try to keep my mouth wet while not breathing, smelling or existing.

'I don't want to cum—'

He's panting.

'—before you do.'

I can't reply because I'm trying not to gag. Also I can't think of a sexy way to tell him that *obviously* I'm not going to cum. That I very rarely do with a new person because I feel so self-conscious and embarrassed and in my head. All the things that might feel nice later, once we know each other better, currently feel like invasions upon my person. His hands and tongue are enemies to be endured until we are . . . I mean, I'd never say this out loud, I wouldn't verbalise it to anyone, but pleasure is only possible once we are . . . connected? Intimate. Once there's safety to let go and— There is no way of making this sound like dirty talk. 'I know my pussy is tight and dry today but in a few weeks after deep conversations and getting drunk and laughing together my insides will be so excited to be near you. All the parts of me that are resisting you right now will be erupting at your touch. But for now, yes, apologies, this is a meat factory and I am a fearful pig.'

Chris grabs the end of his knob and sort of bunny-hops his hips down over my body and then he stabs it into me and resumes pistoning away again, although thankfully it's slightly less painful with his dick. His jerky movements have an epileptic rhythm. I think of fish drowning in air on the wooden deck of a boat.

A pig and a fish.

He's lifting my legs up, it's not clear why. I don't know where he wants them. I bend them in the air for a bit while he speeds up. I point my toes – do men like that? I bet I get cystitis.

Can't believe I'm having sex with Chris.

I'm starting to worry this will never ever end. When I was a child I got into trouble for asking a question in assembly. A woman scientist had been visiting and said we could ask her anything we wanted to know. She said that being curious was where knowledge came from or something like that. So I asked about rigor mortis. If people died while having sex did they stay stuck together? And looking back, she must've been flustered cos she said something like 'I don't understand.' So I thought she wanted a specific example and I made one up: there was a couple doing it in a tree and then they fell out and died. Would they have to have a joint coffin because of rigor mortis because they were forever entwined? I very much wanted to know the answer but everyone laughed so it looked like I was joking. So I never found out. I'll google it on the way home.

I need to work out: At what point in all this are you supposed to ask for a condom? By the time I was sure we were going to have sex we were already having it. Levonelle costs about twenty quid now and you have to answer many embarrassing questions while everyone in the queue pretends they aren't listening to your hussy confessions.

He's still pumping. I'm starting to get sore. I wish I knew how to fake an orgasm believably. It would be awful to do all the squeaking and fluttering about then have someone say, 'I don't believe you, that was so unrealistic.' Maybe I will have to pretend to faint or die.

I make some throaty deep-breath noises to speed him up.

The Fearful Pig and the Drowning Fish. That sounds like a Booker Prize winner. They always have names like *The Silken Butterfly* or *The Brevity of Opals*. Something where you know all of the words but not what they mean in that order. *The Echidna's Parish*. *The Feather of Tenacity*. I'm really good at titles – is that a thing?

Of course Mum was called to the school but she was too busy at work to come in. So my dad had to have a meeting with my form tutor even though I hadn't seen him for nearly a year. And while I sat there, mortified, he told Mrs Smith I'd always had an 'obsession with explicit materials'. And I didn't, I don't! I had one book about the Amazon that I'd stolen from the library and then forevermore was branded a pervert. Those people were naked because they *lived* in the *jungle*, that's not why I—

Oh.

He's gone still on top of me: I think it's over. He squelches out, exhales loudly and then tidily lays himself next to me on the mattress so that no part of us is touching.

'Did you cum?'

Chris is leaning his head on his elbow, a sheen of sweat around his hairline. I use my arm to hide my boobs but style it out like I'm just getting comfortable.

'A lady never tells.'

He's laughing.

'Thought so.'

He's picked up his laptop and sits cross-legged with it in front of him. I'm thirsty. I stare at the ceiling while he checks his emails – I don't want to invade his privacy. I also don't want him to think we're not sexually compatible.

'It'll get better,' I proffer.

I sneak a look at his face and he is smiling to himself, his skin radiant from the glow of his computer. I continue.

'It always does.'

Chris is grinning now but not looking at me. He's typing away while I pretend I can't feel the stickiness spreading under my bottom. I want to get dressed but I don't want him to think I don't want to be here.

'What does?'

Sometimes thirst feels like homesickness. My brain is confused about what I'm longing for.

'When you're with someone for the first time . . . We're just getting to know each other . . .'

Chris stops typing. He breathes like he's thinking about

what to write next, then he moves the computer from his lap, plonks it further down the bed and turns to sit on the edge. I take the opportunity to admire the delicate ridges of his spine. I look at the shorter hairs at the back of his neck. I try to imagine kissing him and even though it was only a minute ago I can't.

'This is what I was talking about. I always ruin things with friends.'

Chris has his head in his hands. His fingers poke through his hair like pale slugs. I hear him swallow.

It's a conquest. I wanted this. I am an achiever – I achieved this just from wishing and working in a pub he could come and find me at.

Chris is rubbing his eyes. Like he wants me to think he's sad.

'You alright?'

'Yeah, sorry, I was just thinking about something.'

Chris stands up and turns to look at me. I look at his knees to avoid his penis's eye.

'We're both sensitive souls.'

Chris shrugs his shoulders like 'What ya gonna do?' then turns and is walking away from me – I don't know whether he's going for the beanbag or the ashtray. He's opened the door. Should I remind him he's naked?

'Chris . . .'

'I'm just going for a quick shower.'

The door closes after him and I feel stupid looking at it so I try to find my clothes instead. It's crazy that he's not worried about his flatmates seeing him like that. Especially when he's stolen an avocado.

I am putting my black work trousers back on when I

see the email he was writing. I don't mean to be nosy; I
didn't do it on purpose. The computer was left open right
there on the bed and my eyes locked onto the word Irina.
Irina is his ex-girlfriend from Australia. I turn away from
the laptop – I don't want Chris to come back in and find
me looking and think I'm a bunny-boiler. As I stand up I
see my reflection in his bedroom window. I ignore my face
to check the overhang above my waistband. Mum used to
tell me the spare flesh was so my sides wouldn't rip when
I put my hand up in school, and then she'd tickle me.

I didn't mean to read Chris's email and I did look away
quickly. But there wasn't that much to see so my eyes
sucked it in all at once and now I know what it says.

I checked out the Visa thing and they'll only take your
passport for 6-8 weeks after our wedding so we can still go
to Bali in May. See ya in 2 weeks love ya X

I'm very stupid.

DEBT COLLECT

——————— UK ———————

1 March 20—

Dear Miss Collins,

14 Days' Notice of Court Proceedings

We are writing to inform you that if we do not receive payment within the next 14 days court proceedings will be undertaken to recover your debt.

We are giving you the 14 days as a courtesy to resolve this matter even though you have ignored all previous communications. If we do not hear from you this case will be lodged with the County Courts no later than 15 March 20—.

It is vital that you understand that any and all court costs will be added to your existing debt of £13,340.52.

Please call 0-800-916-8800 immediately to make your payment.

Sincerely

Fiona Worthington Nee Schultz, Debt Collect UK

I'm looking out of the front window and telling myself to think of nothing. Not the concept of nothingness like nought or zero but like, the void – I am trying not to lay my thoughts on anything. I'm chasing blankness. It comes on all the time without me asking for it – why is it avoiding me now? At primary school a teacher told us that it's impossible to turn the human brain off, that all day long it's whirring away full of responses and notions and then when we go to sleep our brain uses the peace and quiet to think and think some more. And maybe she shouldn't have told us that – maybe that's where it all went wrong for me. That teacher made me too aware of my thoughts. If no one had told me they were constant and inescapable, maybe I wouldn't have noticed and I would be successful and happy rather than standing in a boring pub earning minimum wage thinking about trying not to think.

My mind is like a computer infected with viruses: whenever I try to switch it off I get all these unwanted pop-ups. James's face when he asked me out. The Christians with signs outside the clinic. Sasha dancing with disco lights on her face. Connie whizzing past on a bus, slumped asleep with a mic in her hand. I close my eyes and try to concentrate on emptiness but I see Dana falling off the shed roof when she was nine. I open my eyes but I'm still remembering. She looked so small and spindly on the ascent, her skinny legs dangling down over the window. Then when she dropped, the sound when she hit the floor was – it was sickening. The thunk of it. Of course it was me who'd dared her to climb. As she lay there on the ground, not moving, I thought she was dead. Remembering makes me hate myself and want to apologise and – I want to call her.

Obviously I won't. It's only been a few weeks. We've gone much longer than this without talking.

I wish I could stay angry and annoyed and not soften like this. Wanting to forgive them and wanting them to forgive me back. It takes so much effort to be pissed off with them and the longer it goes on the heavier it becomes. I'm a donkey laden with packages I was supposed to deliver but nobody wants them.

I'm welling up thinking about an imaginary donkey working for the Post Office and sliding those red cards through people's doors.

Another pop-up acknowledges my PMT – that's what's making me such a drippy sock today. I asked Pete if he's ever investigated a murder where the woman's excuse was that she had her period. I don't mind speaking to him at the moment because I have a game: when he talks I look at a spot in between his eyebrows. I read in a magazine that it's an assertiveness technique; it seems like you're being direct and looking into the person's eyes but without the challenging directness that actual eye contact would require. People aren't supposed to notice when you do it, but it's made Pete self-conscious about his mid-brow, he keeps rubbing it with his finger. There's a grubby smear there now, right where his third eye would be if he was in a yoga class. Anyway, Pete's been telling me about a local case, he didn't work on it, but he went to watch a couple of the trial days, apparently. The woman killed her husband and her lawyer said that she wasn't in her right mind because of PMT. But as Pete describes more about her life it sounds much more complicated than that – the husband was withholding money and her passport and stuff; she'd come over from the Philippines or somewhere.

'—that's why I'd never go for one of them mail-order brides, you don't know nothing about 'em.'

Apparently we are still talking about it. I think he's trying to rile me into saying something feminist, so I stare at his forehead. I'm trying to not think so that I don't think about Chris. But the act of not thinking about him means that, apart from the odd pop-up, I am thinking about him constantly. The day after it happened I felt light-blooded with accomplishment. Even the dry awkwardness of the fuck couldn't undermine my triumph, the very fact of it happening. Something I envisaged and then many years later sculpted into existence. I made it. Forced it, created it. It didn't matter that he was marrying his ex who probably wasn't actually his ex at all. I had scored my goal.

I wasn't even that late when I went home to Ian. It looked like I'd had a drink after work and come home. It was nice standing and chatting in our kitchen while he made a cauliflower and coconut curry. I felt relieved that we don't have a cleaning rota or any garden furniture indoors. For the first time in a long time I believed we could get back on track. My night with Chris was some ugly medicine that had made me better and now I could spread that good health. Or rather, my good mood could absorb all the poison and save our relationship.

Even the next day when I woke up I didn't feel ashamed

yet. I was a returned Olympian who'd slept clutching my shiny medal. 'Prepare an open-top bus,' I thought, imagining myself draped in a heart-shaped flag and waving down at the assembled crowds. 'She really did put the work in,' they'd acknowledge, 'and it's paid off.'

'Hiya.'

It's funny to see Nadia in her non-work clothes standing on the other side of the bar.

'Have you come in on your day off?'

That's a very unnecessary question as I already know the answer. It's the kind of thing Pete would have asked. Trying not to think has made my brain stupider.

'This is for you!'

Nadia passes me a small white envelope and waves as she walks towards the office. She looks too happy to be one of our real customers. She's written my name in bubble writing with a star over the i. I've never thought of doing that. It looks so cool – I'm definitely going to do that in future. I can tell people it's because I'm going to be a star one day. Or maybe I'll wait til after I'm a star and tell them then. On *The Graham Norton Show*.

I open the envelope and inside is a piece of paper folded in half like a card. It's hand-drawn with coloured pencils and shows a woman with long hair and no nose holding a baby that's a pink circle above a white egg shape. Inside I am invited to a baby shower. I don't know why I'm crying.

I hear Nadia's footsteps on their way back and turn away to the optics to sort myself out. I pretend to be wiping the Tia Maria.

'Are you wanking that off?'

I guess it looks weird if I'm not holding a cloth.

I thank Nadia for the invitation and she tells me that she drew it herself.

'My pregnancy hormones are making me more creative, it's amazing.'

We are both quiet while I look down at the front of the card again. It looks like a six-year-old did it.

'It's really good.'

'I can't wait for you to meet my other friends – I've told them all about you.'

Nadia begins to list the people that will be attending and I can't listen because I'm so desperate to ask how I was described. Sophie from work, she's . . . What am I? Brunette? Poor? Unthreatening? Nice??? I only know what I'm like from the inside; it would be such a relief to have an objective summary of who I am in the world. Not the things someone might say to my face, like 'You look fine as you are' and 'Of course you're not fat.' I want the truth. I don't care if it's nasty – I'd rather know. Then I can stop the hopeful wondering: 'Maybe I *am* pretty, maybe I have body dysmorphia?'

I think that's one of the reasons I felt so fantastic after sleeping with Chris. Even though I'd seen that email I felt indestructible as I walked home. I must be special, I <u>must</u> be because he cheated on his girlfriend with me, not once but TWICE. He'd kissed me in Australia and then years later come and found me where I worked and taken me to his flat and I should never doubt myself again.

'And my mum, of course.'

Kermit has come out from the office and is using his invite to fan his face.

'She's my best friend on the planet!'

It's not hot in here. He's doing it like an Elizabethan lady as a joke.

'Fag.'

There's no point correcting Pete's language because it just makes him worse. If I tell him how inappropriate he's being he'll start going on about freedom of speech and quoting Ricky Gervais.

Kermit puts his invite down on the bar and does a flouncing curtsey at Pete, which makes me and Nadia laugh.

'You've got something on your face, Pete.'

'Yeah right, not gonna fall for that one.'

Pete swigs his beer and pretends he's not trying to catch his reflection in the back bar. He clocks his smudged forehead and takes another sip like 'So what, I've got a dirty head' but a second later he swings his legs around on the stool and pushes himself off towards the gents, taking his pint with him.

'How's Doris?'

Kermit's girlfriend has a nickname too even though we've never met her. Or maybe Nadia has – she asked that so confidently. Kermit is leaning on the glass wash telling us he took Doris to Chessington World of Adventures and she thought it was a bit boring.

'Whenever we try to do anything we realise we prefer just being at home.'

It's crazy how comfortably Kermit is the main character in his own life. Kermit could never be the leading man in anything, not even an indie film, but to himself he is. And maybe even to Doris?

'We realised we don't have to do all those things, like, er, travel or, er . . .'

Kermit nods at Nadia.

'. . . having kids and that. Cos we just want each other.'

Fuck, I want to cry again. I've got no skin on.

'That's so nice, Kerm.'

Nadia says 'nice' but it's much more than that.

'I miss her when I go to put the kettle on, y'know.'

I can't speak, I am so overwhelmed.

'I have to go back and tell her before it's even boiled.'

This is like the end of *Titanic*, the beginning of *Up* and the entirety of *The Notebook* combined. I never expected to be jealous of Kermit. Does that kind of love happen for all of us eventually, do I just have to wait? I see Pete walking across the pub towards us and remember that poor Filipino woman and the bastard who hid her cash cards who she murdered.

The days after I saw Chris were a lesson in subtraction. The more time passed, the more my positive assumptions eroded. I started with thoughts of 'He likes me, this means I'm special, this means I *will* be happy one day.' Stupid. By Wednesday the nothing was screaming at me, it was all I could hear. I was thinking up ways I could justifiably contact him. I could pretend I'd lost something at his flat and needed it back?

I thought I should use this time to prepare for seeing Chris again. That if I was prepared, then it would definitely happen. I went running but it hurt and I got light-headed so I stopped. Also I kept thinking I saw him – in cars, on movie posters, through shop windows. At home I decided to read *Nausea* by Jean-Paul Sartre so I could discuss it with him; I would give insightful opinions and he'd fall in love with me. This had the unwanted effect of interesting Ian – he found me on the chintzy armchair and asked me how I was enjoying it. He meant the book, and I didn't know what to say because I hadn't been taking it in. I'd been staring at words on a page while daydreaming about telling Chris that I'd realised open relationships are probably really great for women. Then he'd appreciate I was *his* de Beauvoir and we'd have sex again and it would be so much better. Really juicy and sumptuous and afterwards we'd laugh about our crap first time and how we'd tell our grandchildren one day.

I said something non-committal like 'Hmmmm, enjoying doesn't seem the point' then Ian talked at me for ten minutes and complimented me on a fascinating conversation.

As I've got sadder about Chris I've hated Ian more. Not sure why the emotions are connected but they are. I never touch him. I sleep as far away on the bed as I can but still my angry repulsion keeps me awake. It's crowded in my head *and* in my bedroom but not in a nice way, not like I'm popular or in demand. It's like aversion therapy. Or when your parents make you smoke forty fags until you puke because they think it will put you off for life. I'm in the sickness bit – fuck knows how I recover.

You know that thing where you're watching a film for the second time and it's much, much sadder because you know how it ends? The character feels fine but their obliviousness to what's coming makes you pity them. That's what it's like for me to remember walking back to Chris's. I'm living the ending, and everything I did before is so sad and pathetic.

I keep having flashbacks to his bedroom. Getting dressed and seeing the email and sneaking out. Expecting him to call me, chase after me – 'Where have you gone? I can explain.' Now I get it: he wanted me to go. And that – why does that make me want to see him so much? I did lose something at his flat.

At least my depression is making me poetic. I would leave *such* a good suicide note. 'Dear world, a boy won't text me and my haemorrhoids are back. Bye from Sophie.'

Pete's sat back down and is looking at Nadia's baby shower invite. I can tell Kermit wants to take it back but is too polite. Pete is asking nosy questions about how many weeks she is and what kind of birth she's planning and I'm rolling my eyes thinking it's an excuse for him to imagine inside Nadia's vagina when suddenly he starts saying how much he loved being a daddy. He's sniffing and sighing while telling us that he hasn't seen his sons in over a year, that they're not speaking to him. Well, I don't want to speak to him either – his children have my full sympathy.

Pete is telling Kermit what each of his sons does for a living when I'm distracted by someone backing through the main door and shaking an umbrella. At first I think she's famous. Her hair is curled perfectly and unaffected by the shitty weather. She's got a jumper on; it's a plain beige colour with a rollneck and is stretched tight over her boobs. Why am I looking at her boobs? They bounce towards me as my brain tries to compute who she is and why she's here. She's got darker lipstick on today, browner. Ella places her hands flat on the bar in front of me. Is she going to hit me? Would Pete arrest her if she did?

'Nice to see you.'

She's smiling widely; her lips are like glossy Twixes around her white teeth. I'm reminded of those girls at school, pretending to be nice so they could humiliate me later. Has Ella come in here because she knows? Has Chris gone into the golf club and told everyone about my revolting cellulite and my armpits that are hairy even though I'm not a French intellectual?

I've been frozen too long. Kermit flicks me on the arm before asking Ella what she's drinking and turning to pour it. Nadia says she's got to go and I use my eyes to beg her 'Please don't leave, stay and protect me' but the door's swinging behind her by the time Ella has her rum and ginger beer.

Ella is looking at me. Her gaze is friendly, like 'So?' She's inviting me to talk but I can't give anything away until I know why she's here. I want to know where Chris is – where's he gone, what's he up to? The fact that she might know something is tantalising but I have to appear normal if I want to find anything out. But I can't remember any normal sentences. Luckily another customer comes to the bar and I have the reprieve of serving her. She's on the phone planning a holiday to Portugal while pointing at the lager she wants and holding up two fingers.

'Yeah – yeah – no, I have to BACS him the money so he can put down the deposit.'

I can feel Ella watching what I'm doing. I'm in a little one-woman play just for her. The Normal Barmaid in *Pouring Two Stellas and Avoiding Saying Something Dumb*. My customer taps her card and I look around for Kermit but he must have snuck back to the office.

'So . . . have *you* been to Portugal?'

'Mm, yes.'

Ella is nodding and doing long blinks. I was hoping for a longer conversation, if I'm honest.

'I wanted to apologise. You were caught in the middle when you came over – I really hate to imagine the impression I must've given you.'

Oh she's drunk! Her mouth is paying too much attention to her words and she's swaying slightly.

'He quit the golf club so I never got to talk to him 'bout it, y'see, so I just wanted to know if he said anything to you? Chris? To you?'

Ella downs her drink and I pour her a tap water at the sink. Pete is studiously staring into his pint, which is how I know he is definitely listening.

'He quit the golf club. Rang up, never came back in, you see . . .'

She's trying to climb onto a stool but can't quite manage. I give her the glass of water and she squints at it like she's never seen one before. I want to be kind to her. Pete is side-eyeing her arse and thinks he's being subtle. I'm touched she is being so obvious in front of me, that she's being so *vulnerable*. Ella gestures to the outside world.

'What a fucking mess.'

It's like I've passed the baton and she's taken all my shame. Or she's a voodoo doll: all my actions have been pierced into her to suffer with. I couldn't imagine anything making me feel better today, but this being Ella's problem has stopped it being mine. I'm reassured that she can't know what occurred with me and Chris at his flat or she wouldn't be here telling me all this. She'd see me as an enemy or competition.

'I thought we were friends . . .'

Ella has lifted her head to address me and I think it's us she's referring to.

'He said I made him feel understood.'

That makes more sense. Ella shrugs and tries to get on the stool again. Pete holds out an arm to support her and she grips it and looks up into his eyes. They examine each other, two species meeting for the first time.

'I see shlilvelry is not dead.'

Ella's slurring has rendered her compliment meaningless but Pete doesn't care, it's the happiest I've ever seen him. He dips in a small gracious bow towards Ella but she's already turned back to face me. She starts describing her and Chris's friendship – he really leaned on her, apparently, because he was so unhappy to be back in London. Pete is openly listening now and, rather than being annoyed, Ella is turning to him and including him in her outpouring while Pete is shaking his head thoughtfully. I wish I could warn her he used the word fag as an insult earlier.

'—and I told him all about Steve and getting engaged and—'

Pete tilts his glass to indicate he wants another.

'—we even talked about how we'd never sleep together because it would ruin our intimacy—'

I'm glad I'm facing the pump and the spurting beige liquid. This is like a Netflix documentary about a conman, except I'm watching knowing that I fell for it too. For the exact same lines. Ella starts describing how good the sex was, so that's where we differ. It's probably because her bed has fewer crumbs in it. I pass Pete his drink and he looks baffled at Ella's detailed exposition – she's said the word pussy twice so far. I don't want to be listening to it either. I change the subject.

'How is Steve getting on?'

Ella shrugs. She doesn't seem sorry.

'We're going to Relate – you know, that marriage counselling place?'

Pete nods, back on familiar territory. Ella puts her hand
on his arm and wobbles on her stool.

'We're having marriage counselling before we're even
married!'

Ella's started telling Pete about Steve now, how they
met and what he does for a living. I didn't know this stuff.
They've been together since they were at college; he gate-
crashed her eighteenth birthday party. While I'm thinking
how romantic that sounds Ella begins describing their
lack of passion and even though I understand *exactly* what
she's going through I start to feel more and more sorry
for Steve. This is so disrespectful; this is his private business and she's mouthing off down the pub to strangers. Ian
would be spewing – it's his worst nightmare. He has such
an obsessive fear of emasculation. Probably because of his
small crooked penis.

'And he knows about the other fella?'

Pete is so invested in this drama. Maybe it's making him
feel better about his life too. I'm so glad he doesn't know
Chris was the guy in here waiting for me a few weeks ago.
The one scribbling on napkins and being intense and blatant. He came here for me – why do I feel so rejected? It
was *him* who made all the moves.

'Yeah, he knows I'm mates with Chris – he's a bit jealous . . .'

I might say something, defend Steve's honour.

'. . . but he doesn't know I've slept with him.'

'Yes he does.'

I probably shouldn't have spoken but of course he does! He was practically in the room with them.

Ella is shaking her head adamantly. She's deluded if she thinks Steve didn't know what they were doing.

'I denied it.'

Ella shrugs like it's not her fault. Like 'What are ya gonna do?'

'People believe what they want to.'

Oh. It's people's fault, is it? Steve is the deluded one. I wonder what she told him – I mean, we could hear them. We were sat there waiting for them to finish.

'I said we were playfighting—'

Ella slaps Pete on the arm.

'—and had our clothes on.'

Pete laughs. I've never heard him laugh before; it's crunchy like a packet of crisps. I laugh because I don't know what else to do and Ella is giggling like 'What am I like?' She doesn't even hate herself. Because she's beautiful, maybe?

'It's fine, we'll be fine. Steve can't cope without me.'

Lucky Steve.

'I'm going to end things with Chris, a proper false stop.'

I think she means full stop. I make her another tap water even though she hasn't drunk the first one.

'I just need to speak to him, then it's done.'

As I step back from the sink Ella is looking at me beseechingly. I have no idea why she thinks I can help her.

'Otherwise he's always in my mind, I keep running over things . . .'

Ella is my twin! She's my life twin except she's gorgeous and happy but that doesn't inoculate her against insecurity. This is going to sound mean, but I'm so glad she's going through this too. I'm not glad she's suffering, but – it's so reassuring. This self-doubt and obsessing is a natural human reaction to being seduced then ignored. I must *must* remember this when she's gone and the thought-roaches scuttle back in.

I'm also *so* relieved that no one knows what happened with Chris and me. If it's unknown it can be un-happened. I think Ian is protected this way, he'll never be publicly cuckolded like Steve, he has his dignity. I may have cheated, technically, but—

'Did he not tell you when you were round there?'

What oh shit.

Ella is doing that beseeching look again.

'He told me you went round?'

I'm trying to control my facial expression but can feel a nerve twitching under my eyelid.

Pete is looking at me with his arms folded. He's staring and not blinking. I'm in trouble. This was a sting operation. This was a police interview and I had no idea they had evidence against me. I was too relaxed and now I'm busted.

'We had work drinks and when he didn't turn up I called him and he said he was making you dinner?'

What is the question? Ella is waiting and Pete is waiting. I am praying. Please please God I don't believe in or whatever forces there might be controlling things and testing people please please let her not know. The Portugal lady appears at the bar and it makes me jump even though I saw her coming. She asks for two beers and I pour them and I can hear my shoes squeaking on the ground and the chugging of the pump and god I wish we played music and that I had never been born. I squeeze my eyes shut

I don't exist I don't I am a brain in a jar. Portugal Lady taps her card and carries off her pints and I watch her set them down on her table by the window. There's an undrunk pint already sitting there and an empty glass. I could walk and get it and then keep walking to the door and then run. I'll get a job at the golf club – no, that's out. I'll go back to . . . I try to think of any of my old jobs that might re-employ me.

'So I know what happened.'

Ella's face tells me she does know.

'Playfighting?'

No one laughs.

Ella runs her hand along her hairline and I notice her perfect beige nails. She checks her reflection behind me and as I watch her watch herself I realise that I had no reason to be flattered. She's not being vulnerable with me – I'm a nobody. I'm a Pete. I'm just a path she was hoping to take back to Chris's attention.

'I think he's gone back to Australia.'

Ella looks so sad, which is crazy.

'Fucksake. Why?'

'He's still with Irina.'

Ella crumples forward and rests her forehead on the bar, with her arms shielding her face from view. She's making a noise but it's muffled. I've got no idea what she's saying. Pete tuts at me like I'm to blame then pats her on the back like she's choking.

From: MERCPERTH@AOL.COM
To: sscollins@gmail.com
Subject: RE: RE: Happy Xmas luv Dad

Hola Sweet Sophs-

Such a spooky coincidence you asked as I was thinking about
Aiden just the other day, damn shame what happened to him
as he was a good bloke. Of course I recall the RSPCA thing I
was annoyed with your mum for calling them as was none of
our beeswax and as I said he was a good guy. It was his wife
who was the bitch she cheated on him with a bolke she met at
the amateur dramatics a theatre technician I think he was.

Lots of luv Daddio

P.S. got Dana's invite through but she hasn't invited my better
half so we won't be coming could you let her know? Also
whats with asking for money all the time has she gone full
bridezilla?

There's a bluebottle steadily climbing the tiles directly in front of me. I'm sitting watching him with the toilet lid down and my pants still on. Time feels frozen, although Mum's coming to pick me up in half an hour. I should be stuffing my clothes into binbags, not holding this little pink box.

It's a pound-shop one so it might not even work.

Yesterday was like – it was like I was injected with antifreeze. All of a sudden whatever's been slowing me down and making my thinking fluffy evaporated. I walked home from my shift with Ella's words repeating, about how Steve needed her and couldn't live without her. So pathetic – I don't know if that's because he actually *is* or because that's how she treats him. But why do I care why do I care? I kept asking myself. Steve isn't my friend. I don't fancy him; I don't want him for myself, so why do I care? It still hadn't clicked at that point.

Maybe this is clarity at the eye of the storm? The lightness of having no belongings because they're being spun in a tornado. The relief of turning off life support? No, that's too far, shut up Sophie. It's not death, it's just a break-up. A long overdue break-up. And moving back to a parent's house with no ambition, no direction, a huge amount of debt and a very late period. Not the end of the world.

I feel fine today – maybe because I am fine. Maybe my brain knows I'm not pregnant and so doesn't need me to freak out about it. I tried to sit bent over, panicking, but I couldn't be bothered so I'm upright and calm watching this big fat fly.

Okay, pants down, seat up and I'm finally pissing. There's no elegant way to do this – I try not to get too much on my hand. I can never be entirely sure where exactly the urine is going to come from – yes, from my fanny obviously, but it seems like slightly different places sometimes. Like what if I've got more than one hole? I'll never know for sure unless I do a wee very close to someone's face and ask them. People might go through their entire lives not knowing that kind of detail about themselves. Including me. I'm a mystery to myself.

I put the cap on.

I know I'm not pregnant. I have to do this for peace of mind because I'm so late. It's over ten days, but it could be weight loss – I've always read that that can happen but it's never happened to me before. I hope it's not a kind of cancer that makes your period late. I hope it's just stress.

I'm watching the tiny tideline slowly make its journey across the answer oval.

We had a row first. I was putting on a dark wash because I'd had a Red Bull thrown at my work trousers, that's why Kermit'd let me leave early. I was getting more stuff out of the basket: Ian's Metallica T-shirt, a pair of his jeans – and I hate these jeans because they are so faded and should be thrown away. They had a white stain on them and I thought 'It can't be.' But I took them to him in the living room where he was watching TV and I held them up and pointed at the white and said, 'What's this?' Then I stormed back to the kitchen like I was annoyed. And when

I put the washing in I WAS annoyed – why was I doing his chores when he's been doing that? He doesn't want to touch me but he's watching porn? Waiting til I'm out or gone to bed. Probably lesbians or bondage or something gross like strangling people.

I was stood by the washing machine as it started working, the water all running down inside, and I looked out of the window and there was a massive bird flying past and as I watched him I realised it was a duck – a goose, probably. He was flapping his huge wings and it was like I was right inside a Chekhov play. Not that they had washing machines in their cherry orchards and drawing rooms, but I had exactly the right kind of weary melancholy.

The first line comes up but it's very faint.

After I couldn't see the goose anymore, it had flown out of view, Ian came in and was really upset. He said how dare I but when I tried to answer he said, 'No no no, you listen, you LISTEN.' So I listened as he told me that it wasn't working and he felt trapped and disgusting while I looked out the window again like it was a play but this time the sky was empty. And I remembered Steve and Ella and now it was obvious that I was not avoiding hurting Ian by staying. I have not been avoiding hurting anyone.

And I sat down with my back against the saucepan cupboard and I told him that he was right and I was sorry and 'What do we do?' And Ian cried and said he was stuck because he knew I had nowhere else to go. So I cried and said, 'I'll be going.' We shared a mug of wine on the floor and discussed logistics. It's the most I've ever liked him, actually. We cried and smiled and kept saying sorry and holding hands. He's gone out all day today so I can sort my things.

A second line is coming up. I'm glad I did the test at home this time. I'm not in a public place where I need to hide my devastation.

The packet says three to five minutes but that was only forty-five seconds. But once the second line has come up you don't have to wait anymore; it doesn't go away. Not by itself.

The devastation hasn't hit me yet.

I need to hide this away somewhere that Ian will never find it. I could wrap it in toilet paper and walk down to the high street and throw it in a public bin. But I don't want to throw it away, I want to keep it – the test, not the baby.

I wipe and pull my knickers up with one hand, gripping the test in the other.

I wonder what the biographer would think if they found it with my other things . . . They'd wonder who got me pregnant and they'd want to know how I felt. It would be a gap in their understanding of me; I would seem so enigmatic. 'She left me so much, but she still had her secrets,' the biographer would write.

Shit.

What do I think?

I walk into the front room, thinking about Ian. That he was once a tiny growth in his mum, and then I realise that I was once a tiny growth in *my* mum. How can it be true? That someone is right this minute a tiny, minuscule growth in me? This is existentialism. I put my hand on my abdomen and pretend I have to be careful sitting down. I lower myself with my hands, like an actor pretending to be pregnant would. But I am <u>actually</u> pregnant. I don't have cancer.

I reach for my phone and google 'I'm pregnant what should I do'. The answer is the same again and again: take folic acid. Apparently that's all you can do.

This is not like last time.

I cried when I found out, and I cried every day waiting for it to be gone. I was even crying when I woke up from the procedure. A nurse brought me a cup of tea and told me that anyone who gets pregnant does it on purpose really; subconsciously, they want it even if they can't have it.

I am really in me, in the living room. Ha. Living. I watch my fingers stroking the test, which is still damp and quite unhygienic. I am the goose and I am flying away free.

Dear Mum

Hope work is good please answer as honestly as poss:

Are you angry bout your hairbrush still?
- ☑ YES
- ☐ NO
- ☐ Havent decided

Do you still like me?
- ☑ YES
- ☐ NO
- ☐ a bit

Am I your best friend?
- ☑ YES
- ☐ NO
- ☐ maybe

Do you like this picture of you? (see overleaf)
- ☑ YES
- ☐ please don't say no

'The instructions say to put it on dry hair but I tried that and it wasn't as good.'

Mum is telling me about a hot treatment I should use on my split ends.

'Dry hair is more porous and you want to get the best use out of it because it's so expensive.'

She stops wiping the sink and turns round and poses at me.

'Because "you deserve it", as they say.'

I haven't told her yet and holding it in is a minute-by-minute struggle.

Mum turns back and wipes her yellow sponge along the kitchen surface. She reminds me of me at the pub. Now that I've got a little me at my centre I'm so aware of all the me in Mum, or Mum in me. We are matryoshka dolls. My nose fills with synthetic orange as Mum sprays her surface cleaner. I sniff deeply and Mum recognises the compliment.

'It's anti-bac but I buy it for the fragrance.'

It is extremely hard not to tell her. I'm not waiting until twelve weeks or anything like that – I've realised I'm scared of how she will react. That she will say the wrong thing and break my heart and I'll have to leave and I've got nowhere else to go.

I've already made the wrong decision once: I told Nadia. I thought she would understand and would share her happiness with me. I thought she'd enjoy being the same, but she reared up and reacted like I'd copied her. She asked me question after question like she was trying to catch me out, like she was about to accuse me of lying. She asked, 'Who got you pregnant?' like she meant who *on earth* did that? It reminded me so much of school I nearly forgot I was telling the truth. Like when I told Stephanie I'd lost my virginity and she told all of 3A and a gang of them found me in the playground and asked me what cum tasted like and I said washing powder.

I don't trust Nadia not to tell anyone.

I really expected her to understand. I told her it gave me a reason to sort my life out and she said that was 'the most depressing thing she'd ever heard'.

Mum's finished wiping and has started slagging off Dana and James for doing a Kickstarter wedding. She thinks it's tacky and grabby and that it shows us all up as a family.

'Sorry, I know she's your sister but she's shown her true colours.'

Oh I absolutely love this. She's been giving variations of this speech all week, even occasionally calling James the C-word when she's had a wine. I just listen and nod. I know better than to join in and risk another Christmas. I'm really enjoying being Mum's current favourite – she's being so nice to me. Letting me wear her pyjamas and putting on the heating when I want a bath. It's because she thinks I'm broken-hearted. She's told me several times to 'let it all out'.

When she went to work yesterday I put a quiz in her bag like the old days and I found it under my pillow when I woke up this morning. It's like this baby has changed our universe, has exerted a gravitational pull, even though it's only the size of a kidney bean. I wonder if Jesus was healing people before he was even born . . . I doubt it. More likely causing rifts when Joseph found out it wasn't his.

'I've already spent eighty quid on a really nice set of plates from Next and Ron's given them his old rowing machine – all they have to do is collect it from his garage – and then Dana, or Lady Muck, should I say, was telling me she wants SIX GRAND and I said excuse me, it's FATHER of the bride who pays, not the mother, why don't you ask your father?'

It's so hard not to tell her! My tongue is like a goldfish jumping in my mouth and wanting to talk about the baby.

I've been thinking about the Mona Lisa, the woman in the painting, because people always talk about how she had a secret and you can see it in her face. I've been looking in the mirror, checking if I look like I might have a secret and if anyone could guess it. Then I wondered if anyone ever found out what the secret was and solved the Da Vinci Code or whatever, so I googled it – and I found all these articles saying she was pregnant! Apparently there are signs in the painting and the way she was dressed and – I couldn't believe it, except I can because it makes perfect sense. That little smile and the composure, that's exactly what it feels like because you – she – *we* – have this purpose now. And the hormones – I'm usually so moody and weepy and, I swear, pregnancy hormones work as antidepressants. Because I am the most together I've ever been. I make lists of what to do and I actually do it. I sit with my little decaf before Mum gets up and I set my aims for the day and then I work through them. So many things I've been avoiding, now I just get them done.

This pregnancy, my baby, makes sense of everything. THIS is why I was so drawn to Chris – even though he is not the most handsome guy or very nice to me and we never even really got on; he was so IMPORTANT and now I know why. This new person needed to be made. They were the bacteria acting through me and insisting on it. My obsession with him was all so they could be made.

I know it sounds *Handmaid's Tale*-y, but I'm not like some dumb vessel or something – it's more. Maybe there are always two plots? The one that you're in control of, the things you want, and then the one that's necessary. The things that just happen whether you like it or not.

And the timing – what makes sense to me now is that my timing was completely off. I went after Chris TOO EARLY. I flew over to Australia and he *had* to reject me because if we'd slept together at that point I wouldn't have got pregnant, I'd have wasted my chance. Or if I did get pregnant it would've been the wrong baby, not this one. It wouldn't have been her.

Before I knew about the baby I was so disappointed and embarrassed at how I'd behaved, and at how Chris was behaving towards me. But now I'm giddy with the perfectness of every scene and line of this story. I'm applauding this denouement. All my mess has had a purpose after all. If I'd been anything else or had done stuff differently, my <u>now</u> wouldn't be happening.

This is why people believe in God. Because sometimes things work out so perfectly that it's impossible someone hasn't been planning it all along. Some benevolent force watching you cry on the way home from work on New

Year's Eve, or on a tube train after you've thrown up, or
when you find out your sister is engaged to your ex, and
they chuckle to themselves: 'Hang on in there, Sophie –
this is just preamble. It's going to get good in a minute.'

'Mum . . .'

I've decided to tell her.

This feels momentous to me but Mum doesn't know
what's coming. She carries on talking about my sister
while checking sell-by dates in the fridge.

'I had her for <u>you</u>, y'know. The best gift you can give
anybody is a sibling. Someone with the same memories –
to go through life with you.'

I make a non-committal noise. I am not going to say
thank you for Dana. We do not have the same memories.
We don't 'go through life together'.

'I always thought you'd get on better once you were
older.'

'We've got nothing in common.'

We share a parent and we shared a bedroom but that—
Why is Mum laughing?

'What?'

'*We've got nothing in common.*'

Mum is putting on a high-pitched squeaky voice and
moving her hand around like she's voguing. I think it's
supposed to be an impression of me.

'We haven't.'

I'm adamant about this. Mum returns to her own voice
for the slam-dunk.

'Except the same taste in men!'

She's really enjoying her little remark and smashes the
fridge shut and spins while spluttering with laughter. This

observation bursts inside me like a delicious firework: we should *laugh* at this, why have we not been laughing?

Maybe because I'm smiling and seem fine, Mum becomes solemn. She pulls out a chair and sits opposite me.

'It's been hard for Dana, being your sister.'

No. I don't agree. But I'm not going to say anything.

'You needed so much—'

She's stroking my hand and I want to pull it away but recognise that I shouldn't.

'—because you're very sensitive and you always wanted me all to yourself—'

Untrue.

'—and then resented what little she got. If I gave her a bath or—'

'Stop, Mum.'

She squeezes my hand and lets me pull it away from her grip.

'Okay. But you are a bit much.'

And I can't help it, I'm laughing because I am, god knows I am. I am too much, even for me.

Mum gets up and goes back to sorting the fridge and I bite the skin around my thumb for a bit. It tastes of the garlic I helped chop last night. Mum made a bolognese for Ron and I helped her. I was like an advert for the perfect eldest daughter: I washed up the pans while they ate and I was even nice to Ron. I asked him how his case was going and if he knew Pete the policeman. He said my description of 'creepy and lonely' could be anyone in the Met.

Mum's pouring some green soup down the sink. There'll never be a good moment, I just have to—

'Mum . . .'

I've made my voice quiet but serious. I don't know how to finish the sentence, though.

Which words?

'You going to keep this one?'

Mum has turned to look at me, the soup container in her hand still with slime at the bottom. How did she know?

'I knew the second you came home. Could see it in your eyes.'

I'm not as inscrutable as Mona Lisa.

'Is it Ian's?'

I nod my head, but not convincingly.

'Well, it's none of my business, but if it is, don't tell him. You don't want to be stuck seeing him every two weeks for the next eighteen years.'

She comes over and hugs me around the shoulders. Her hair smells of the hot-oil conditioner and is tickling my neck.

'Have you got folic acid and have you been to the doctor?'

I shake my head and Mum puts an out-of-date yogurt down in front of me.

I haven't got a spoon.

Dear Sophie,

Well I was very surprised to get your letter — partly because no one writes letters anymore and you could have asked James for my email address!! As far as I considered it, the whole matter was completely forgotten — I didn't think you owed me anything. At the time I merely wished so much to help, as it was a sad thing that happened to you both. James took a very long time to get over it as I think he was quite keen to be a daddy!! Of course it all worked out for the best in the long run, and he's very happy now. I hope you are also. A family wedding to plan for is always a crazy time, it is over here for sure!!! You must pop in for the evening — do if you fancy? It would be lush to see you again after all this time. And please don't worry about the money, James paid me back in instalments and was very responsible about the whole thing (you know what he's like!!!)

Lots of love Stephanie xxx

Decaffeinated coffee tastes much worse than normal coffee, and normal coffee is already quite disgusting so I don't know why I'm drinking it. But as I sip it now I realise I do *like* the taste, even though it's not nice. How is that possible?

I bite my pencil and try to remember what I have to remember to do today. First I've got the doctor's appointment where I'll have a urine test and they'll confirm how far along I am. The leaflet says to write down any questions you might have so you don't forget. But I can't think of any yet. All the emotional questions seem inappropriate – 'Oh please tell me, Doctor, will this child provide a sense of peace and purpose that I've never felt before?' And there's no point asking medical questions because everything's on Google.

I've been thinking a lot about birth because that's the scariest bit, but it's all quite disconcerting. My body isn't mine anymore; she's borrowing it for all of *her* needs. Some of that is quite screwed up to think about, like I read on a new-mums' forum that if you don't eat enough calcium the baby will steal it from your bones. I've been drinking lots of milk so she won't have to cannibalise me. I've never eaten so much in my life, actually, and I'm not even weighing myself. I've bought some really stretchy leggings and I'm weirdly looking forward to seeing myself grow.

The women on the forum complain a lot about haemorrhoids, which makes me laugh. At least now I'll have

them for a reason . . . I'm not sure what the reason is exactly, maybe because the baby needs more space so pushes
your intestines out the way? Mine aren't even bad at the
moment, but I'm already getting some aches as my hormones are changing. I've been having these deep tummy
aches that the internet says are 'round ligament pains' as
my womb gets bigger and pulls into a new position. It's
crazy that this is all I think about when a few weeks ago
all I was concerned with was boys and whether I was in an
experiment I didn't know about. That me was a completely different person.

Oh yes, knickers, that has to go on the list. I need big
white sensible ones for wearing to all the appointments
and examinations. Wouldn't be appropriate to wear a lacy
thong.

I'm having such vivid pregnancy dreams. Last night it
was about after I died, and my baby, she was grown-up
and going through my things. She was talking to me even
though she couldn't see me and opening all these boxes in
my bedroom. When I woke up the meaning was clear: my
biographer isn't some professional writer that I've never
met, it's my daughter! She's the person I've been keeping
all these letters and emails for. All those moments I was
compelled to document, it's so she'll have a shared story
with me even though she wasn't here.

This all makes so much sense.

I remembered that thing about hysteria. That the original meaning was about how the womb moved around a
woman's body and caused all her problems. Like it would
be up in her brain or down her legs, pressing on her bits
and bobs and making her act mental and annoying. So the

doctors used to suggest her husband got her pregnant to stop the wandering womb, to tack it down and – obviously that's bollocks, none of that is true, or possible. Except that it would be quite a good description of how I feel. Like there was an organ inside me causing mischief and scrambling me up and now it's been fixed in the right place and I am enjoying the calm.

My tummy is aching a bit this morning, actually, but you're not allowed to use hot-water bottles or take Nurofen when you're pregnant as it hurts the foetus. It feels a bit like period pain but it's the ligaments and everything stretching.

'I'm going now.'

Mum is looking at me from the doorway. She's wearing trainers with her work skirt like someone from the eighties.

'Good luck at the doctor's.'

I wave my list at her and she gives me a thumbs-up and leaves. I love having her house to myself while she's at work.

I finish my list – it's only a few things. There's no point putting things on there for the sake of it.

Something psychosomatic is at work and the decaf has gone through me like regular coffee. I walk into the downstairs toilet and am surprised by the huge photograph even though I know it's there. I grin at us before pulling down my tracksuit bottoms and taking a seat. I'm still smiling like an idiot when I notice the sliver of pink blood on my underwear.

Sophie Collins
124 Arden Crescent
Harold Wood
Essex
RM9 0UH

8 Feb 20—

Dear whom it may concern,

RE: Independent Voluntary Action

I am writing regarding debt consolidation having spoken with your company and I would like to use Baines and Ernest's services to pay off my debts in manageable sums. I enclose the most recent bank statements from my accounts and credit cards and understand that they will all become frozen within seven working days. The agreed amount specified on the telephone was £135 per month until the debts are repaid and this is the amount I would like to be/am able to pay going forward. I understand I will not be able to take out any loans or lending for the foreseeable future and that this will affect my credit rating. I give you permission to contact my banks on my behalf. Thank you for all of your help and I will look forward to hearing that the action is confirmed.

Sophie Collins

Nadia is blindfolded and has her arms tied behind her back while someone called 'Ems' is holding a nappy over her face. Nadia is sniffing enthusiastically.

'It just smells chocolatey!'

Cue screeching and yelling from all the others. The one with silver streaks at the front of her hair starts a chant:

'Eat it! Eat it!'

And the other women join in. It's like *Lord of the Flies* if poor Piggy had been five months pregnant and all the other boys were screeching harpies. Much to my surprise, Nadia does start licking what's been smeared inside the nappy—

'IT HAS LUMPS!!'

Nadia has brown goo skidmarked down her nose. Mum was right: I shouldn't have come.

Two of Nadia's friends are pregnant too. One, her sister-in-law, I think she said, is full term. Stretched and ridiculous-looking. Wobbly boobs shivering and swelling up above a floral wrap dress. I am trying not to stare. Nadia is wearing a stripy black-and-white top and blue dungarees and her hair is in plaits. She's barely showing; she looks like a wholesome children's TV presenter. She looks like one of the non-pregnant models they get to wear the maternity clothes on ASOS.

I should send the leggings back but I can't bear it. They're under my bed.

I'm the only person who didn't bring a present because I didn't know we were supposed to bring presents. I've never been to a baby shower before but everyone else seems to know exactly how to behave. The non-pregnant ones are drinking prosecco and getting very into the games. The pregnant ones are less excitable and keep trying to move the conversation away from ruined vaginas or 'baby names that are child abuse' and onto 'colostrum harvesting' and 'doulas', whatever the hell that is/they are. And me, Nadia's friend from work, halfway between the two. All the hormones but nothing to contribute.

Nadia has worked out it was a Snickers bar smeared in the nappy she's been nosebagging and now it's her mum's turn. She hired a limo to get here and is wearing a white tux, which is a bit OTT for the basement area of an All Bar One, but she's clearly a very interesting woman. There was nearly a fight a minute ago when one of the pregnants asked her to stub out her cigar.

I'm currently listening to Karen, Nadia's friend from school. She told me she was seven months 'gone' and I told her I liked her dress. I don't – it looks like underwear. She just pulled the straps down on it and whispered how it was for feeding so I don't know what kind of restaurants she's planning to go to. I couldn't help pulling a face and now she's turned around and is leaving me.

I'll keep my eyes soft and not look directly at anyone and it'll seem like I'm fine standing here by myself. A few yards away, Nadia's mum is still holding the cigar and it stinks worse than when it was alight. My sense of smell is still really sensitive and I feel sick and . . . I didn't ask them when those symptoms would go away and I can't type any more questions into Google because I keep landing on the saddest places on the internet and the pleas and requests for reassurance are seared into my brain forever and I want to reply to every post 'I hope you're okay now? Did you get over it? Please tell me that you did and that I will be okay one day.'

I had to come. I shouldn't have, but I had to because I didn't know how not to. What excuse to use? I didn't want to lie and I couldn't tell the truth. My fear, and this is strange, is that Nadia would think I was lying all along. That I would do something like this for attention. I – I don't want attention. I don't have any words for this and I didn't want to tell her.

I seem like a liar because I always used to tell lies. They construct themselves and leap out without my instruction. Telling someone that my dad was gay and lived in Sydney or that I had a twin. That's something, I suppose. Chris didn't reject me – he didn't even know me.

A woman with a shiny bob is setting up a karaoke machine. All the songs have 'baby' in the title. I think about leaving, picture myself going outside and walking away down the high street. I could go to Boots and get Nadia a present, some Sudocrem or something. I take the prosecco I've been holding for an hour without drinking and go and look at the table with Nadia's gifts on it. There are tiny soft clothes in light greens and yellows. There's a set of balms and oils called The Tummy Rub Set. There's a weird cushion thing with a strap on it . . . for haemorrhoids?

'It's for breastfeeding.'

Nadia's mum has appeared next to me.

'No one needs all this crap – didn't have it in my day.'

I nod respectfully. I'm glad she's not my mum, and even as I think that I realise she's pretty similar.

'She'll regret it when she sees what her tits look like afterwards.'

Nadia's mum, to my astonishment, is making low-flying hammocks with her hands and I reassess. My mum wouldn't talk about me like this to a stranger. Since it happened she's been letting me sleep in her bed. She's been brushing my hair and making me hot-water bottles. She even offered me a foot rub during *EastEnders* but I said no. I don't want to be touched, I'll evaporate. But I do like sitting watching soaps with her in the dark, pretending I'm crying at the fictional people's badly acted lives. The only thing I hate is one of the adverts that keeps being shown during *Coronation Street*. It's for a bank and shows a couple looking at a white stick and being disappointed and the tagline is about trying again and – I shouldn't be thinking about this. I shouldn't have come.

I nod at Nadia's mum and walk away. I don't know where I'm heading until I reach the opposite wall and am forced to stop. I'll lean here. I'm still holding this full glass. I'm allowed to drink now – there's no reason not to except it's like, if I drink, it's all over. I'm admitting she's gone. And she's not yet, I'm still bleeding. It's a process. I prefer it to be happening than done.

The hospital make you do another test after two weeks. To make sure all the baby hormones are gone. To make sure it isn't secretly growing somewhere outside of your uterus. I must've looked too hopeful when she said this because the nurse changed tone from kindly to alarmist to reinforce how DEADLY this'd be. But it didn't work: I'm still rooting for her.

I'm trying not to stare at everyone's bodies. People making people, while being people who were once made. Ems and Nadia's mum are dragging folding chairs into a line for another game. They're putting envelopes on each seat. I imagine standing up and noticing I've left blood on the chair and screaming until I faint. They'd have to let me leave the party then.

So maybe I do still like attention?

When I first googled 'pregnant bleeding blood' I was reassured. Lots of medical websites describing implantation bleeding and how some people bleed throughout their pregnancy and it doesn't affect the baby. 'Get it checked if you're worried!' the websites said. I wasn't worried, because I knew this was meant to be. I thought she was implanting, digging deeper into me, her home. I was too stupid to be worried.

And now I don't know anything anymore.

I smell the prosecco; it's vinegary and unappealing.

'No one <u>wants</u> to, Mum – I told you already.'

Nadia is shouting at her mum about the chairs but is guided over to the karaoke machine by someone I haven't met. She doesn't look pregnant.

Is this all I am going to wonder about everyone now?

A song is selected and the electronic intro elicits an excited high-pitched scream from Ems while Nadia smooths her hair smugly. It's a Justin Bieber song and by the chorus everyone is screeching in unison. I'm embarrassed for them. Then I look down and see that one of my feet is tapping along like a traitor. Do the extremities of my body not comprehend what's going on at my heart?

I should leave. Go for a walk, get Nadia a present, drop it off, then go home. I could tell Nadia I feel sick but, no, I can't.

As if I could walk down the baby aisle.

I never noticed before that everyone in the world has a pram, that everyone has a bump, a sling and a toddler on their shoulders. Babies keep looking at me like the dogs used to – like they know. The nurse told me it wasn't my fault, that there was nothing I could have done. She also told me to put my trousers and pants back on and that I had to leave.

I had no idea what was going on. I'd walked around all morning thinking the aches in my abdomen were due to bonding, a fusion rather than an exit. It was only when the blood started whooshing and glooping and I was bent over myself on the toilet that my— that I understood. I rang 111 and they gave me a quiz. I asked him, 'How can I stop it?' A man, it was, being kind to me and my shaking voice. He sent me to the hospital and told me which ward to go to and what to say. When I got there I had to sit opposite a woman who already had a baby but was pregnant again. She was the only person chatting in the waiting area.

They do a scan thing, with a wand. And the nurse pulls a sad face and says she can't find anything. That's what they say – not that it's dead, or gone. They gave me a leaflet too. Saying they couldn't find it. But still this glimmer of hope because it could be in your fallopian tube causing internal bleeding and preparing to kill you – fingers crossed.

She told me to take ibuprofen and I told her I couldn't

because I was— Even though she'd just told me I wasn't anymore.

I walked home. I finally managed it, thought of nothing. Didn't even breathe.

I had to call the doctor's and say I didn't need my appointment anymore. The receptionist was matter-of-fact.

When I got back to Mum's—

'You've got to sing!!'

Nadia is pulling on my arm.

'I don't feel well.'

The music is too loud. Nadia's mum has started singing a song by Britney Spears and is flicking her hair like strippers do. I remember Steve. From back when I was a different person.

Nadia is looking at me sympathetically.

'You want some ginger tea?'

'No. No thank you.'

One of the pregnants looks over at us. I texted Nadia and said please not to mention it but – but she's put her hand on my abdomen and—

'I'll just go to the loo.'

I'm not coming back. I leave my cardigan, I don't need it. I hate everything I own and will shed it all like a snake sheds its skin and then I'll scrape off *my* skin and my meat and float away. I concentrate on one foot in front of the other towards the toilets. There are three small stairs and I remember I'm holding the prosecco glass and noticing I'm holding it makes me stop. It smashes but the sound is drowned out by the karaoke so I keep going, up to the main staircase and towards the daylight and the quiet.

When I got home after the hospital, back to Mum's, she was still at work. I wandered into every room and tried to be who I had been when I woke up that morning. Someone who searched for YouTube videos of prenatal yoga. There were vitamins on the table; on the label a woman in cycling shorts and a vest smiled at her round stomach. I threw her in the bin and hated how stupid I had been to believe. There were special teabags too, and a cream to help stop stretch marks. I threw it all away and stayed a curled-up lump on the kitchen floor until Mum got home and put me to bed.

Admissions Department
Barking & Dagenham University
Dogbar Road
DG13 4DU

13 February 20—

Dear Sophie Collins,

This is to acknowledge your recent application for our teacher training programme, we are thrilled to have received a record number of applications this year and will be letting all successful candidates know by 1 May.

Your request for financial assistance will also be assessed and you'll be contacted about that separately.

Thank you for your interest in Barking & Dagenham University.

William Carter
Head of Admissions

Well, this is embarrassing. My eyelids are closed so I don't know if anyone is looking at me or how obvious it is. The far corners of both eyes are leaking wet warm streams into my earlobes. This isn't even like crying, it's too relaxed. It's more of a seepage. The teacher is telling us about smoothing our foreheads and letting our tongue be loose and I don't understand any of these instructions, yet somehow I'm the heaviest I've ever been. Starfished on a smelly yoga mat, serenely weeping.

What witchcraft is this? Is this the bit it's all about? You have to put up with all the discomfort and contortions and then when it's over you cry with blessed relief. My sideburns are damp now. I didn't even like the stupid class – have been cursing Imogen, who told me to come. The teacher kept making us do 'downward dogs', which is like the bit before a handstand, but you freeze there and your legs and shoulders ache and then your back joins in and starts aching too. And she was like 'We will hold here for five breaths' but her breaths lasted at least two minutes each. I kept looking at the clock, thinking 'It must be over soon', but it was only ever a minute since I last looked. Also I hated her voice – she was like a robot pretending to be sympathetic. Exactly what a machine would sound like if you programmed it for kindness.

'Push your thoughts away and let the floor support you.'

Except robots are way too logical for this crap. That is

the most nonsensical thing I have ever heard a human say. How does anyone 'push' a 'thought'? They can't. All of the words of yoga don't mean anything, but – but she's done something to me. My muscles have been hypnotised; my whole body is pretending to be dead down there. And I'm still crying. Jesus.

Is it sideburns on a girl? Maybe they have a different name. I've never heard any woman refer to that part of her hair. If I ever go back to a proper hairdresser I'll ask them – even though they'll probably pull a face like I'm a prat and I'll see them in the mirror and wish I could leave but I won't. Push thought away, fuck off. Get out of my head. She's telling us to breathe now – maybe someone's body has relaxed too much and they've gone blue? I hope it's the man next to me, I hate him. He smells like milky salmon and our eyes met when he looked through his legs. I don't think men should come to yoga – is that sexist?

The teacher wasn't as skinny as I was expecting. She has big strong thighs and a firm belly and I was relieved I wasn't going to have to watch a bendy ballerina for an hour. So that's sexist too.

Okay, we've got to sit up now. It's over. I shield my face and reach down for my rolled-up socks. I am being as subtle as I can drying my ears, but everyone still has their eyes shut anyway. Even the teacher. They're all cross-legged and praying-hands and making a humming sound. I have the world to myself for a moment. I put my socks on and now people are politely clapping and getting up and spraying their mats with a green spray. What will I do if someone tries to make friends with me? I'm looking for the easiest route out of the room when I meet the teacher's gaze. She smiles so nicely. She is nice. It must be hard to remember all the moves and keep your voice calm without sound-ing a bit robotic. Maybe that's what happened to Stephen Hawking with all the physics – that must have been even harder to remember.

I don't want to clean my mat, I can't be bothered, but the milk-fish man has passed me the spray bottle and now I'm doing it. He's got a beard; he looks like a smaller ver-sion of Robbie Coltrane. Like a Shetland pony version. He's given me a big paper roll now to wipe off the spray and I should say something . . . I should say thank you. I've sprayed too much. I wipe it all off and when I stand up he's hanging up his mat and leaving. I send thank-you vibes to his small, broad back and also sorry vibes. I can send vibes now, apparently; yoga has really changed me.

I am very sleepy as I put on my shoes in the corridor. I'm relieved no one is talking to each other or trying to make this a social occasion just because we all shared a room for an hour. The teacher made a joke as we were rolling out our mats at the start about 'all the love in the air on this special night' but I'd completely forgotten it was Valentine's Day. I don't need to feel sadder because it's— because I'm not supposed to be alone. I am alone but that's not any sadder today than on any other day. I'm going to have a Pot Noodle and go to bed and I've been out to yoga so I have something to talk about at the golf club tomorrow. I am more of a Kermit there, the older funny one. Imogen will like hearing about the Shet-land version of Robbie Coltrane. I always point out to her when people look like elderly versions of celebrities.

I found an ancient Billie Eilish last week. I think it might be my truest talent.

I'm walking out of the community centre and a car beeps, making me jump. I carry on walking but my heart is beating a lot, and I'm looking straight ahead and purposefully ignoring it when it pulls up beside me. I'm really hoping it's not the man from the class asking why I didn't thank him for his help. Or the teacher asking why I was thinking so much when she told me not to. It's dark even though it's only seven o'clock and the car is crawling next to me and for a split second I imagine: What if it's Chris? Hope cuts through fear then dissipates limply as it's not strong enough anymore. I can't even believe my own fantasies. And he'd never drive a jeep. Nor would the yoga teacher. This is it – this is how it feels to know you're about to get murdered. It's happening.

'Get in, stupid.'

It's a woman's voice coming from the other side of the car, a woman in the passenger seat. This is what the Wests did, wasn't it? So the victims would be more likely to accept a lift. You have to trust your instincts in these scenarios. I keep walking, pretending I can't see or hear them. It gets darker between street lights and I want to speed up but I don't want them to know I'm scared. I hear the electric whizzing of a descending car window.

'Your money or your life?!'

It's not Fred West, it's Ron. I look into the car and Rose West is in fact my mum. I'm too weary to trust my instincts. Ron thumbs behind him and I open the door and throw my rucksack onto the back seat followed by myself. A willing kidnap.

I'll give him this: the jeep is very smooth and it's nice to be up high once you're inside. I keep this compliment to myself, though.

'Where are you guys off to?'

Maybe they have to travel further afield so Ron's wife doesn't see them.

'We came to get you.'

Mum has turned round in her seat. She has backcombed her hair and fringe. She looks like an old Amy Winehouse.

'How'd you know where I was?'

'Insta.'

Ron and Mum are laughing, pleased with themselves. She turns back round and puts her hand on top of Ron's as he changes gear. She used to do that with Dad. It's mental to remember it. That this is the same life and I am the same person. Dad's green Escort that always smelled of petrol. Dana being carsick on any journey longer than twenty minutes.

I did put up a lot of stories about going to the yoga class. Pointing at the poster on the way in. Taking my trainers off and adding them to the row outside. The Himalayan salt lamp in the corner. I do it more now, whenever I'm doing anything. In case he looks, or wonders. If I pop into Chris's mind at all and he thinks to check what I'm up to, I want to be up to loads. Main grid is all golf club so that he thinks 'How did she end up there? Did Ella get her a job? Do they talk about my penis?' He'll have to look at some point, and I'll be prepared.

'Where are we going?'

We're driving through back lanes away from town. The headlights yellow the trees on either side of us as we pass.

I stop myself from acknowledging how nice this is.

'It's called third-wheeling, sweetheart.'

Must be a car term I don't know but I don't ask Ron to clarify.

What if he never ever looks? Chris. What if he never thinks about me ever again? If nothing ever reminds him of me or occurs to him? We could have been parents. Together. For the rest of time connected and mixed up in someone's genes and bloodstream. That must be why it feels so bad after you sleep with someone and you know they don't like you. Even if you don't like them. There could be ramifications and—

A small brown rabbit hops into the lane up ahead of us and Ron slams his emergency brakes.

'Off you go, Bugsy.'

Mum's laughing.

'Thanks for the whiplash.'

How will I accept that I still exist, even if I don't exist to Chris?

The bunny disappears into a hedge and we're moving forward again.

I just want to work out what the point of it all was.

Gravel crunches deliciously under our fat tyres as Ron turns into the driveway of the most beautiful pub I've ever seen. Squat and white with black timber running unsymmetrically across it. Roses around the front door. Candlelight flickering through the tiny windows. As we get out of the car a cocker spaniel runs from the beer garden towards us, wagging his tail excitedly. He sniffs around the car a bit then licks my hand.

'That's Sheila the landlady.'

Mum is in hysterics. Ron must be good in bed. They walk on ahead of me and I'm surprised that I am following them willingly. With gratitude.

Ron's all business when we get inside. I'm not used to being around men. Here's my booking, we'll need an extra chair, no not that table, one near the fire. No please or thank-yous. Yet the waiter is being all matey with him and Mum has her arm through his. We sit down and I look at my menu while they both check their phones. I wonder where his wife thinks he is on Valentine's Day? I'd be a bitch to ask. Mum catches my eye and smiles. She has mascara gloop in the corners of her eyes. She looks so happy.

'It's romantic, isn't it?'

I nod, but I don't know what part of this she means. Ron shouts to the barmaid to bring us a 'decent Malbec' and I watch her facial expression as she reaches up to a shelf. It doesn't change when the customers can't see her – very professional. She holds a bottle tilted at Ron.

'Not a screw-top, this is a special occasion! I'm out with two birds on Valentine's Day!'

Mum hits Ron on the arm but she's laughing. Even the barmaid is smiling. Is he charming?

Mum starts telling us about an uproar at her work involving the canteen cannelloni. Apparently the ingredients were changed without anyone being warned and the cheese tastes vegan now, even though the canteen are denying all knowledge.

'Head Office are having the same problem. Apparently it's delivered frozen and out of all control.'

Ron's now talking about when people found out lasagnes all had horsemeat in them, when, thank heavens, some wine is brought to the table and poured generously without ceremony. I have a very big slurp, like Bridget Jones would do on a bad day. Or someone from *Sex and the City* who's just been dumped or carjacked. It tastes like furry vinegar. My taste buds are taking ages to reacclimatise, but the bleeding stopped last week.

I miss it.

'I thought you might be one of those people who wants to sip a little bit first?'

I must be drunk already. Ron doesn't seem annoyed with my question.

'Think I'm a right twat, don't ya?'

Ron goes into a skit, pretending to smell his wine glass. He's huffing his nostrils and rubbing his fingers together like a chef.

'Ooh yes, melons and pine trees. And a touch of SIM card.'

I'm laughing with Mum and my cheeks feel hot and I remember I've done exercise and not eaten. Mum gets up to go for a wee and I want to go with her, I don't want to be alone with Ron at the table, but it's too late, she's walked away and now I am. I look around for the spaniel.

'It's nice, isn't it?'

Ron thinks I'm admiring the pub. I nod and he looks smug. I resist the urge to snark and have a sip of wine. It's much nicer when I sip it. I love wine. If it could always feel and taste like the first glass then—

'Like it?'

Ron's gesturing with his glass.

'Lovely.'

Ron is laughing at nothing. This is basic small talk. My

dad does this sometimes. Is it nervous energy? Or is being a middle-aged white man continually joyous?

'It was sad what happened at Christmas.'

Oh shit I thought we were small-talking.

'Sorry.'

'It's not me you should be apologising to.'

I can't believe I'm getting lectures from Ron. RON. Ron with the wife and the shit clothes who represents criminals and gets them off because the police forgot to put them in the right interview room.

'Sorry.'

I hate being told off. I glug my wine again and regret it. But here's Mum striding back purposefully.

'Guess who I found?'

She's holding her left arm out like a model on a game show. Presenting nothing, until after a few seconds from the other side of the bar slinks a mortified-looking Ian.

'He was using the hand dryer in the ladies!'

Dana and James's Wedding Part Two

Hello to our beloved friends and family,

It's super-exciting to be able to tell you we are the luckiest betrothed people in the world and we are bringing our wedding FORWARD! Yes, you read that right, one of James's friends from work has broken up with his fiancée (it's for the best don't worry!) and as they had already paid for their venue and it was non-refundable we have kindly stopped it going to waste.

The new date and address are on the card, and this means we can spend your donations from the Kickstarter on making it an amazing day to remember (or night if you're only invited to the evening disco) and an even more amazing honeymoon.

Love Dana and James.

P.S. There has been some confusion about the 'plus-one' situation. Some of you have been invited as a couple, and other people have been invited by themselves as it's only them we know. It's really not the big deal some people have made it out to be. <3 <3<3

It's like one of those kaleidoscope toys – when you shake it and the shards and crystals rearrange to create a totally different picture. I'm at a table, a patron, enjoying my evening. Someone else is behind the bar, someone in kitten heels with much better customer rapport. And rather than staring across the room at Chris, it's Ian I am watching. Ian on a date. On Valentine's Day. He doesn't believe in Valentine's Day, was very sneering about any mention of it. But now he's over there with Fake Ella sharing a cheese plate and drinking prosecco.

I look down at the hairs on my arms, who are all lying down and behaving normally.

I look back up to see that Ian is choking on some cracker and trying to dislodge it with water. Maybe I'm a witch.

'Don't watch them, Sophie.'

At least this pub plays music, even if it is Savage Garden.

'I don't care, Mum.'

When she arrived I thought it *was* Ella. I thought this was all a set-up like *This Is Your Life* and that's why Mum had collected me and everyone I knew was going to give a speech. Then when she walked over to us and took Ian's hand, my brain melted into itself. Mum and Ron were making fun of Ian cos he'd been trying to dry a hot chocolate spill on his crotch and had looked like a perv rubbing himself in the ladies. It wasn't until I focused on Ella that her features arranged properly and I could see it wasn't

Ella at all. Just a girl with curly brown hair and lipstick on. She seemed shy and tugged Ian away from us to their own table.

'You might be making it weird for them.'

It *is* weird. When coincidences like this happen it's no wonder life feels like a script or an experiment. I turn my head back to Mum and Ron.

'What's Dana up to?'

I don't really want to know the answer.

'They've gone pictures. He had a voucher.'

Of course he did.

'And Plus-One-Gate rolls on.'

Ron tuts sympathetically as Mum begins listing the family members whose partners Dana has excluded from her wedding. I sneak my eyes back over to Ian and Fake Ella. He's talking and she's listening and stroking his fingers. I hope she's made him feel more confident about his penis.

Real Ella says she isn't into men anymore. It was quite dramatic. Steve broke up with her during a therapy session and after a week-long breakdown she decided it was the best thing that could have happened. And now she's enjoying a supremely busy sex life with women she meets through an app. I wouldn't say we were good friends, but I hear her talking to Imogen about it at the golf club. There's a tension when she talks to me; she's more guarded. I don't think I'm her enemy, more that she doesn't like what I remind her of. Or what I know. Anyway, apparently orgasms with women are much better than normal ones and especially ones with Steve. She says she's happy. A lot. But she doesn't seem it because she's had her forehead and laughter lines Botoxed by Imogen's sister.

My timing with the golf club could not have been more perfect. I knew they were a member of staff down and called them about a job a day before they advertised, so – yeah, they thought it was fate. Imogen is the manager but she doesn't act like one and is going back to Brighton to finish her degree in October so she doesn't care if people don't mop properly or if they drink unfinished drinks in the slop room. Imogen's having a sabbatical for her mental health and is really good at giving advice you didn't ask for, like 'You should take Ritalin' and 'Have you thought about yoga for your anxiety?' Her sister Beth works Saturday nights, mostly to scope the older wives as possible clients.

Beth is the only one who ever mentions Chris. I think she slept with him too; she has this sense of ownership – 'Oh remember how Chris would do this' or 'Hahaha when Chris said that.' I cannot picture him working there, wearing a clean shirt and a black apron. I cannot imagine him wiping down their mirrored bar. I have thought a couple of times about what happens if he comes back. If he comes in for his old job and sees me and— Blah, I can't really fantasise about him anymore. I did it for so long it's still a habit, my mind still tries to go there, but it's extinguished now. An old volcano – nothing satisfying or convincing comes up.

I'm so tired. I roar a big unattractive yawn without covering my mouth but Ron and Mum are whisper-bickering and don't notice. I knew the wedding was dangerous territory.

I couldn't go back to The Slipper so I didn't. I emailed them. Dana very sweetly took my uniform in so I could get the deposit back. I did not want to see Nadia again. I couldn't tell her what had happened and I couldn't watch her going through it all. Not with my phantom due date loitering a few months after hers. I sip the last dregs from my wine glass. Mum's eyes are red and brimming. How does Ron not know the signs? The soft emotions and the slackness in her cheeks. This could turn very bad very quickly; I decide to change the subject.

'Mum, I'm sorry about what happened at Christmas. I should've apologised before. It was really shit, and an upsetting thing.'

Mum says she doesn't know what I'm talking about. Her tone is warning me and her eyes are blank. Ron is looking at his shoes under the table.

'The Jesus monkey thing?'

'Never heard of him.'

The angle of Mum's head – it's like she's daring me to describe it in more detail. I can barely remember, truth be told. I know there were hungry babies and robots.

'We should eat.'

Ron's taking charge again. Mum's shaking her head. She tips the bottle into her glass but it's just drips remaining and then empty.

'I want to go home.'

She slams the bottle down and the barmaid looks over at us.

'What's the point of having a nice time now, hmm? If you're never going to leave her?'

Shit.

Ron gets the car keys out of his pocket and plonks them on the table. He doesn't look at either of us, although my mum's face is stretched up towards him as he stands,

awaiting his reaction. He walks away. We watch him as
he goes around the bar, then I feel a hand squeezing my
thigh.

'He doesn't like confrontation.'

All of a sudden Mum seems fine. I was worried she was
going to bawl.

'No one likes confrontation, Mum.'

She shrugs.

'I do.'

I shake my head at her and see Ian and Fake Ella in my
peripheral vision – they're looking over at us. I wonder
what he's told her about me, about my family. If they've
had post-coital heart-to-hearts. Naked and sipping tea
while he described me as a mental bitch. It doesn't even
piss me off, that's the stupid thing; it's so reassuring to feel
like I exist. My staff badge at the golf club has my real
name on it and I like running my fingers across and feeling
the grooves.

'Another one, please.'

Ron is at the bar ordering a shot of something dark
brown which he swirls in a glass, waiting for Mum to turn
around. I can tell from her posture that she knows he's
there. She rolls her eyes at me and I squeeze my mouth to
stop from smiling.

'The trouble with having kids is that they only remember the bad stuff.'

Ron's downing his shot. I try to make it feel like an episode of something, with a coincidental ex showing up and
a brewing row between the main characters, but I don't
have the energy. I'm warm and blurry. Is this living in the
moment – am I present? Or am I slipping into a coma?

'The fights and mistakes and spills and yelling, even though the other ninety-nine per cent of the time was absolutely fine. But you don't remember it.'

Mum tries to fill her glass from the empty bottle again.

'So we all think we're fucked up when we're not.'

I try to imagine being a baby and it's impossible. How is something so ordinary also absolutely mental?

'Another one, please.'

He's louder this time. Turns out Ron is quite the little attention-seeker. It astounds me to acknowledge that they are very well suited. Ron swills his glass when he receives it, empties it down his throat and lines the empty glass up along with two others. Mum smiles sweetly at me before speaking over her shoulder at him without really turning.

'Think of the carbs, babe.'

Ron nods. He hands his card to the nice barmaid, who doesn't try to smile at him this time. He's looking glumly down at his hands, then he rubs a finger along where his wedding ring should be. He must take it off when they're together. God, we've only been here for twenty minutes – he can still get home and do a full Valentine's night with his wife.

Mum and I help each other on with our coats. I do feel pissed when I stand up. I love wine. I wish I'd taken a picture of my full glass and the open fire. Chris might've seen and wondered who I was out with and—

And what?

I thank Ron because I think I like him now. And then we trudge outside to the jeep and the spaniel reappears but doesn't seem as pleased to see us. He's over us already, old car-park news. It's very dark and the sky is cloudless so there's very good star visibility. I point upwards to Mum and she nods without looking.

Ron clicks a beeper and we try our doors but they are still locked. Ron presses it again, but I'm still holding the handle so it doesn't work. I suddenly realise the point he was making at the bar. He's done this on purpose.

'Have you had too much to drive?'

Ron ignores me and clicks to release the central locking. He raises an eyebrow at Mum over the roof; she gives him a look that means something. Something nice, maybe sexual.

'Oh come on, you're always talking about how you want to die.'

Mum and Ron open their doors and get in, absolutely guffawing.

'How long is it to walk?'

I can see Ian nosily looking out of a window from his table. It looks so twinkly in there but I'm glad to be going. I am an outside person looking in, but I wouldn't rather be on that table with him. I think about giving him the finger but we've probably ruined their night enough already. Or maybe he thinks we're leaving because I can't bear to see him romancing again? Yeah, I hope he thinks that – it's nicer for him to believe I care.

'I'm going to walk.'

I start across the car park and Mum shouts from the car, 'Don't come crying to me when you get raped.'

'Mum!'

They're laughing at me. They're sitting in their lofty seats, joined in mockery of me.

'MORE WORK FOR HIM, EH? REPRESENTING MY RAPIST.'

I probably shouldn't have shouted that outside such a lovely pub but it's worth it to see Mum laughing through the windscreen. Ron headbutts the steering wheel and toots the horn. I walk back towards them and get in the back. I make sure to put my seatbelt on. We crunch out slowly and Ron tells me he's got an old bike I can have if I want it. I do want it. Maybe I will cycle everywhere and get strong legs and that can be my personality.

'Be careful of the rabbits.'

I've never been in a drunk driver's car before. We had a whole assembly on this at junior school, on just saying 'No' and reporting people to the police. But I suppose it is nice to find out that you *don't* want to die very much, if at all.

Good luck in your new home, its much nicer living without a bloke you'll see.

Love Mum xxxx

I enjoy imagining I'm being interviewed by someone like Jonathan Ross or Graham Norton. And as I tell them what happened to me they laugh at my jokes then look sad at the sad bits. My eyes would glisten with tears, I'd look at my hands in my lap and seem like I'd drifted off . . . drifted back there for a moment. Then I'd collect myself. I'd turn to the audience and confide, 'Oh it was the worst thing that ever happened to me.' Then the audience would spontaneously start clapping because I am so brave and so brutally honest. 'We should talk about these things more,' I say on the interview, even though in real life I never talk about it ever.

Sometimes I feel relief for her. Not existing is the definition of not suffering – eh, Sartre, Camus et al?

I look at my italicised name on a little card in the centre of a dinner plate. My mind skips over a quip about being so hungry I could eat myself but there's no one else at the table to say it to. They are mingling. Out of their chairs and leaning on the backs of other people's or at the bar or, in Dana's friend Katie's case, sitting on a man's lap. I sip my lemonade and try to remember what it felt like to fancy someone.

James's friends are behaving like it's just a party. They're drinking disrespectfully quickly and one of them has turned the music up too loud. Mum told me the playlist was a combination of both Dana and James's favourite songs, but it's all been Black Eyed Peas so far so maybe there's been a mix-up.

She's married him and I'm sitting here waiting for an emotion to hit me.

It's been very strange to have Dad here. He's staying at Mum's in the spare room. We didn't expect him to come because he told us he wasn't. But last night Mum confessed she'd threatened to give the taxman his Australian address if he didn't 'do his duty'. So he realised it'd be cheaper to fly over and give his daughter away than be taken to court by HMRC. Dana doesn't know that – she thinks he wanted to surprise her. She's absolutely fuming about Belinda being here, though, and keeps calling her 'The Gatecrasher'.

This morning at the house, Mum, Ron, Dad and Belinda were all drinking Buck's Fizz, eating croissants and roaring with laughter. Teasing each other, raking through the years and finding everything hilarious now that decades have passed. The betrayals and recriminations so far behind everyone that they're teeny-tiny on the rear horizon. It was unexpected. For such a long time there's been poisonous resentment but for some reason Mum was now telling Ron about Belinda leaving her things behind, like it was a joke, and Ron said, 'Don't try that at my house!' and then all four of them guffawed and slapped the table or their legs while me and Dana sat on the stairs listening like we were kids again.

Maybe it's something magic about weddings. James seeing Dana at the altar and his eyes looking like a child watching a magic trick. I could write a poem about it. About how purely I want him to love her. He knows what's happened, obviously – he tried to give me a hug at Mum's, which I suppose is sweet. Dana reminded me that he had been upset about the abortion. I wish I'd had space to acknowledge that at the time. Not that I'd have known how to commiserate. It *is* a loss, I see that now. I haven't spoken to him yet today. Maybe we can politely ignore each other forever? I think that's the mature thing to do.

I try to imagine telling Jonathan Ross or Graham Norton 'My sister married my ex-boyfriend' but I can't picture them laughing. They squirm and seem embarrassed, so I look out to the audience for reassurance and they're all tense and so I regret bringing it up. Other people will never laugh because they won't believe that I'm okay about it, so I'll never bring it up. Maybe one day there'll be another wedding. One of Dana's children marrying . . . not one of mine, that would be incest; they'll marry someone they're not related to and James and I and Dana will all roar at a table because our heartbreaks are so ancient and ossified that we find them hysterical. Like the *Titanic* becoming a theme park – we can just enjoy the rides.

I was expecting today to be easier because with all the people and noise I wouldn't have a chance to dwell. But it doesn't work like that, apparently. I didn't know I had the capacity to care this much about anything. Except maybe the dog next door. Maybe this is what happens when you can't use words to tell someone how you feel? You can't ever put them down and leave them behind.

A new song is starting. It's the Black Eyed Peas: they think tonight is going to be good, apparently. They sang the exact same thing a few songs ago. Either the playlist has restarted or the band have more than one song about their high hopes for a good night. I try to remember that feeling, the flip-floppy tummy while getting ready to go out. Having a drink while putting my make-up on, sucking my belly in as I looked sideways in the mirror. I would never have thought of that as happiness.

Something's going on by the bar: shouting, people running over. Oh, it's an older guy – I think it's one of James's uncles. He's just been informed it's not a free bar after handing out a round of sambucas. James has rushed over and is patting his uncle on the back and glaring at the barmaid like it wasn't entirely his own responsibility. They asked me to work the bar as a wedding gift to them. I shouldn't have been surprised, but I was. I felt like I had to do it as my penance, until Mum found out and told them she wouldn't allow it.

I'm enjoying watching this drama unfold.

The uncle has stormed off without paying, which has revealed who was standing behind him in the queue. Ian. His face is very serious – maybe he's worried he'll be asked to pay the man's bill? I knew he was invited. Dana's kept me updated about his and James's friendship – the Sunday-afternoon paintballing and competitive pub quizzing. I think he'll marry Claire; we're all that age now. She's not here, of course, because Dana thinks she's boring, although she pretended it was out of loyalty to me.

All my daydreams are much weaker now. My imaginings are not fooled by themselves. I drink the end of my lemonade and disguise my burp as a cough. It's simpler to be me now, even though it's worse.

Oh, someone's switched off the Black Eyed Peas and without their rhythmic nonsense the chatter of guests sounds too loud and people are shushing each other. The women from my table, mostly Debenhams Book Club members, return to their seats and fill their wine glasses in preparation for the speeches but – hang on, no – someone's just changed the track. Oh man, I try not to laugh but I'm smiling as Dana and James start swaying in the middle of the room to 'Every Breath You Take' by The Police. Dana looks absolutely hammered; James is having to hold her up.

This is such a stalky song.

She offered to lend me money, so that I could move out of Mum's. That was nice, I know she wanted to be nice, but I've learned my lesson after what happened last time. I told her 'I'll do a Kickstarter' but she didn't get my joke.

In my peripheral vision I see Dad going up to Mum. He points at the dance floor and pulls on her arm, trying to lead her to it. She's dragged a step or two by his momentum before she pulls her arm back. Mum's looking over at me like 'Did you see that?' while Belinda rushes over and escorts Dad towards where Dana and James have been joined by three other couples. The thing about watching real people, not TV or a film, is that you realise how ugly we all actually are. Men with big bellies and short legs, women who've put the wrong-colour foundation on, their too-tight bras digging into back flab. I love them.

'He may have abandoned me with two kids but I got the last word . . .'

Mum has crept up behind me and is loudly whispering in my ear. Her breath smells like a hangover.

'. . . told him to go fuck himself.'

I can't tell if she's joking. I turn round to look at her

facial expression but she's already dancing over to Ron, pointing her fingers out ahead of her to this awful song. The injections she got off Beth from the golf club have increased her confidence as well as freezing her eyebrows.

I didn't tell Dad what happened with me. He'd only have said something insensitive like 'Lucky escape.'

I don't want to watch couples dancing. I look down at my hands and realise I've wrapped my cutlery in my napkin.

I have checked in on Chris, of course, I'm only human. Every few days I go on his Instagram – he's started a microbrewery business, which he is promoting heavily. The beers have his dog's face on the label. He never posts pictures of Irina. Even on their wedding day the only photographic evidence was a toilet selfie. I thought once I knew he was married it would feel like an ending, but it's just another detail.

Ha! Ron's danced Mum over to Dad and swapped her for Belinda in a debonair move I would not have thought he was capable of. Dad's spun Mum under his arm before she can get away and – oh, she's grinning.

Ron's dipped Belinda down like a ballroom dancer and— Oh shit he's dropped her! Another dancing couple, oblivious to the trip hazard, have been felled by my step-mum's body and now there are several middle-aged people laughing on the floor. Dana pretends to fall over to join them and James gets out his phone to take pictures. This is perfection.

I turn my head to take in the entire room. I'm the camera, recording all of the people with their skin and ears and hair and teeth. I'm *watching*, that's what I do; I was confused for a while but now I understand my purpose. I unwrap my cutlery so that I can wrap it again. Maybe this is what celebrities mean when they say they're content to be alone?

I catch the eye of another woman scanning the room – perhaps because we're the only two people still sitting down. I spend a moment pondering her backstory: What happened to her, why is *she* alone? Then with a lurch of recognition – HA – this is so funny – it's a mirrored pillar. She's me, as am I. My twin. Ahhhh, it's so obvious. This is the most *obvious* thing . . . I felt someone watching me all the time everywhere I went and ha ha DUH of course: it was me.

OH MY GOD I've just had the wisest thought.

I *am* the experimenter, I'm my own biographer, this is *huge* and—

I have no one to tell. So I get out my phone and text myself like a lunatic.